Commitment

A Blade Holmes Western Mystery

Book 1

Neil A. Waring

Old Trails Publishing

http://oldtrailspublishing.blogspot.com

Old Trails Publishing
http://oldtrailspublishing.blogspot.com

To readers of western and historical fiction everywhere and to my wife Jan, for her patience with this project as my first reader.

Commitment

"Trust instinct to the end, even though you can give no reason."
-Ralph Waldo Emerson-

Chapter 1 – The Prologue

If the young cowboy had but one wish, it would be to live. He would be thinking of nothing else.

However, it was then obvious, he did. He thought back one minute to his unfortunate attempt to force legendary lawman Blade Holmes to draw. It was likely the worst decision he'd ever made. If present conditions were not so grave, he might have laughed but instead his mind flashed scenes of his impending death. The cowpoke felt the cold from the barrel of the Colt pressed under his chin and shivered, but not from the cold.

From the bony tip of the cowpoke's shoulder, blood had started a slow seep through his threadbare shirt. The blood tickled his skin where the pain was still bearable. No longer standing tall, he seemed to tilt slightly backward, frozen.

Afraid to move, even to take a much needed breath, his eyes bulged, his face became an artist's palette of changing colors, from bright red to what now was a hopeless blue-grey. Still conscious, or so onlookers believed, he slumped against the bar, fighting to stay upright. With the help of the bar, he was motionless except for the ever so slight in and out of his chest. The cowboy's feeble breaths moved him so little that, to the untrained eye, he appeared more a poorly constructed cowboy manikin than a man under arrest. He didn't have many years on him, but was old enough to know it might be best not to move, not even so that he could fall to the floor.

As for the celebrated lawman, he looked business-like and appeared relaxed holding the six-gun tight under the chin of the wobbly young cowboy.

The moment had been magical; Blade Holmes reacted so fast to the situation that time may not have moved. Years from now people would swear, actual clock ticking time, had been stopped. Blade Holmes, already a legend in the West, made the impossible happen, for a moment he'd stopped time. And for a moment one young cowboy likely wished he could go back in time, to a time before he'd handmade the unfortunate circumstance that led to his present calamity.

The once tough-talking cowboy Blade held against the bar now looked even younger than his nineteen or twenty years, more a boy than a man. The beaten cowboy lowered his eyes, careful not to move any other part of his sweat-streaked face. His trembling right hand hung beside an empty holster. Bending forward, but only from the neck, he took in a long slow breath then focused both eyes on a grimy back smudge a few inches in front of the toes of his worn-out boots.

The young cowpoke appeared afraid to look up, afraid if he did it might be for the last time. Betrayed by unsteady knees he could no longer stand. His breathing changed to gasps; the young trail-hand looked like he might be sick. Onlookers, most now standing, backed off a step or two, waited for him to throw up, slump to the floor or both. The bars gambling clientele might have bet on how long it would take for one or the other to happen if there had been time.

Blade Holmes held the big Navy Colt with a steady hand, the butt of the gun pressing hard against the cowboy's breastbone the barrel wedged tight under his peach fuzz chin. The ongoing nervous state of the cowpuncher may have reached the extreme point several seconds back. It should have been about then when the realization had come to him. He'd not drawn his six-gun. There had been no time to touch his holster or gun.

To the young cowboy, everything in the barroom stopped when he went for his gun. However, time must have moved, maybe a fraction of a second passed, but not enough time for him to touch his right hand holstered forty-five. The wannabe gunfighter now looked timid, swallowing over and over, with his chest heaving, he licked his lips and then again, he looked to be only moments away from running or dying.

The tense situation eased and Blade's mouth curled into an uneven smile. He knew nothing more would happen, not today. Blade relaxed his grip, and the young cowboy slumped to his knees then stood back up and grabbed the edge of the bar with both hands. Raindrops of sweat ran down his face, dripped from his chin and speckling the front of his shirt. Blood widened the crimson spot around the newest hole in his soiled shirt. His face brightened and flushed with embarrassment as he stood fighting back fear, tears, acute nervousness, and worst of all, thoughts of dying.

Now an epiphany reached the young would be gun hand. His empty holster could only mean one thing. The gun under his chin, before he fell to the floor, belonged to him, not the sheriff, it was his gun. His mind produced a blurry picture of what must have happened. The thought took his breath away, he gagged, puked down the front of his shirt and on the chair beside him, and felt no better at all.

The shuddering cowboy's mind started to clear, much too late. He realized the man he had challenged to draw, a man he did not recognize, was not just another small cow-town sheriff. The man he challenged was a mythological figure in the American West, the greatest, lawman, gunfighter, tracker and army scout in history. People wrote books about him, a man seemingly everyone but he knew all about.

The cowboy's shaking now became uncontrollable, his knees buckled and he started to go down, again. This time Blade caught him in the middle of a slow-motion collapse, laid the kids six-gun on the bar and grabbed his belt and elbow keeping him upright.

Blade Holmes had shot him, only a shoulder nick to stop him, and then had taken two steps pulled the cowpunchers gun and pinned him to the bar, in how much time? Maybe, but the blink of an eye.

Blade relaxed his hold as the young cowboy started to come around, regaining some of his equilibrium, he took one small shuffling step back away from the bar. Paused, trying to take a deep breath, but instead gulped at the air setting off a coughing fit, hoping all the time his next breath would not be his last. A little braver now, he took a long blind backward step, caught a chair leg with the heel of his boot and toppled over. Hitting the floor with a groaning thud he rolled to his hands and knees, crawled a few feet, grabbed an empty chair and pulled himself to his feet. Looking around he thought for the first second in the past thirty, he might live.

His hat lay on the floor inches from where he stood. Bending straight legged from the waist, all the time his eyes set on Blade, like the quarry watching the hunter. He waited for something to happen and prayed nothing would. Scooping up the trail worn hat he adjusted the feather in the band, straightened the brim, and then placed it on his head as if this might be his last living task.

Moving as fast as he could, without running, he straight-armed the batwing doors and stumbled outside. Taking in as much of the dust-filled fresh air as one breath would allow, he took a long step, hitched up his pants and yanked the battered black hat down to his ears. Stepping down from the boardwalk he stumbled, tried to run, but settled for walking, walking as fast as he could, away from the bar, and out of the life of Sheriff Blade Holmes, forever.

Within a minute of the young cowhand's exit from the bar the patrons started moving again, most through the doors and away from the scene of the thirty-second altercation. Many had expected a shooting or at least a decent brawl, but Blade seemed to have a way of making this small prairie cow town more peaceful, much quieter, since his arrival in town a few weeks back.

The stories preceded Blade, stories about how quick he was with a gun and how good he could be with a knife. The stories seemed to be nothing but tall tales, bigger than life because, until today, no one had seen him in action. No others had tried him, all the rest, and there were a half dozen or so, backed down knowing Blade's reputation. The young cowboy, likely riding hard, minus his gun, and probably still shaking, had been the first to try Blade since he started Sheriffing in the small Kansas cow town.

Sheriff Blade Holmes had not only drawn his gun. In what seemed to be one fluid movement, one moment when time stood still, nicked the young cowpuncher, holstered his Colt, pulled the punchers gun and held it under his chin.

Three minutes after the young cowboy left town the bartender, Blade, and an old timer drinking coffee were the only ones left in the bar. The familiar stench of stale beer, cheap tobacco, and untidy customers hung heavy in the air. But the usual commotion, sights and sounds of the bar had vanished with the customers.

Blade turned, scanned the room and noticed the old man in a rumpled black suit for the first time. Catching Blade's eye, a knowing smile bending his weather-beaten face, he raised his cup in salute. Blade noticed the clerical collar, wondered momentarily why a parson would be in the bar, then nodded and turned back around. Almost as an afterthought Blade turned again, the old man, despite his age, seemed to beam as he sat at the corner table with his head down both hands wrapped around his coffee cup.

Blade Holmes stood tall at the bar, relaxed as if he'd only now awakened from a pleasant afternoon nap. The bartender did not look comfortable, instead he looked like a man in shock, or maybe it was disbelief. He stood nervously patting droplets of sweat from his forehead relieved the fight, or near fight, was over

It started like it always did in small towns along the trail. Confrontations like this were a way of life in the Kansas rail and cow towns Blade frequented for most of the past few years. The cowboy, a young man who might have been on his first trip up the Chisholm Trail, only a few months removed from life with ma and pa. The boy, eager to impress, and maybe prove something about his manhood had drawled. "Draw your Colt if you have the nerve, sheriff."

The young cowboy, who may have fancied himself a gunfighter, had likely never been anywhere before and never heard of Blade Holmes. A cowboy trailing cattle because it was all he could do or wanted to do. It had not been about anything, a young man feeling too brave or feeling too many drinks under his belt and trying to show the sheriff he was the better man. But he was not, not even close.

Blade supposed in another place and in another circumstance the young cowboy's bravado might have backed the law off, but today it could have got him killed. Blade Holmes never backed down, not part of his nature.

The young cowhand committed a simple mistake, a young man's mistake, and Blade recognized it for what it was. When possible, Blade liked to end things in a hurry without serious harm to anyone. The one-sided duel following the deputy sheriff being called out may have been an embarrassment to the cowhand, but it left him alive and in reasonable health. In a few years, he might make up an amusing little story about the day he met Blade Holmes. However, for now, and in the near future, he could always blame it on too much to drink, go back to the herd and forget about it.

Blade laid his Kansas-dusty hat on the bar, changed his mind, took it back and sat it on the stool beside him, crown up. He reached both arms behind his back and stretched, then stepped his own version of a worn out boot up on the wooden bar-rail and asked for a cup of coffee.

The bartender squinted at Blade forced a wry smile, took the grimy dish towel from his shoulder and patted beads of sweat from his forehead, again. Turning to face the pot belly stove behind the bar he reached an unsteady hand for the ancient looking coffee pot. His senses returned quick enough, and he pulled his hand back wrapping it in his sweat-dampened towel before taking the pot off the stove. Fumbling a chipped gray cup from under the bar he spilled a cup of coffee into it. A small stream of the thick coffee missed the cup, pooled on the bar, crept across and dripped to the floor. The bar-keep watched the black liquid move along the bar top then pushed the steaming cup through it toward Blade. He forced his second smile in the past half-minute and stared at the sheriff, now with a renewed respect and more than a bit of awe.

"Dang sheriff, you sure know how to clear a room, gonna have to quit yer scarin' my customers away, that's the first time since you got hired you emptied this place, the other times you just looked at em and trouble took off."

Blade sipped at his coffee like a man without a care in the world. The bartender stepped back blotted his forehead and turned pretending to rearrange the back bar.

"Didn't mean to, out of the office making my afternoon rounds, don't know what it is about this star, but it sure seems to bring out the worst in those punchers," Blade said, tugging his shirt loose trying to use the extra fold in a weak attempt to polish his badge.

"Especially the young guys," he continued, "think they need to call me out, try to scare me off." He set his cup down, pinched his lips together and shook his head.

Blade blew across the cup, took a second small sip, frowned from the heat, sat the cup back down on the bar and gazed into it as if it were a crystal ball. Lost in thought, Blade continued to stare into the cup, looking like he was waiting for an answer from the dark liquid. But his thoughts had nothing to do with the now completed altercation or with the cup of scorched coffee he moved from right to left hand. His mind wandered much farther away than the cup sitting on the worn bar top or of the nameless cowboy riding back to the herd. His thoughts were of other places and other times, better times, things he should have said or done.

He fought the melancholy.

The bartender faked a smile, his back still to Blade, took the damp towel away from his face and patted his chest as if fighting off an impending heart attack. For a moment, he looked a bit like he'd been the one Blade had held a gun on.

He turned, adjusted the tall stool behind the bar and took a seat across from Blade. "Don't worry about it, you might a saved me a peck a trouble, scares me when I have to drag the double barrel out and run Cowboys out of here. Since you been here, I haven't needed to do it, no, not a single time. When it used to happen I would worry, stay up all night sometimes, thinking they'd come back after me, plus it tain't no good for business, no good a-tull. I'm glad it's my side you're working on.

How'd you do it, take away the kids Colt so fast and move so quick, makes me cat nervous and I'm only thinkin' about it?"

"Don't know, guess I always could," Blade answered, taking a third sip of coffee and frowning.

"I heard stories about you being fast, but you drew your gun and you drew that cowboy's gun, and he didn't have time to move. Not sure he even took a breath or had time to blink, don't think I wanna see you draw against someone in earnest, glad you're on my side. Still don't see how you did it, how anyone could move so fast – be so quick. Heard tell you was faster than the mornin' light itself now seems like weren't no exaggeration at all. Might not of even told the real story, I've seen the rays of the morning sun coming down a might slower than your gun, no sir, no exaggeration at all."

The bartender patted at his chest again, made a mental note that he was still alive and went back to mopping his forehead, then as an afterthought, ran the grimy towel over the coffee spill and tossed it toward the storeroom door. Leaning back on the stool he took a new towel from the back bar and alternated patting his face and keeping his heart beating with the marginally cleaner towel. Tiring to relax he locked his eyes in a stare, watching Blade drink his coffee, black, no sugar, and no cream, black.

Blade took a last sip from his coffee cup, stepped his boot down off the bar rail, dropped a nickel on the bar for the coffee, tipped his hat to the bartender, turned and walked toward the door. Pushing open the batwings he held them open for the stooped elderly man dressed in preacher's garb. Before letting the doors swing shut Blade stopped, looked back and said to the bartender, "Practice, used to practice some back in my younger days." Blade turned to say something to the old man, but the rumpled preacher was gone.

The bartender stood wiping at a few imaginary spots from the bar top waved a fistful of towel toward Blade shook his head and slapped the towel over his shoulder not knowing this would be the last he would ever see of Sheriff Blade Holmes.

Early the next morning, without a word to anyone, Blade unpinned his star, wiped it on his shirt, laid it on top of his letter of resignation and placed it on his sheriff's office desk. He walked the two blocks to the livery stable, saddled his horse and rode north.

Three weeks later, wearing the best suit of clothes he owned, Blade sat with his back to the wall playing stud poker on the third floor of the Cheyenne Club on Seventeenth Street in downtown Cheyenne, Wyoming Territory.

Chapter 2

On this day, Blade Holmes rode in near silence hearing only the faraway cry of the hawk, the halting music of an occasional Meadowlark and the delicate whistle of the breeze in the canyon. Looking at nothing but the trail ahead and thinking about nothing but his past.

Blade Holmes was renowned throughout the West; he didn't always like the notoriety, but most days he knew he couldn't do a thing about it. He was liked and respected up and down the western trails and throughout the rough and tumble cow towns from Texas to Montana. A gifted man of 26, a man others talked of when he was not around and whispered about when he was. Conversations stopped when he stepped into a room. Heads turned when he walked the sidewalks of Kansas City or rested on a boardwalk bench in downtown Cheyenne or any of dozens of other western cities and towns.

Blade was a shining knight on horseback riding the dusty streets of a new city. People everywhere knew who he was, and some lied, claiming him as an old friend while quietly wishing they actually did know him. An inch over six feet tall and a nudge under 200 pounds of lean muscle, he was taller than most and stronger than just about anyone a man might meet in a lifetime. Respected by everyone he met, even men he'd sent to jail held a grudging admiration for a man of his talent and skill.

Lightning quick with a gun, unbelievable with fists or a knife and the best horseman and best rifle shot of his generation, folks thought he had it all, and he did. However, Blade Holmes was never sure, not of his skills but his life. Today he rode, unsure of many things.

When left alone Blade, at times, became brooding and unsure, thinking more about imagined faults than his considerable gifts and today seemed to be a brooding day. He thought about many things and worried about most of them, thinking more than anything else about bad things crowding and complicating his life. Blade never liked to stay anywhere too long and often told people he liked to leave before he wore out his welcome. Deep inside Blade knew that was not it, not really, he just couldn't make a commitment to do anything or stay anywhere for long. He didn't know why. Blade only knew he couldn't do it. He was a drifter, but he didn't want to be. Sometimes he felt like faults, and bad habits were what kept him moving.

Blade liked to play cards when he felt the melancholy come on, stud-poker, five-card when he could find it, but he would play three-card if it were the only game in town. Loved to play, but in recent months he started to see the foolishness in playing. Playing poker is only good if you win, and Blade did not win much, matter of fact, he could not recall the last time he won a significant amount in a game. He liked to play but wasn't much of a player, cards were possibly the only thing he was not good at, and he was just now starting to understand. Poker and staying, he wasn't good at either. He liked to keep moving, especially when the melancholy was with him, and then he felt best with strangers or by himself.

On days like this Blade's thoughts snarled with too many things, too many bad things. Thoughts, where he conjured up some, make believe inner fault or his mind placed him in the middle of something he could not get out. Couldn't get out of because of the made-up defect. When the gloomy thoughts came, they overtook him like a quick moving spring storm takes over the prairie.

Blade did not care for the gloomy feelings but when he was alone and taking it easy, the melancholy sometimes rode along. The glum was generally short-lived, the spells seemed to be getting better with age, but on his worst days the misery sometimes took him from the day. Today he felt somewhere in between his usual good days and a bad one. Riding and thinking, and today he started to like it, liked being alone, and he began to feel better as he covered the miles, everything seemed to be getting right in his mind.

Blade might have been like many men his age, lost in life some days and sure of everything on others. His mood improved as he sat in the saddle with the warmth of the sun striking his face. This day, riding easy, he might look like any other lonesome cowboy or out of work saddle bum, riding north across the Wyoming sagebrush plains. Maybe commitments didn't matter, but good or bad, he knew they did. Blade Holmes knew he would never be just another cowboy. He was bigger than life, a dime novel hero to people across America, especially here in the west. He was not sure he wanted to be anyone special; sometimes he liked being, just another cowboy, another cowboy riding the big lonesome. Riding without a care enjoying a storybook spring day.

An hour later Blade stopped on a small rise and twisted back and forth in the saddle. His smile faded, and his face contorted in pain when a new throbbing soreness moved through his lower back causing him to blow out an aching breath and gasp for new fresher air. He twisted again and relaxed in the saddle, looked down the back trail shielding his eyes. Blade squinted into the heat of the lowering sun, checking for someone, anyone, following. He flipped open a saddlebag with his left hand and pulled out a worn pair of field glasses. Holding the glasses out at near arm's length he looked at them for a moment before putting them to his eyes. Pulling them down he scratched his thumb against the grey-green patina revealing an old U.S. Army mark, he dabbed at the outer lenses with his neckerchief, held them out for inspection and decided they pass muster.

Peering through the binoculars tiny eye sights, he took a lingering more careful look down his back trail, scanning the ridges on both sides of the rock-strewn gravel valley he had ridden a few minutes earlier. Three minutes later, after seeing nothing of consequence, Blade blew out another sigh, this time of relief, then bent low over his saddle horn, his aching back reminded him it was time to stop for the day. Then he saw it.

A quick flash, a glint of sunshine in the rocks, a miniature bolt of lightning jumping from the sandstone, maybe a flash of mica or broken glass, but it looked too large, much too large. Blade concentrated the glasses on the area and searched again. There must be something, but he could not find it. Maybe he was overreacting, but he didn't think so. Blade decided he needed to be even more careful tonight and for the next few days.

No one was following, no man or horse he could see anyway. Blade twisted in the saddle one last time, in a now hopeless effort to ease the dull and constant pain in his back. A pain born of too many hours in the saddle over ground better suited to Buffalo and coyotes than to a man on horseback. The last few nights of sleeping on the ground or not enough nights in a bed the past few days may have also been part of the reason for the most recent pains. The meaning of this was understandable. The pain was his doing and maybe a needless doing. No one ever suspected Blade of being soft, but spending most of the past three years in town, sleeping in beds, eating in cafes and spending his day's playing cards or wearing a badge might have softened him up some.

A few years ago when night came, the ground and the sky were the only bed and the only roof he needed. The prairies and mountainsides he slept on felt better than the best hotel feather-bed and the sky over his head, well the sky was still the best bedroom ceiling he could think of.

Blade pulled out the front of his dirty, once-white, shirt and used the corner to wipe the field glass eyepieces. He held them out in front of his eyes a few inches and took a look, then wished he hadn't. He reached deep into the corner of the saddlebag and pulled out a strip of red flannel and took his time wrapping it around the field glasses before sliding them back into place. Turning back hard against the saddle's cantle Blade took one last look back. Satisfied, pushed his heel into his horse's flank, rode a few yards reined hard left and rode up a crumbling shale and sagebrush bank.

The bank rose some thirty to forty feet above the wash and would be a steep climb for most men on horseback and impossible for many. However, Blade Holmes, late of Kansas City and several unnamed cow towns, was an extraordinary man on a special horse, and in a quick moment they were on the ridge. When Blade reached the top, he slowed Medicine, his big Appaloosa stallion, to a walk, and looked around for a place to camp, and to think. Then he took yet another look back. No one followed.

Blade was a man alone, he knew it and accepted it, but he didn't like it, not right now. At the moment with the sun wearing out for the day Blade thought he would prefer being a man of action, of people and cities, bright lights and shiny new decks of playing cards. Then his mind formed a picture of a man sitting in a rickety chair in a dusty room surrounded by walls cluttered with yellowing wanted posters and wearing a tin star engraved Sheriff or Marshal. He was a complicated man, someone who'd done much and been many things the past ten years. Right now, he was none of those things. Now he rode a lonely trail, a man, and his horse, riding, looking back, worrying, aching and part of the time brooding.

Blade felt the hair on the back of his neck bristle; even daydreaming didn't seem to get his heart to slow down a few beats. And the nagging feeling of being followed would not go away. Blade didn't much like the tension he felt, and it had been eating at him for the past day and a half. Just maybe there might be someone behind him, following, for what purpose, he did not know. Blade tried to sort out what he thought and how he felt, alone, but maybe he wasn't all alone after all. He thought about circling back then decided to wait until morning to make up his mind. A good night's sleep would do wonders for his aching body and perhaps his mind.

Two days ago in Cheyenne Blade had learned a valuable lesson. Never rent a room expecting to pay for it playing five-card stud. He'd never been real lucky when it came to cards, the problem that plagued him was sometimes he felt like he had it all figured out, and Cheyenne had been one of those times. The Cheyenne Club may have been a bit much for his meager cash supply, but he won some money the first two days and enjoyed playing with the wealthy Wyoming cattle barons.

His luck changed after those first few nights at the club. Maybe they'd played him like some cheap harmonica, a greenhorn sucker, but he didn't think so. No, he just lost his streak and then lost his money. The valuable lesson he learned, one he'd been taught before, he had learned some variation of this same lesson from Kansas City to Dallas and now north to Cheyenne. Yea, what a lesson Blade thought, I can't make a commitment to stay anywhere, that's one lesson, and I can't play poker, a second lesson. Before riding out of Cheyenne he put most of what little money he had left on his boarding house bed, to pay his bill, then left at three in the morning with four bits and a dime in his pocket.

Now he rode north, north for Fort Laramie, again. No commitments and sometimes feeling sorry for himself that's who he was right now. Couldn't even make a commitment to stay in the same town or stick with a job for more than a few months, sometimes a few weeks. All it took to get Blade out of town this time was a third straight evening watching his supply of cash growing more meager with each hand he played, followed by two sleepless hours on a boarding house bed.

No money, no prospects for a job, and no idea why he rode toward Fort Laramie, maybe to enlist this time. He really didn't think anyone followed him, not anymore. The sixty cents in his pocket didn't seem to make him much of a target for robbery. If someone was following him, following to rob him, they must be in sorry shape, he thought, or they didn't know he was thinking about signing on for a twenty-five dollar a month Calvary Scout job. These thoughts brought a smile to Blade's sullen face and for at least a brief moment made him feel better.

The feeling of being followed came back again, and it left him on edge, something felt wrong, if he had to explain it he couldn't, but it was there, hanging over him like early morning fog. Blade felt the heat rising on his face and his pulse quickened. He'd had feelings like this before, and been right about them, right every time. But this time he tried to chalk it up to a guilty conscious for leaving, leaving Cheyenne and leaving Kansas City, and the little town in between, and all the other short time stops. He tried to let it go. But he couldn't.

Depending on how he looked at it or felt at the time, his life seemed to have lasted either a long time or a very short time. It had been either worthwhile, or a waste. Blade hated it when he started analyzing his life, but over the last forty-eight hours he could not help it. For two days in Cheyenne, he felt relaxed and wise beyond his twenty-six years and then it turned. Now over the last two days, maybe for the first time, he realized what a mess he'd made of his recent life. Moving from one job to another or one town to the next with a few bad poker experiences and a few hard-working lawman days along the way didn't seem like much of a life. At each stop he hoped no one would recognize him from some other out of the way place, but they always did. After all he was Blade Holmes, people wrote stories about him, but most days he didn't feel like the dime novel Blade Holmes. Running from every commitment he ever made as soon as he got too involved. Not in the sense of leaving before the job was finished, but leaving as soon as he felt like he should stay.

His mom might have been right. He'd been born with wanderlust. Always needing to see what was over the next hill or around the next bend in the river. However, he knew there were other reasons and wanderlust was not the only thing keeping him moving. He was afraid. Not of outlaws he followed and arrested, or troubles he might face, no it was commitment he was scared of, anything lasting seemed to make him run away. The trouble he could take care of, if someone followed him today, he would handle that too. If he had to stay too long or settle down too much, he couldn't do it, couldn't do it no matter how bad he sometimes wanted to. When Blade felt down or felt like he was running away, he worried what others thought of him, and it bothered him. He was a powerful man with dark piercing eyes, creating a striking contrast to his shock of wheat straw blonde hair. He rode a great horse, and now wore the only clothes he owned, a pair of black wool pants, a white silk shirt with a ruffle down the button line, and what was once a beautiful buckskin jacket, made for him by Emma's Haberdashery in Kansas City, Kansas. Blade's once shiny dark brown boots were dull and scuffed, the soles so thin his feet felt like they were in moccasins instead of boots. Worn through again, about wore out Blade thought, sounds like how I feel right now, about wore out.

Blade stopped and swung down from his big Appaloosa, stepped back and took a look at the near seventeen hand black stallion, still the best-looking horse he had ever seen. Medicine stood a full three hands more than the average for his breed, and his perfect blanket markings and striped hoofs were a striking contrast to the rest of his shining midnight black body. Blade might not be sure what others thought of him, but he knew what they thought of Medicine. People recognized a great horse when they saw one. More than once Blade had watched people turn a half circle to watch as he rode past. Medicine, tall with a broad chest the dappled rump and four matching white stockings shimmered in the sunshine like a night sky full of stars. Moreover, the horse was proud, so proud he seemed to prance more than walk, always with his head up and brightness in his eyes that seemed to confirm the intelligence of the great animal.

Today Blade wished he had a treat for Medicine, but he didn't. He looped the reins over a scrub juniper then stretched his arms above his head and groaned. He pulled off his jacket and shook it hard, squinted through the dust and shook it again, it still did not look anywhere close to the beautiful off-white color it had been a few weeks ago. After a third and last snapping shake he watched a small cloud of dust float from the jacket and disappear tumbling sideways in the high plains breeze.

Yes, this was Wyoming, where the ground cracked from drought and dull red dust escaping his jacket was nothing like the black soil back where he grew up in Ohio. The cold breeze reminded Blade it was still early spring, and anything could happen this time of the year.

Rain, snow, blizzard, wind storms, heat, anything could happen.

Maybe it was the weather making Blade feel on edge. He tugged the reigns free of the juniper and started walking, leading Medicine along the ridge, careful not to skyline either of them. He liked the feeling of the blood, once again, circulating through his legs as he walked along the flat gravel strewn hilltop. After twenty minutes of walking, and feeling some better for it, the two went up a gentle rise where Blade remounted and trotted Medicine along the high sage prairie. After five minutes, they slowed to a walk allowing plenty of time for daydreaming and Blade thought back to his many trips to Emma's Haberdashery and his recent six-month stay in Kansas City.

His relationship with Emma was complicated, and Blade still wondered if he did the right thing when he left in the middle of the night. It's possible all the complications were mine, Blade thought, seems like sneaking out in the middle of the night or leaving when it was least expected were the things he seemed to be getting best at doing the past few years. Being tied down to a steady job, living in a tidy city home, and sitting on the porch in late afternoon sipping lemonade, talking, and watching buggies pass by might have been more than Blade thought he could take, and he just left. No words, no goodbyes, no tears, no nothings, Blade rode off trying to forget Emma and everything else in Kansas City. But he had not forgotten, and he knew he would never forget because he couldn't. Blade would go back someday, but not yet, not today, but someday. He hoped she understood, and deep inside; he hoped she waited.

All Blade dreamed about as a kid growing up was to live out west and be a cowboy, but as a grown man things kept getting in the way of the simple life of a cowboy he'd dreamt of. Things like wandering, wearing a badge, a card game here and there and always riding off when things got too comfortable. Riding along Blade wondered if owning a horse, he felt was smarter than him, was a good idea. Seemed like Medicine could tell when he had it good and knew when he wanted to stay or go.

A working cowboy's life is an excellent life; Blade thought, riding the high lonesome, looking out for cows and minding his own business. But Blade had never lived the cowboy life, never looked after cows all day long. He had lived the life on the high lonesome, for a while, a few years ago. But now town life suited Blade better, he liked the pace and the action of the city life and felt like it was where he belonged. Maybe childhood dreams were just dreams.

He had been an excellent lawman in several cities; some newspapers called him great. Stories of arrests he made were so popular they were reprinted and read throughout America and even in Europe. An old gentleman in Cheyenne told him; a Mr. Beadle wrote a book about him and lots of people were buying it. Blade was self-conscious about that thought and even with no one around blushed, shook his head and looked around. A book about him, he guessed it would have to be a pretty short book. And not too long ago he'd been told he was a first-rate handyman. Blade smiled as he thought about that complement, bet it would never make newspaper headlines or a book. He rode down a wash looking for a place to spend the night.

It wasn't the thinking about being a good handyman that brought Blade out of his gloomy mood; it was who told him he was first rate at it. When Emma mentioned it to him, he smiled and laughed it off, but now the thought relaxed him and made him feel contented. He started to enjoy the day as he daydreamed his way north. After an hour of deep thought, he concluded that there were two things he was good at, enforcing the law, and at least Emma thought he made a good handyman. And today, for some reason, those two things seemed important to him.

As for poker and commitments, those were the two things he was worst at, atrocious. The poker table, it would have to be left behind, someday. Poker was something he was good at sometimes and winning sometimes was not enough in poker. Good poker players make their living from sometimes good players. Then Blade smiled big, heck he was never much of a poker player, occasionally lucky, maybe, but never much of a player.

A few weeks ago Blade had been a big deal, popular, well-known and happy in Kansas City. He had friends, he'd become prominent in the community with money to spend, and well, he had it all, and he left, he left it all.

Loneliness set in as soon as he left Emma and Kansas City. Six weeks working as a deputy sheriff in a small trail town west and north of Kansas City was six weeks of wanting to go back to Emma and the six weeks of not being able to go back sent him north again. He ended up in Cheyenne and then left again and now, here – all alone. Wondering about life and wondering why?

Three-quarters of an hour passed as Blade rode letting his mind wander away from the most recent months and back to the past few years of his life. He circled back to a secluded area that looked like a perfect campsite. He'd passed the area ten minutes earlier, then made a careful circle and eased Medicine down near a small stand of aspen picketing him fifty feet away near a stand of scrub cottonwood. A single, larger cottonwood stood guarding an almost dry streambed dappled with pockets of water left behind as the days of spring lengthened and warmed. The little bit of melting snow and ice was starting to renew the season of the stream. It was dry for so early in the year in the high country, more so than any year Blade could remember.

This year an early spring started the melt, but it seemed cool and the uneventful and dry winter worried Blade worried he could get caught by an overdue northerner. One of those spring storms that were never anticipated yet should have been. Seemed like this kind of weather often brought on the unexpected, he looked west and could see snow on the peaks but sometimes snow never melted, not that high. However, worries about the weather passed, Blade knew bad weather might slow him down but would not be any real hindrance. He had lived, for a time, in the high country and knew what could happen this time of the year.

Blade Holmes was a man of more than considerable skills, a man who had been put in positions where he survived because he had to. The time he'd spent up here prepared him for anything that Mother Nature might throw at him, he knew what could be in store for someone alone on the high plains or in the high country. He wasn't worried, not at all, not about the weather.

Blade took some time before filling his canteen from one of the little pockets of water, a puddle that would have a hard time being recognized as part of a creek. But it was drinkable. The intermittent stream, meandering and nameless, might be swollen and formidable in a few weeks when the first of the big thaws melted the snowpack up high, but today it was a puddle, clear and sweet. Blade took another look at the snowcaps to the west and shook his head, cold as it had been none of it would melt until July at the earliest. But for now this looked like a perfect campsite, food, water and shelter for his horse and at least water and shelter for him, what more could he ask for? "I'm glad we didn't wait till the middle of June to have to cross this stream," Blade said to Medicine as he started to brush the Appaloosa.

Blade patted the big horse on his nose, wishing he had something sweet for him, all the time talking in a soft voice, one so soft it was little more than a whisper, talking to the big horse like he might be a real person and an old friend. Blade took his time rubbing down and brushing the big stallion then spent another ten minutes picking out his hooves. Once he was satisfied Blade stretched, walked over and sat down.

Medicine walked an ever-widening circle, munched what green he could find. New green shoots punching their way to sunlight as soon as the frost allowed sprinkled the area, and the big stallion seemed satisfied with the fare. Blade readied the camp, taking his time picking up firewood and clearing a place to sleep. All of this to fight off a creeping feeling of loneliness, it didn't work. He tossed another branch on the growing pile then kicked at the top of a rock with the heel of his boot. He was frustrated and discouraged. Camping alone in the mountains didn't make him feel better.

Then the feeling came to him again, like a chill on a summer night, just as the sun started to set. The air had not changed, but Blade felt cold and nervous. He felt his heart picking up the pace as he looked over the area again before walking back over to where Medicine was grazing. He pulled off the braided picket rope and looped his worn saddle rope over Medicine so the big stallion would have more room to graze on scattered green shoots and so he could reach more of the tender scrub cottonwood leaves.

Blade reached in his jacket for his pocket watch, thought he might wind it and let the ticks put him to sleep later. No watch, but he found the sixty cents, and then remembered he lost the watch in a game. He looked at the sun, now in the closing stages of setting, but he didn't need to, he knew the time, around six o'clock in the afternoon. Blade always knew what time it was, but didn't know why, just always knew. The watch, the only one he had ever owned, he'd bought on impulse, and more often than not he let it run down, letting it go for days without winding. At the time of purchase Blade thought it made him look more like a gentleman of the city, wiser, but out here, when it mattered most, he knew what time it was, and most of all, out here, he knew it didn't matter.

Deciding he still had time to build a fire, not a fire showing his location when full darkness came, but a small warming fire. Blade walked into the aspen and broke off another armload of dead sticks then picked up a handful of pinecones near a pair of ancient pines. One more foraging trip and he had enough fuel to last for the time he needed. It would be a small fire with as little smoke as possible, and a fire he would put out long before full dark arrived. He might be worrying too much, being too careful, after all no one was following him, but he still was not sure.

Blade wasn't certain why he needed the fire. It had been hours ago when he drank the last of his coffee and ate his last meal. That is if anyone would call a stale biscuit and a piece of jerked meat a meal. And that had been about twenty-four hours ago. He was hungry, but at least Medicine seemed to be enjoying the break from the trail as he worked in an ever-increasing circle near the Cottonwood eating everything green in sight. Blade unhooked the coffee pot from his saddlebag, filled it from one of the clear mountain puddles and put it over the fire to heat. Maybe warm water would help fill his growling stomach, but it did nothing for his disposition.

Blade liked to tell people he didn't know a lot about most things. He felt that way sometimes, but most of the time when he said he didn't know a lot, it was to cover up, he used it as a ploy to get out of the conversation, or as a poker playing excuse for losing. Today he knew something for the first time, he could not keep running away from commitments forever, and he knew sometime and somewhere he needed to settle in and get his life in order. Maybe the army was the answer he needed.

On his worst days Blade lamented about being found dead by someone watching buzzards circle, finding his body, eyes pecked out and his alkali white body half-eaten by coyotes. A victim of gunshots or stab wounds the result of someone robbing him for his poker winnings; Blade laughed at himself, no winnings, ever. No, more likely killed because of someone he'd arrested, a man who felt crossed by law. Or worse yet he might fall victim to a stray gunshot in some smoky nowhere bar, sitting at a table with all the money in front of someone else and an extra card or two up the sleeve of one of his playing partners. "When you call someone out for cheating there's decent chance they are not going to fight fair either," Blade said to the sky and trees as he sipped the hot water.

Blade had seen enough bad things happen and had been told enough stories about shots in the back or under the table ambushes to know cheaters cheat and gambling is a dangerous way to pass the time of day, let alone making it a full-time profession. Then again he also knew arresting and putting people in jail may not be the safest way to make a living either. Make a living, Blade started to wonder if running away to Fort Laramie and drinking hot water for supper constituted any part of living. He never liked being alone and never thought about danger, dying or loneliness except when he found himself in the kind of predicament he was in right now, broke, hungry, tired, hurting and alone.

Blade relaxed in the deepening shadows away from the dying embers of the small fire with night cascading down on his camp. A saddle made a fair pillow and his two green wool blankets still made a passable prairie bed. He looked up at the early night sky. The moon was full, but the sky was dim without stars, cloudy tonight, looked like possible rain by morning. Blade walked over to check on Medicine one more time. Maybe this was not too bad a way to live after all. The eerie call of a nighthawk interrupted his lonesome thoughts and the breeze rustling through the trees sang a night song as Blade turned a slow circle checking everything, one last time.

Kneeling on the ground Blade spread his rain slicker over a pile of pine needles and leaves he'd arranged for a makeshift bed. Covering the slicker with one of his two worn blankets he felt relative comfort on the ground against the stand of scrub aspen. Bending forward he groaned, pulled off his boots then turned and lay back pulling the better of his two green wool blankets up to his chest. With his head comfortable on the saddle he plucked a long stem of brown grass, stuck it in his mouth and daydreamed back to another life and another person. Perhaps it was another lifetime, the lifetime of a child growing up in the rolling hill country of central Ohio. "It's a place where a man can put down roots," Pa said, more times than Blade cared to remember.

Chapter 3

"Matthew, Matthew, it's time to get up. Hurry up if you want breakfast," Virginia Holmes called up the stairs in her soft voice sounding more like she was asking than ordering.

Then she added a little louder, "school starts today."

"Matthew your breakfast is going to get cold." Blade took the stairs three at a time, and his mother tried to frown at him as if she was irritated when he slid into a chair at the breakfast table. Grabbing up a knife and fork Blade devoured the hotcakes and side pork washing it all down with a tall glass of milk.

Blade smiled remembered back to his life on the farm ten years ago; it seemed longer. He tossed the stem of grass he was chewing and locked his hands under his head. He never wanted to be a farmer and he wasn't sure he would ever feel the need for the roots his pa needed. When he turned sixteen, his father gave him the 45-70 Sharps he still carried, a few days later he said his goodbyes and left. Now the only part of the farm he needed were the memories and two smooth rocks from the creek his mother gave him the night before he left. "Mathew, carry these with you, part of this place, and remember your home will always be here, don't forget."

Blade continued to let his thoughts ramble through his mind, drawing a picture of his mother. Small and wiry, a pleasant lady in a flowered dress with her red hair tied back and the smile that never seemed to leave, like it was a part of her she could not, or would not, change. And he could see his father, a tall, lean, hard man with dark, penetrating eyes, and a man who worked too hard and expected the same from everyone around him, especially Blade.

Blade liked working with his dad and learned much from him, but he didn't want to be like him. No, farming was not part of his makeup, even if his father, grandfather, and great-grandfather farmed in the same Ohio creek valley. "I was born to be a farmer, born to it," he told Blade dozens of times.

Possibly Blade was born to see around the next bend in the river or on the other side of the mountain. He seemed to be born to wander, but he wasn't sure why. Blade never felt the relationship with the land and crops his father did. The log home where he grew up looked similar to many others in that Ohio farming valley. The front faced east and the morning sun warmed the front kitchen and his bedroom above it.

Kicking part of the wool blanket from his legs Blade closed his eyes to see more clearly the days from his past. His mouth curled into a kids smile dreaming of a house looking out on a clear meandering stream and the fields beyond. Bright peeled log walls, cedar shingles and windows framed in white paint. In his mind, it looked more like a painting than a real place.

A cast Iron cook stove, fired with corncobs from last year's harvest blazed in the center of the kitchen and a basket of apples leaned on the wall near the kitchen door. The house was always spotless, and Blade remembered more than once getting in trouble for tracking mud or blood from his latest hike or hunt into their rather spacious log cabin. None of Blades friends had a room of their own like he did, and most of them thought of him as a rich kid and just a little lucky to live in a house with five rooms. A house like most of his friends lived in but bigger. And the thing Blade liked best about the house was his bedroom with the morning sun and the smell of his mom's baking bread to wake him up and put him to sleep every day.

Those were great days, an excellent place to grow up. His parents were terrific parents, parents who cared about him. And he had books, along with school, hunting, fishing and friends and oh yes, one enemy, Roy Tibbs. Blade chuckled, even thinking back about Tibbs, a kid Blade never got along with. Today, on reflection, it was just kid stuff, stuff he was sure Tibbs had long since forgotten. He's probably married with a farm and a family by now, Blade thought. "And here I am sleeping in some trees a thousand miles away thinking about him." Blade smiled, then laughed out loud and thought he might stop by to see Roy Tibbs someday when he went home for a visit.

Darkness settled in, the Wyoming skies cleared, and the moon lit the sky illuminating the hillside where a drowsy Blade now readjusted his head on his saddle. He watched through sleepy eyes as each new star appeared, disappeared again and then came out of nowhere to stay lit, the sky becoming a picture of twinkling candles in his darkened outdoor room. It looked to Blade like there were a million stars in the sky as he slipped into a light sleep with thoughts of life as a boy growing up on that Ohio farm.

Chapter 4

A slight sound, something cracking or something tripping woke Blade up as sudden as if it were a clap of thunder. A twig snapping, maybe a toe catching a rock, not much of a noise, but a noise that didn't fit - not here, not now, animals did not trip in the dark. Without a sound, Blade was on his feet backing into the deep shadows of the Aspen surveying the dark area in front of him melting his body into the trunk of a tree. His eyes darted from side to side searching for the source of the noise. Then he slowed, took a deep breath and searched a few feet at a time into his line of vision. Any movement at all, even in the dark, Blade was able in to see or sense. Blending in with the grove of trees Blade could see nothing. But he was sure, sure something or someone was out there, merging with the darkness.

Blade felt the dampness and realized why it was now near total darkness, the night skies had clouded over since he lay down for the night with moonlight and stars. A light mist hung in the still night air. Blade squinted into the darkness where he thought the unwelcome sound had come from. He had the eyes of a sharpshooter but even blinking and refocusing he could not find the source of the sound. Blade's legendary eyesight was part of what made him one of the most celebrated men in the West, that and the eyes themselves, piercing and cold to all but his closest friends. His natural look could be menacing enough when he needed it to be. He backed down enemies and could since his youngest days, but tonight no matter how hard he stared into the darkness, even his great eyes could not find anything out of place. Nothing seemed out of the ordinary, everything was as it had been when Blade fell asleep a few hours ago. Other than being a bit darker now and a few hours later, nothing had changed. It was the quiet bothering him now, too quiet for Blade's taste. Quiet like the absence of sound after a battle, and that worried Blade.

He relaxed a little but did not re-sheath the knife he had pulled from the back of his shirt when he stepped two steps deeper into the trees to wait out, maybe nothing, for a few more minutes. Medicine, his big stallion, grazed nearby, and all seemed fine, or almost. Maybe the tension he felt this afternoon finally caught up and awakened him or maybe he had been dreaming. But Blade knew better, someone had been behind him for at least the past two days, and he had heard something. A meaningless noise from a forging animal or a bird landing or leaving were possibilities, but he knew what clumsy sounded like in the dark, someone was out there. Blade tried to relax a little, sitting down a few feet from his bed but still back in the deepest shadows of the pitch black night. He even exaggerated an unconcerned look for anyone in case they could see him, which they could not. Blade slid his knife away and carefully lifted his Colt with his left hand, clicked the hammer back and waited, leaning against one of the smaller trees and waited. He knew it wouldn't be long.

Blade preferred knives to guns since he was a youth in Ohio, even though he packed a Colt on his left hip since he'd left home. Blade wore the gun with the butt pointed out so he could cross draw with his right hand if needed. He rolled his thumb over the hammer of the Army Colt one last time and loosed the hammer string from the 45.

He was fast with the Colt, lightning fast. His pa taught him how to use the gun and then told his wife. "Maybe I shouldn't have taught him, he's faster than a scared rabbit, shoots straighter than the road to Hell, a road he will be riding if he ever uses his gun in anger." However, he was quick to add, "But he never will, not our boy."

Growing up he was so talented with the gun that he frightened people with his skill, even his friends, who should not have been afraid. People shuttered when they saw him draw and shoot coins out of the air with the Colt when he was thirteen. Only his closest friends saw him practicing shooting coins flipped in the air holding the gun upside down and fanning it with the back of his hand and hitting every coin. Blade also carried a 45-70 Sharps, old but true, only two men had seen him shoot it, his father who gave it to him and an old mountain man he spent more than half a year with seven years ago in the mountain wilderness near Laramie Peak.

With a knife or a gun Blade Holmes just might be the best, the strongest, toughest man in the entire American West. As good as he was with a gun he still preferred the knife. His pa started calling him Blade after he gashed open his thumb sharpening his first knife when he was seven years old. Funny he thought, from that day on everyone except Ma and his schoolmate and grammar school enemy Roy Tibbs called him Blade, his mother, preferred his Christian name, Matthew, possibility because she named him, and never called him anything else.

Roy Tibbs was another matter; he never liked Blade. Tibbs saw everything they did in school as competition, competition Blade always won. Blade could run faster, skip rocks farther and jump wider streams than Tibbs. Blade even won the fifth-grade spelling bee with Tibbs finishing third. As they got older Tibbs often shot in local contests against Blade, but he never won, at best he proved to be a fair shot with a pistol and not bad with a rifle. He blamed Blade for his losses, but his marksmanship suffered even when Blade was not around. Tibbs often avoided Blade shooting in contests in the next county, but still never won, not once. Blade was friends with everyone else growing up and to all of them he was just Blade. Tibbs thought it brought Blade down some if he called him Mathew, which he did every time they spoke, but Blade never minded. Today only Emma called him Mathew and he liked it.

Blade spent most all of his non-working and non-schooling time, from age seven to age eleven throwing knives then his father started him shooting guns. From age, eleven on Blade practiced with both, for hours if allowed, every day. He seldom spent time outside without a knife flying at something. Later Blade started making his knives; the two he carried now were special with perfect balance and handles made of Ohio whitetail deer antler. The blades were hand forged by a family friend in his blacksmith shop. Hand forged from a chunk of meteorite like the one Jim Bowie once carried and Blake read about in one of his favorite dime novels, *The Knife Fight at the Mexican Sandbar.*

Blade spent weeks grinding and honing the knives to get them perfect. Today he still polished them every few days and sharpened both often. His guns were treated the same, oiled and cleaned about every other day, even when he had not shot them, they were always perfect.

CRACK, it was not much of a sound but for Blade it might have well-been cannon fire. Blade spun, dropped to one knee with the shoulder knife in his hand targeting a man outlined near the remains of the dead campfire about thirty feet away and now with his hands up. Blade had already started to snap off the throw when for some reason he stopped with his arm in mid-action.

"You could have got yourself killed, what's the matter with you," Blade shouted, but only half loud, at the stocky dark figure, now about twenty feet away and moving closer, hands high above his head.

Blade stayed in the shadow and cover of the trees, he could see the man better now and was conscious of the fact he remained hidden from the stranger, his camp and horse had been found but Blade knew he had not been. The shadows kept Blade in a position that made his new visitor nervous, Blade could see him fidgeting and his head swiveling left to right and back again. He looked like he wanted to put his hands down but fear kept them up. Fear and talking to a shadow somewhere in the dark made him nervous, more than he wanted to show.

"I'm, sa, sa, sorry, maybe I should have called out before I approached your camp," came the answer in a thick, almost comically nervous British accent.

"Maybe, there is no maybe to it, don't ever do that again, or you'll find yourself on the ground dead," Blade barked, twenty feet from the nervous man who still had not located him.

Thirty seconds of night silence later and with more of a normal level and sound to his voice

Blade continued. "Now, who are you? And how did you get so dumb as to try and sneak up on me in the dark? Where did you come from, and why have you been following me for two days?"

The man moved closer, and Blade could see a baggy suit and hard-boiled derby hat on a rather young squat man. His stocky build made the derby hat look funny on his round head, but Blade was not ready to laugh, not yet. The closer he moved to the fire the more his thick body looked fat rather than solid. The rumpled suit he wore might have looked all right on a banker behind a desk but looked far out of place on the Wyoming high plains. The closer Blade looked at the man, the longer and baggier the suit seemed -it was too big. Maybe about thirty pounds and four inches too big and on the dirty, bedraggled man, the suit looked like it belonged to someone else.

Blade couldn't tell in the dim moonlight breaking through the damp night what color the suit should be, brown or gray. So much dust clung to the jacket that it all looked the gray-red color of the high country. This stranger didn't look dangerous to Blade, but something told him not to put away his weapons, not yet.

Chapter 5

"My name is Luke Templeton, and I've hoped to catch up with you since you were so quick to remove yourself from Cheyenne. I have been in America a few weeks. I work as a school headmaster in England, where I am from. I'm on a working holiday in your country. And I would like to put my hands down now, please."

Blade kicked a piece of dry wood on the dead embers of his fire and rolled a small rock out of the way with the toe of his boot all the time glaring at this odd British school teacher. He bent warily at the waist and pushed dry kindling on the old fire. Striking a match he rekindled the fire. In just a moment, the fire flared belching thick gray smoke with the two men looking at each other over a flickering red and yellow kaleidoscope of light.

The Englishman kept his hands up and despite the cool night air rivulets of sweat ran down his pockmarked face. He now looked even shorter than at first and trembled from either cold or fear standing near the fire with his eyes down waiting for Blade to say something. Blade stared at the man until he looked away and then asked, in a quiet but accusing voice, "If you're a school teacher what are you doing following me, halfway through the middle of Wyoming? And put your hands down before you draw lightning."

Blade took his time sliding the knife back

into its sheath behind his left shoulder and motioned for the British dandy to take a seat on a log near the smoldering fire. Blade picked up a small stick, tossed it on the fire, and took a seat on the ground opposite the still standing Templeton. Blade sat in silence waiting, waiting for the Englishman to say something. Time had come for him to go free or hang himself with his next few words. "I had wished to speak with you in Cheyenne City before you left town." Templeton turned his back to Blade and pretended to brush the ashes and dust off a log with his hat before sitting down and continuing his story in an attempt to stay alive.

"I am writing a book on the great American last frontier, and I wanted to use you as an example of the dying breed of America's real cowboys," Templeton answered in a stern, teacher sounding voice. He looked at Blade, this time looking him right in the eyes as if hoping, hoping Blade would buy this story about him being a school headmaster just in from England?

Sitting on the log and now with his hands down it looked as if Templeton might be trying too hard to appear relaxed. He jammed one hand deep into his coat pocket and used the other to Jester while talking. He didn't look casual and unafraid as he talked but instead seemed stiff and forced. Like a man caught in a lie, Blade thought.

What Blade did not know was that Templeton sat with a hand in his coat pocket because he liked to run his fingers over the badge in his pocket. The badge he'd pulled off his jacket lapel and pushed deep into his pocket moments before he had the misfortune to step on a small stick and alert Blade of his presence. The badge in his pocket was something he thought Blade might not want to see, not right at this moment anyway. The words on the badge were not sheriff or Marshal, instead embossed in the metal were the words, Pinkerton National Detective Agency. Templeton was not just another guy in the west with a badge; this badge had the name, T. Pinkerton engraved on the back, and Terry Pinkerton's father was Robert Pinkerton one of the most famous crime fighters in the world, Robert's father Allen had founded the legendary Pinkerton agency. Terry Pinkerton, fresh from the East already had found respect as an agent and other Pinkerton's considered him a fast-rising star among their detective agency.

Blade watched Templeton with his frozen fake smile decided to stay somewhat obscured near the trees, even as he sat not ten feet from the fire. Templeton sat mopping at his brow with a grimy bandanna every few seconds. What Blade couldn't know was Templeton's mind racing along with his heart reminding him over and over; "keep the English accent, keep the English accent."

As a kid Blade liked to think of himself as some sort of western hero and as an adult sometimes, he'd almost became a real western hero. His kid daydreams turned him nearly every day into the greatest cowboy, sheriff, hunter, trapper, Indian chief, Marshal or gambler in the West, but those were dreams of a ten or eleven-year-old, and now he was an adult. Tonight Blade felt more than a little skeptical about why anyone would want to write about him. There had been times in the past few years when Blade had lived out or almost lived out some of his childhood daydreams but not lately. "Why would you want someone the likes of me in a book? I'm out of work, out of money and may be close to out of time to ever make something of myself."

Templeton stood up, contemplating the question and trying to look casual moving closer to the remains of the smoldering campfire to get a better look at Blade Holmes, who remained closer to the shadows than the fire with the big Appaloosa stallion behind him. He explained he was writing an anthology of the American West, and Blade was the type of carefree, colorful person he wanted to put in his book. "People in Britain are so interested in the West, and I hope to take advantage of that fact and sell lots of copies of my book. You have been the subject of several newspaper stories since I have been in America, and there is mention of a new book about you and your adventures here in the mountains, to go along with a previous book I believe."

The story sounded so good Blade wanted to believe it, but something about this British schoolteacher, turned author, didn't seem right. Maybe his yellow crooked and chipped teeth, the missing little finger on his left hand or the scar in the middle of his forehead. Or the awkward fit of his suit, the overdone English accent, something was not quite right about the guy. Blade smiled his mind racing, maybe everyone in England looks like this guy, heck he might be the best-looking man in the whole country. He looked over at Templeton, shook his head and then kind of nodded. Neither was sure what that meant.

The awkward conversation started to lose out to his need for sleep Templeton said goodnight to Blade with a promise of more talk in the morning. He laid his head back on a clump of grass to catch some much-needed sleep; he pretended immediate sleep, but real sleep did not come for an hour. When sleep did come it would not be deep or long. Blade was not the only one worried about being followed. Unlike Blade, Templeton didn't think someone might be followed him, he knew he had been followed, and the people behind him were armed with colts, rifles and worst of all they might have ropes, ropes for hanging, hanging a murderer.

Templeton fell asleep both surprised and relieved Blade hadn't asked him about his horse. People don't walk around Wyoming like they were in downtown Kansas City, in suits and dress shoes, without a horse. He knew Blade had not forgotten to ask about his lack of a horse, he just had not asked.

Chapter 6

Templeton had a simple plan, one he had thought through over and over as he trailed Blade from Cheyenne. As soon as this storybook hero with the fancy knife and gun falls asleep— kill him, then take his horse and be gone from here. He smiled to himself and rolled over to catch a couple hours of sleep, and to prepare for his flight on Blade's horse, wouldn't be long now.

Sleep came quickly as he thought about a job well done, he'd found Blade and fooled him with the fake accent and the new suit. He knew he didn't look or act perfect for the role, but it had been good enough to fool Mr. Holmes, and that was good enough for him. Now he would kill him, take his horse and guns and maybe the fancy knife before heading back to Cheyenne. This would not be as hard as he believed or as hard as those close to him thought when they tried to talk him out of it. Cheyenne would be nice again, getting out of this middle of nowhere place would be great. He put his hand over his pocket where he could feel the Pinkerton badge and fell asleep with the smile still firmly anchored on his face, thinking how much he hated being outdoors at night, then he dreamed happy dreams of killing Holmes.

Templeton's body clock awoke him a half hour later than the two hours or so he wanted. He took his time rolling over trying to be as quiet as the dead silence of the night. He would make sure Blade was still in a deep sleep. He'd learned as a kid to set an alarm in his head and it usually worked, unless he had too much to drink. As a kid in Chicago, he often awoke in the middle of the night to sneak out of the house to plunder, terrorize and raise havoc with his friends. He also understood the significance of silence and he used it tonight to his great advantage.

After a slow rollover, Templeton bent his arm under his head to take a look at the sleeping Blade Holmes and plan his attack. He was careful to the point of even opening his eyes one at a time, slow so he would not be noticed in the dim light. He knew he couldn't be too careful. Surprise was on his side. Thinking about outsmarting the great Blade Holmes made him smile again.

He was all alone. No Blade, no horse, no nothing, only poor old Luke Templeton in a bad suit with a badge in his pocket on a dark Wyoming night. He sat up and swore under his breath and then out loud. And then he screamed at the night.

Blade figured he had ridden three or four miles from Templeton and the camp by now and allowed Medicine to slow down to a walk and a few minutes later a slow walk. For the first time since he left the snoring Templeton, he could see well enough to let his mind wander and not concentrate on watching the terrain every step

Medicine took. Riding by moonlight was never easy and in such a wild and uncivilized area almost impossible, but this was not a first for Blade or Medicine, and likely would not be their last.

There are a lot of men who are restless, even some as restless as Blade. Maybe a lot of men were as troubled as Blade felt today out here alone on the prairie, but few had his awareness, his intuitiveness and the type of thought patterns allowing him to know and feel danger. Instinctively he knew Luke Templeton was not who or what he said. Knew it the moment he stepped into his line of vision and particularly when he started to speak. Blade tried to push those thoughts out of his head, but he couldn't, try as he might, he couldn't.

Why would someone posing as a British schoolteacher be walking in the middle of Wyoming? How did he catch up with me walking, not possible, which meant Templeton had waited there for him? Or did he hide his horse for some reason and walk into camp, didn't seem likely, but maybe. The suit didn't fit, too big; he had on city shoes and a derby hat that didn't fit, too small. He had an accent, but it sounded more than a little made up. Writing a book didn't seem to fit either, the man didn't appear to be well spoken or particularly smart, he didn't give the impression he could write much of a book. And then once again he thought about the man's horse or the lack of one. How many times had he heard, "a man without a horse is no man at all," and he knew it to be true, especially out here?

Blade stopped to let Medicine drink and to fill his canteens from a rather large stream he figured must be the Laramie River. After both, he and Medicine were watered Blade re-mounted turned his back to the rising sun and loped west along the river. He liked riding close to the river and if he didn't have so much on his mind, it could have been just another pleasant ride. Trees along the river were not leafed out yet, but the branches had a pastel of green about them as the buds filled and primed to open into leaves. It was a time of year Blade always enjoyed. He tapped his heel to Medicine and decided to speed up his trip to Fort Laramie a bit.

He liked the sound of the river and the cover along its banks. He remembered stories of Indians trekking over these banks not too many years ago. Riding along his mind filled, thinking, thinking, where are the connections, what am I missing? Why this man, called Luke Templeton, followed me and why was he on foot? Somewhere Blade knew there must be a connection between this man and him, but what was it, who is this guy? Blade didn't think he had seen him before but if he were dressed differently and in a different setting, a city maybe, he could have.

Templeton rolled over and slept until well past daylight then walked back, with his feet hurting every step, to the cut in the high bank a half mile backtracked in a deep wash from where he slept. He hated walking, but he didn't want Blade, or anyone else for that matter, to see the horse he rode. The horse itself was alright, a nondescript brown, no, the horse wasn't the problem, it was the fact he was riding without a saddle, and the horse was stolen, with a botched JG brand on its left hip. Anyone who had been around livestock at all could tell the brand had been changed, and not long ago. He rode a stolen horse. And he was the one that stole it. Worst of all if he got caught the horse would be the least of his worries, horse thieves were never treated well in Wyoming territory and murderers were treated even worse.

Templeton walked the horse over to a large flat rock, stepped up and then mounted the brown. He thought back to his botched attempt to change the JG brand, he had gone about it all wrong. Before thinking about what he was doing he heated the cattle thief's greatest tool, a running iron, to a red-hot glow and then started altering the brand with no real plan as to what the brand would be when he finished. He tried to change the JG to UQ, but it looked bad, as a matter of fact, he thought, even a seven-year-old greenhorn could recognize the brand as changed. So he tried to make an OQ and now it had become a mess, a festering mess of a fresh red sore on the brown horses flank.

"Should have used a cinch ring the way I learned," Templeton said out loud bouncing along the prairie on the brown.

But without a saddle he had no cinch ring and he didn't carry an extra the way skilled stock thieves did. He needed to get rid of this horse as soon as possible. Templeton took a few seconds to look around and convince himself no one was around to see him or the brand or the stolen mare, but he still needed a different horse to be safe. He wanted the big stallion Blade rode and after letting him get away last night he was convinced he would be riding the big Appaloosa before the next day saw darkness.

One of Templeton's two Kansas City mentors, a two-time Missouri Chain Gang member and a no-account con man and thief, much like Templeton, had told him "a changed brand is a work of great art, it takes time and skill."

The brown horses OQ brand did not look like great art, it looked more like an artist spilled paint on the canvas and then left it there to dry.

Templeton had taken no time and had come up with no art. When he stole the brown, it was the second horse he had taken in a quarter of an hour. The first he stole from a gambler had a fair saddle, some useless ammunition; three decks of cards a running iron and some traveling provisions. But the horse had run off when he tried to tighten the saddle. Templeton jumped the next horse he saw, the saddle-less brown complete with bit and bridle hanging on a fence post. He found it in a small corral behind a white clapboard house on the northernmost outskirts of the city. Someone's buggy horse, he thought, he was riding a brown buggy horse and a stolen one at that, with a bad brand to boot.

The brown horse drank readily as Templeton studied the tracks on the soft ground where the mud gave way to sand near the Laramie River. "It looks like my boy's been here and turned west, can't believe he left tracks so plain," Templeton muttered as he mounted and turned toward the still snow covered mountains of the Laramie range he could see in the West. He kicked the brown and frowned thinking about how cold it would be up in the snow, he had to get out of here.

Chapter 7

Blade stood beside Medicine in a tangle of waist-high cottonwood and junipers looking for a place to sit and rest. The bigger trees, except for a few ancient looking giants, were gone, cut down three feet above the ground. The timber along both sides of the river looked the same, small trees and hundreds of stumps. Blade figured to still be at least a few miles from Fort Laramie, ten or twelve at the most.

He stood looking up and down the river in an area where the army had sent wood cutting details for decades. From the looks of the landscape, this seemed to be out as far as the cutters came. The men were often allowed to clear-cut close to the fort as a safety factor but as they ventured further away they cut only the log ready trees, leaving the largest and smallest. Scanning both sides of the river with his field glasses Blade could see no sign of firewood cutting more than a quarter mile past where he now sat watching Medicine graze. Blade decided he must be on the far edge of where the cutting crews from the Fort came. Crews tried to stay within an hour's hard riding distance, but Indian troubles were less and less now and it looked like the crews were comfortable a little farther out than they were a few years ago. This would put him about ten miles south and west of the fort. Blade had been riding toward the fort for two days, the two days since he lost the

Englishman, riding hard and all the time thinking, thinking about joining the army when he got there. But now he had a burr under his saddle that he could not seem to move and it put a twist on his thinking. This guy Templeton wearing a bad suit with a fake British accent had been following him, but why?

Blade walked Medicine to the flat river bank pulled the saddle off and watched him starting to eat the new shoots of green popping from the sun-warmed mud inches from the water. He found a place nearby in the shade to rest and think. Blade lay down, stretching his feet out to a small mound of blackened dirt that might have once been a campfire. He fought to keep his eyes open, but only for a moment.

Blade danced with Emma. It was a warm summer night and the downtown Kansas City pavilion was packed full of people in fancy clothes whirling, laughing and smiling. As Blade spun Emma he couldn't keep his eyes off her. Others were looking around and checking everybody out. But not Blade, everyone at the dance could see he had eyes for Emma and no one else and it had been that way for most of the last four months.

Blade's dream flashed ahead and the couple walked hand in hand under a canopy of overhanging elms, the heavy branches filtering the silver glimmer of a half moon. An eerie yellow circle of light cast from one of the new city gas lights illuminated each street corner. The two walked as if no one and nothing else mattered. And nothing and no one did. They walked, they smiled and they talked about everything and then talked of nothing at all. The couple passed from the filtered moonlight to the yellow of the street corners, watched buggies and saddle horses pass and held hands letting the troubles of the world find others on this perfect night.

Blade had never been in love before, didn't know what it felt like and wasn't sure what it should be. But he knew it that night and it scared him worse than he had ever been scared in his life. They had kissed for the first time on their fifth date several weeks before. The first kiss extended Blade's stay in Kansas City from one month to six months and as the time had worn on their relationship deepened, growing stronger and stronger by the day. Blade hadn't worked since he arrived in Kansas City. He'd came to pick up his reward for catching Big Ed Whitten on a riverboat upstream from Kansas City near Saint Joe, Missouri and planned to leave in a few days, decided to stay for a while. Then he met Emma.

Months later, he had spent half of the two thousand dollar reward and started to wonder if he needed to look for a job, or if and when he needed a job. And he didn't know if he had any real skills or could do a regular job. Emma looked over at Blade as he seemed to be marching in a straight line in a world of his own; a mood that sometimes engulfed him. "You've turned quiet, what's on your mind, something you don't want to talk about."

Blade went blank for a moment trying to remember what she'd asked, then answered. "Just thinking about a job, not sure if I could handle a regular everyday job or if I could do anything someone would want to hire me for, but it might be time for me to get one, or at least look around for something."

"Blade, you have more talent than anyone I have ever met, you've worked for the Army, been a sheriff and a town Marshal, worked for the government and you know how to fix things, everyone is amazed at the beautiful counters you built in the shop."

Then she smiled knowing Blade did not want to hear what she was going to say next, "and you grew up on a farm, I'm sure you could do some kind of farm or ranch work if you wanted to."

Blade nodded in the dark but didn't answer, unsure of what to say. He felt pretty proud of the new front counters he had built and thankful his father had made him help build furniture during the cold dark winters on the Ohio farm. But he never took to the work, never liked it, even if he was good at it. And he especially didn't want to do any farm work, not now, not ever, and Emma knew it. Blade liked the way she teased him, but he still was self-conscious about hating farm work and felt his face flush with embarrassment when she mentioned it, he was glad it was dark.

He'd been thinking about doing some work, maybe getting back to playing cards, maybe winning some money. He knew how Emma felt about his playing cards. She didn't say anything but didn't approve and Blade realized he cared deeply for her approval. Maybe a more normal work a day life would suit him someday. They turned the corner and walked a few steps before Blade opened the waist-high wrought iron gate. The pair walked up the red brick, flower-lined sidewalk to Emma's Haberdashery. Blade fumbled around in his pockets for the key, even after several months in the city he still had a tough time digging around in his pockets for a key. In the world where he lived when he reached in his pocket, it meant reaching for guns, knives, badges or cards.

Emma lit the small kerosene lamp in the store window that served as the only illumination for the window sign. In bright red and gold the sign proclaimed, "Emma's Kansas City Haberdashery," and then in smaller letters underneath; "Also Specializing in Wedding Apparel and Fine Women's Dresses," and near the bottom of the window, "Emma Fick owner......all work guaranteed." The sign, made by one of Kansas City's best sign painters, covered most of the large window to the left of the front door and made the store look prosperous and important, which it was.

Blade's room was in the rear of the building, a building now shining with a new coat of white paint trimmed in green. Blade had completed the paint job a month ago and still smiled every time he looked at it. He had never painted before, but the job looked professional. No wonder Emma saw him as some kind of great handyman. But all the handyman chores around the shop may have started to be too much domestication for Blade.

Blade's tiny room, behind the showroom in the front and the workroom in the center had been used for storage before Emma invited Blade to move over from the Mary-Etta Hotel as their relationship entered its fifth month. The storeroom had once been reserved for, extra bolts of cloth, sewing machine parts, and wooden boxes of thread, needles, sewing machine oil, old books, and back issues of Kansas City newspapers, several boxes of cloth dye and several boxes marked miscellaneous. Now only a few of those items were left and sat in and on top of an old bookcase in the corner of Blade's eight by eight bedroom. The rest were stored up high in the workroom out front. Blade liked the fact the back door to the building opened to the alley from the back wall of his room. When Blade started to feel too domesticated, he could always step out the door to the alley and look at the night sky or walk to the saloon four blocks away for a drink or some cards. As of late Blake didn't seem to be using the back door often, thinking more of Emma and his new life than anything else.

Emma's upstairs living space had a small parlor with two matching formal chairs and a library table, several books on top. She had a tiny kitchen and a bedroom in the back. Built for efficiency, not comfort, it suited her and her lifestyle, before Blade. She never liked the back bedroom looking out over the alley, but the past few weeks she had started to like it because it was over Blade's small accommodations. Knowing he was close only a few feet away made here both comfortable and happy. Until Blade came into her life Emma often thought being married to her job would be enough and she would never settle down with a man.

Not that she hadn't been given enough chances, as a matter of fact, the past two years she had started to stay away from the budding Kansas City social scene just to avoid all the men wanting to spend time with her, she had begun to think she might not be the marrying kind. Then the tall, charming and now well-dressed, Blade Holmes, came into her life. Blade came into the shop looking to get some new clothes. He had tried the dry-goods stores and felt they never had anything to fit his build or anything he liked or felt comfortable in. Blade didn't mind the work clothes the general stores sold, but he had enough of them growing up, and needed more and wanted more, he liked the way he looked in finely made clothes and liked the way he felt in them. And that's how he came into Emma Fick's life.

After taking her time lighting the front shop light, Emma turned the wick up a bit looked around the shop and then turned back and smiled up at Blade. Taking him by the hand she led him past his room to the stairs then upstairs, to her room, for the first time.

Chapter 8

Blade woke after what may have been one of the best night's sleep he'd had since he left the Ohio farm and his cozy life with mom and dad. He didn't know what to do; he opened one eye to peek at the other side of the bed where Emma slept. She was gone. Blade felt like it was late he looked toward the top of the bureau with the ticking mantle clock. He rubbed his eyes and looked again making sure he saw it right, he took a deep breath. Ten after eight—Emma had already gone downstairs to her shop. Today was the first time in his adult life Blade had lost track of time, his life was changing. As much as he hated it he was becoming citified which embarrassed him. His life was changing and he had no doubt why, he was in love.

Two weeks later Blade stepped out the back door of the shop an hour before daybreak, walked the half mile to the livery stable, saddled Medicine and rode north and west, north and west toward Wyoming.

The breeze had freshened into a cool wind and the sun sat lower in the sky than Blade expected it to be when he woke up from his nap in the cottonwoods. He hoped the nap would replace his lack of sleep last night but didn't feel like it worked. As Blade stirred himself back to consciousness, he hoped the dream of Emma and Kansas City was real and sleeping on the ground in Wyoming was the dream. But it didn't take much time to see the reality of his situation. Emma and Kansas City were far away and he was stiff and sore, sleeping on the ground in Wyoming. In the past few weeks he had done a lot of soul-searching about why he left Emma and Kansas City behind, he didn't know.

Blade had felt hunger pangs for the past hour and needed to eat and needed a fire before it got too dark. He crept west along the river bank keeping back far enough to not be seen but close enough to carefully survey the river's edge as he slow hunted the bank for supper. It took fifteen minutes but immediately ahead a single green headed mallard sat in a puddle a few feet away from the flow of the river. Blade reached for his Colt then thought better of it and slid the knife from behind his shoulder. A quick flip of the wrist and the duck was pinned in the shallow water and mud. Blade made quick work of cleaning and skinning him, picking up a handful of dry kindling as he walked back to his camp. If he would have needed to use a gun Blade likely would have chosen to skip another meal, safe was worth being hungry for a while. It was the perfect time of day to build a fire; late enough the wind would soon die with the setting sun but still enough light so the small flames would not be seen from any distance.

Blade fired the kindling and walked back away from the river gathering a partial armload of small dry sticks. Picking only dull gray ancient looking sticks, the ones that looked to be somewhere between living and petrified, smooth and stone dry would allow the fire to burn with little or no smoke. It often took Blade a little longer to do things, even simple things like gathering wood, but being careful was a part of him out here. In less than three-quarters of an hour the duck had been roasted and eaten, as he ate Blade worried, disturbed by his dreams of Emma and Kansas City. Not that the dreams were new, they were not, but the past few days the dreams seemed to bother him more than he felt they should. Roast Duck was a favorite of Blades; this one was alright but not filling, maybe because Blade was preoccupied with thoughts of more importance. Or maybe it was his cooking bothering him tonight. About half the duck was burned to a crispy black and part still raw but warm enough to eat.

The more he considered it, the more he thought joining the army seemed like a bad idea. He'd visited the fort several times in the past few years and sometimes believed the disciplined army life might be what he needed. A few years back he spent two months working as a scout for the army tracking Indians outside of the reservation where they were ordered to stay. He spent two months up in the Powder River country and then on north into Montana. After those months, he'd almost signed on as a full-time scout but changed his mind, something he was really good at and left the next morning. The last few hours dreaming, sitting, cooking, thinking and looking up and down the river every few minutes had made him re-think a lot of things. Blade stretched and took a handful of steps to the river washed his hands and splashed some of the ice cold water on his face. He looked up and down the river again then saddled Medicine before starting to cover his sign.

Blade led Medicine out into the shallows of the stream and tied him to what was left of an ancient log jam in the six-inch deep water. The jam had small plants growing from the moss covered limbs giving the entire log pile an odd, dead but almost alive, look. Medicine seemed to enjoy the tiny plants as he licked and nibbled on the mossy shoots. Blade used a small juniper branch to brush away all signs of his having been camped on this site. He stepped back and surveyed the area several times, each time going back to redo something he did not like the looks of. Satisfied Blade walked away from the river through the scrub stand of trees careful as he walked to leave no boot prints. After clearing the trees, Blade turned and walked a quarter mile upstream, looked around again, stepped into the river and walked back to where he had tied Medicine.

Having spent the last ten years being careful about leaving sign he'd became pretty good at covering up his trail, but today he was more careful than usual. This Templeton guy had him worried, and he wasn't sure why. The sooner he could forget the rough looking ill-dressed schoolmaster, the better. Blade mounted and rode downstream for a quarter of a mile, east toward the fort until he found a solid rocky area to bring Medicine out of the water and onto the prairie without leaving much sign. Blade nudged his heel against the side of his big Appaloosa and started in a trot turning away from the fort and instead toward Laramie City, several days to the south.

Luke Templeton was lost, lost so bad he was almost without hope, how had he let this happen? He could follow a man and had yesterday and the day before, but he couldn't track. If someone were dumb enough to leave tracks in the sand, he could follow, but maybe those tracks he found were left there for him to find.

Templeton exploded in a fury; he had been played for a fool. He cursed Blade Holmes and the ground he rode on and swore to the heavens he would find him and kill him. He steamed just thinking about it, that big cowboy with the knife had played him out for the greenhorn city boy he was and he had played and won. In frustration, Templeton kicked his horse with both heels causing the big brown to rear then stumble and almost go down. Templeton brought the stumbling horse under control, crawled down holding the reins tight. He stepped back and took a good look at the horse, she was about done in. Wouldn't go more than another couple of days and might take some amount of luck to hold up that long. Templeton needed to rest and let the horse rest. He didn't care about the welfare of the horse, didn't care if she dropped dead on the spot, but he hated walking even more than he hated the brown horse he rode. Templeton stood and looked around, nothing, nothing anywhere, a good place to rest for a few hours. He reached down and tied the brown to a clump of tall sage, moved around to the shady side and dropped to the ground. Time to rest and to figure out a few things, he thought back to Cheyenne and what he was doing out here in the sagebrush. Templeton sneezed, sneezed again then again, he hated the smell of sage. Rubbing his watering eyes and sniffling he pounded his right hand against the sandy ground and cussed himself, cussed Blade Holmes and then cussed the Wyoming plains.

"Roy Tibbs it was Tibbs's fault, all his fault, and Holmes, yeah Holmes too," Templeton muttered as he leaned back on his elbows sneezed again and cussed the brown horse.

He couldn't believe what a fool he'd been. Tiring to sort things out, he was lost, lost out here with the pitiful brown horse, hungry and angry all because Roy Tibbs had promised him a job. When Tibbs made the offer, it seemed like an easy deal, kill Blade Holmes he would be paid and then set up with a job, a job with the Pinkerton Detective Agency. When he saw Holmes on that stunning horse, he wanted it so bad it all seemed easy. He'd killed people before and the reward for this killing would be worth it. A job with the detective agency would give him an aura of respectability and allow him to ply his trade as a petty criminal under some amount of protection. The five hundred dollars promised for killing Holmes would give him a good start and he would get the Appaloosa to boot. "Should have killed him in Cheyenne, had plenty of chances, should have killed him there," Templeton mumbled to himself as he dug into his coat pockets looking for the makings.

He moved away from the sage to a sand blowout, trying to get comfortable and took his time rolling a smoke. While he built the smoke he talked out loud about where he went wrong or where he could catch up with Holmes and make up for all his troubles. He sat on a ridge of sand smoked and tried to decide what he would do next. As for Tibbs, he would take care of him when he got back to Cheyenne. Maybe demand more money or it might be possible things would still work out. His mind flashed a daydream building a smile on his pudgy face. He would ride into Cheyenne on his new horse get his five hundred from Tibbs and go to work for Pinkerton. Templeton took one last drag from the cigarette, tossed it into the nearby sagebrush, spit on the ground, shook his head and said, "yeah maybe, maybe things will work out."

But he did not look like a man who believed it.

Chapter 9

Templeton thought there was a fort around here somewhere. Which one, he couldn't remember the name. Being in the west felt nothing like hanging around the south side of Chicago when he was growing up. But he'd left Chicago for a chance at a new life in the west. Or the truth, he had left Chicago with the law chasing him for everything from petty theft to murder.

There had to be some ranches, some people around here, he had not seen so many cows in his life, not the live walking around kind anyway. He grew up around cows, but they were in the plant, skinned and hanging on hooks, his father, and all his uncles were packers and he had worked for two different packing plants but got fired both times. Wasn't my fault either, he thought, the boss hassled me, always after me, he deserved it when I clubbed him and took his wallet. "And I was smart about it," he said out loud, as he blew out a stream of smoke then spit little bits of tobacco into the grass.

Templeton continued talking to the prairie, "I waited more than a week after he fired me to get him, by then he had forgot about me, smart, even if he only had six bits and a few pennies on him, that's why I hit him a couple more times." Remembering the killing Templeton burst out laughing, "He deserved it, he really did," then laughed again, this time for the better part of a minute.

Chicago was full of packing plants, cows, and stockyards with hard-working laborers— and railroads. Maybe it was the packers and railroads, maybe it was their fault he was out here in the middle of nowhere, lost and hungry, he thought. It was their fault, the stupid packers and the railroads and most of all it was Blade Holmes fault, big dumb cowboy, wouldn't last a minute in the city.

Seemed like every hill looked like the one he had just ridden over. Each hillside he rode down looked like the one before. The past two days Templeton had seen nothing but sagebrush, short grass and barren rocky spots of shale, gravel, and rocks. The sun came up the sun went down, yesterday and the day before. Occasionally he crossed a small stream or rode by a pothole of water but most of the land was bone dry. Now riding for several hours through bottomland valleys, where snow piled up for weeks in the winter, the grass should be greening but instead it was dry and brittle and his horse kicked up puffballs of dust with every step. The sun warmed him some despite the cool breeze coming off the mountain, he pulled up his collar to fight off the chill one minute then let sweat drip from his face in the sunshine the next. He hated everything out here, even the weather.

If he were heading north, which he believed he had been since he left Cheyenne, the fort should be close, he still couldn't remember the name, he kicked the worn out brown in frustration and nearly was unseated for his trouble. He regained control of his horse then blurted out—"Fort Laramie," and laughed like he had learned somebody's best-kept secret.

Templeton was still laughing when like an apparition a small winding river appeared in front of him. Scrub cottonwood and serviceberries lined the banks of the running water, so blue it looked more like an artist's idea of a river than the real thing. He rubbed knuckles in his watery eyes and looked again but it was still there. Riding down to within a few feet he decided to turn west paralleling the Platte, he hoped it was the Platte anyway and not the Laramie River, but he didn't know for sure. The North Platte and the Laramie Rivers were the only two rivers he'd heard of in this area. Maybe he hadn't been tricked. He might be following this Holmes straight to the fort if that's where he headed two days ago. He felt pretty sure now the fort had been Holmes's destination. "Maybe I really do track alright, good as most out here anyway," Templeton said as he pushed his heels into the brown and trotted toward the mountains to the west.

Three hours later he could see buildings surrounded by crumbling adobe walls. Small pieces of Fort Laramie's old cottonwood stockade stood a jagged line of ancient sentries. The logs rotting and leaning at odd angles served now only as a reminder of a troubled past. The river ran near two sides of the fort. The only guards he could see were active in the front or what looked to be the front as he rode. It had been a few years now since the last Indian problems in Wyoming and the fort looked old and tired. Templeton didn't think it looked much like a real fort, only a few scattered buildings looked occupied. He wiped at his burning allergy eyes in an attempt to try to get a better look at Fort Laramie. Riding into the setting sun with the breeze blowing sage pollen and dust at him had kept him sneezing and rubbing his eyes for the past hour and a half. He sneezed again and wiped a grimy sleeve across his face, spit, then spit again, "it's been a long time but tonight I'm sleepin' in a bed."

Looking down from a small rise he watched soldiers in blue coats riding guard on horseback. Now close enough he could see the ramshackle log and adobe buildings of the foothills fort. A rare smile turned his dry weather checked lips upward, he flinched when he felt the skin crack in the middle of his lower lip. Seeing civilization for the first time in days Templeton eagerly anticipated his accommodations in the next few hours, he would be put up in an army cot inside of a building tonight and army food. Something cooked by anyone else would be good, yes this would end up being a good day, a very good day. Army food and a cot would be so much better than sleeping on the ground and living on jerky, those thoughts made him lick his lips. The pressure on his cracked lips made him flinch then he relaxed, rolled his eyes and laughed when he thought about hot army food. Now a hundred yards away from the fort Templeton looked down at the ground and in a deep British accent said, "So you thought you could lose me did you, but here you are and here I am Mr. Blade Holmes."

Templeton had been through many disappointments in his life, most he brought on himself but knowing Blade Holmes was here and the fact he had followed him here made him feel good. He did have ability out here in this wilderness. After suffering through the past few days, or maybe the past few years, when it seemed like everything went wrong, today had been a good day, no, it had been a great day. Maybe his bad luck had changed, about time. Within the next twenty-four hours, he would have two of the things he most needed. Blade Holmes dead and he would be riding a new horse, Holmes's horse.

Templeton needed a smoke. He reached into his jacket pocket for the makings before realizing his pockets were as empty as the hills he'd been riding through. He kicked both his city boy shoes against the brown horse's sides and bounced along toward the camp. When he was close enough to smell wood burning from cookstoves and bread baking, he said under his breath, "Think I'll call my new horse Lucky or maybe Blackie."

Templeton puffed out his chest as proud as he could be. He had followed his man directly to Fort Laramie, just like the Pinkerton's. Holmes had to be here, he was heading north the last few days and this is the only place he could be. Templeton rode up to the gate, adjusted his dusty derby hat, straightened his back on the worn out, saddleless horse trying to look taller and more important. He identified himself to the guards as a Pinkerton Detective flashed his badge and the guards without a second look waved him past and moved on circling the fort. There was no gate to be waved through, but Templeton touched the brim of his derby and rode toward the biggest of the buildings straight ahead. The two boyish-looking soldiers on guard duty, one with a single stripe and the other with two didn't seem as impressed by the badge as he believed they should have been. A private and a corporal, he understood some things about the army and inside with the fort commander this knowledge might help him out. Templeton had treated the two as if they were of little importance when he had asked for the commanding officer. He assumed, because of his Pinkerton badge he would be ushered straight into the office of Colonel Henry Clay Merriam. But he was quite mistaken.

He reached the front door, but that was as far as he got. The grizzled looking guard standing in the door, this one wearing sergeant stripes, asked him to take a seat or told him to take a seat then motioned with his hand toward a crude wooden bench near the door. Templeton took a seat but not on the porch. Instead he sat on the top of the four steps, where he waited for at least three-quarters of an hour. While he waited, several uniformed men, some with a stripe or two and one officer went in and out of the Colonel's office. Templeton sat, wishing he had a cigar and watched army life. He didn't mind the wait. The rest was welcomed and he liked taking a little time with his first view of the army of the plains. Spending some time sitting on something flat instead of the worthless brown horse felt good for a change. The last soldier to enter the headquarters building was the guard duty private, the one he had asked for directions to Merriam's office.

Finally, after a wait which seemed longer than necessary, the office door opened and he was motioned inside. Templeton's usual bravado was lost as quickly as when Blade drew the knife on him when he walked into the office, shook the Colonel's hand, introduced himself and then saw the framed Medal of Honor on the office wall. The guy was a certified hero and this was the guy he was going to try to con. He had been thinking about it for the past few hours. No time to change now. He had to go through with it.

Nerves were about to get the best of him, he ran the back of his hand over the beads of sweat starting to run down his forehead, hoping his south side Chicago charm and con might work on a certified war hero. Templeton crumpled the derby hat in his hands as if he were wringing out a newly washed shirt then felt his knees wobble and his face flush, warm sweat rolled from his neck, dripped on his collar and ran inside his shirt and down his back. He stepped his right foot a few inches ahead of his left then switched them and tried to look at the Colonel's forehead instead of his face. "What can we do for you, Mr. Templeton?"

Templeton swallowed, felt his eyes burn again from perspiration and looked around the Colonel's office. Log walls, beautiful pine desk, straight back chair, stove in the corner with a coffee pot and a shining round table, no chair for him. He wondered why the Colonel hadn't offered him coffee or a place to sit. Then he noticed a fancy looking three-legged stool in the corner near the door, he stepped back picked it up plopped it down in front of the Colonel and sat down. No pictures on the wall, just the Medal of Honor and an old calendar with a photo of Ulysses S. Grant on the top and the year 1886 on the bottom under the thirty days of April. Templeton started to feel surer of what he was doing; his old bravado began to return and he faked a smile. Adjusting his backside on the polished oak stool he unconsciously wiped the palms of his hands on his pant legs and looked across the Army desk at the old war hero. A two-year-old calendar on the wall made him think this place may be a little behind the time in other things, more than just a calendar on the wall. His nerves faltered again when he got a no-nonsense look from the Colonel letting him know he needed to state his business and get out of here, and sooner better than later. "Good afternoon General."

"It's Colonel," Merriam stated flatly, and then glared at Templeton.

"Excuse me, must have been thrown off by this odd little stool I'm sitting on, looks like somebody run out of wood and forgot the last leg, sure is strange, this one, only three legs." Templeton laughed nervously and fidgeted on the stool waiting for the Colonel to say something.

"Yes, I suppose it is, what can I do for you this afternoon Mr. Templeton?"

This was a hard man, a forget about the formalities, and get down to business, army officer. Maybe that's the way all officers are, Templeton had no idea. He moved his eyes downward from Merriam's and concentrated on the Colonel's mustache trying to keep from looking away and giving the appearance he was not comfortable looking the Colonel square in the eye.

"As I'm sure you've been told I am with the Pinkerton Detective Agency. We need your help I'm looking for someone, he's a horse thief and a killer, and I tracked him to this area and believe he may be here, at your fort."

"This sounds pretty serious, but you're the first civilian visitor here in more than a week. The Fort belongs to the United States Government, not me. Are you looking for one of my men?"

"No he's a civilian, big guy, wears a white coat, eyes look right through ya, carries a fancy knife, rides a big black horse with some spots on its rear end."

"Sounds like a guy I know pretty well, been here a couple of times, does he wear a Colt on his right front hip, butt in, fancy buckskin jacket and the horse, is it a big Appaloosa stallion?"

"That's him Colonel, stole the Appaloosa from me and killed one of our men, left me with his ol' worn out buggy horse to get here on." Templeton worried he may have said too much, but he couldn't spin it any other way now.

He waited. It seemed like minutes before the Colonel spoke. Templeton's stomach turned over then turned again and he felt the burning inside, why he said the horse had been his he didn't know, but he knew it was a mistake. He'd just blurted it out before realizing the Colonel knew the man and he knew the horse.

Colonel Merriam thought for a moment before answering. He sat staring at Templeton twisting his wedding band around several times on his finger. Templeton squirmed when Merriam opened his right-hand desk drawer, but he only came out with his pipe, took his time finding a match in his uniform pocket, struck the match and drew deeply from the pipe. He blew out a stream of smoke, slid his chair back a foot and tipped it back against the log wall. He stared right into Templeton's eyes, Templeton felt like a kid in elementary school caught in a little white lie. But he wasn't in grade school anymore and this was not a little lie it was a big lie and he knew he'd been caught. Now if he could only find a way to save face and get out of here. He felt the Colonel's eyes bore right through him or into the depths of his soul, he wasn't sure which, before he leaned forward and spoke. "I don't think we're talking about the same man, although the description fits him," Merriam said, then leaned back silent again, puffing on his pipe.

Almost like an afterthought he stared at Templeton with a look. A look so icy it froze him in place before he continued, "But the man I am thinking about is honest as the day is long and would never steal, might kill someone if he had to, but steal a horse, no not this man. Mr. Templeton, I think it's time for you to show yourself out."

"What, you know him, how do you know him, he's wanted, a wanted man, he stole my horse? We at the Pinkerton's need to catch up with him, are you refusing to help? Who is he to you anyway?" Templeton knew he had overreached his bounds but a life of telling lies trapped him again.

The colonel tapped the still warm pipe in his hand, cleared his throat and let a wry but almost threatening smile cross his face. "His name is Blade Holmes as I am sure you must know. He caught raised and trained that magnificent horse and it certainly never belonged to you. Blade Holmes has worked for me, the army, on more than one occasion. Mr. Holmes has never stolen anything or even treated anyone badly, to my knowledge, in his entire life. Blade Holmes is better with a gun, knife and a horse than anyone I have ever met or ever heard of in my whole life. He can track a man across bare rock, survive on nothing for days and has instincts like no one else on earth. If you are going after him, I hope you or Mr. Holmes is carrying a shovel so he can bury you—Mr. Templeton, of the Pinkerton Agency, or whoever you are. Blade Holmes is a legend out here and I am proud to say he is a friend of mine, you are not, and never will be. I have no idea why you are trying to find Blade, but I can tell you this, you will catch up to him when and if he wants you to, not before. I should throw you in lockup because you lied to me, I can't because you're not in the army, so the best I can do is say goodbye and good day, now get out."

Templeton got up without saying a word, his face flushed, felt like his body was on fire, he walked out the door. Once outside he pulled his wrinkled derby hat down so hard on his head he could feel the top of his ears burn. He walked to the stable with more speed than normal but not fast enough to show he'd been scared into hurrying. With every step, he tried not to show how furious he felt. What he really wanted to do was pull his gun, go back and shoot Merriam, shoot him in the gut so he could bleed out slow. He knew he couldn't, but he boiled over with anger and it took everything he could muster to keep walking toward the stable.

The post wrangler on duty had already put up the brown horse with the bad brand and grained him expecting the visitor to stay the night. It was now the time of day where the sky held as much dark as light, the red in the west had started to fade and would be taken over by darkness before he could ride out of sight of the fort. And out of sight he wanted to be as fast as he could. He felt like choking the kid in the stable when he asked, "why ya leavin' now, it's almost dark out, aren't you stayin' for supper, cooks are pretty good here, cept for the bread, usually burnt on the bottom, no one watches the coals much."

Templeton said nothing at first then took a deep breath and told the young wrangler to go ahead over to the hall for chow he'd get his own horse. As soon as the Wrangler left he grabbed a Calvary saddle from a long line of dark brown polished saddles in the barn, strapped it on the old brown and left the fort at a lope. Night started to settle over the fort, he was hungry, it was getting cold and he needed to get out of here before someone started after him, again.

Chapter 10

The eastern sky began to show signs of night approaching although the western skies still blazed with warming spring sunshine from the setting sun. It was an odd time of day, late, still light in the west, dusk. Blade had pushed Medicine pretty hard today the horse didn't mind, but Blade did, he felt tired and in need of a real night's sleep. He rode past the area where he would camp, as he had done for years in the wild, then circled back the half mile and unsaddled Medicine tying him near a patch of new grass. Being cautious had become a part of Blade since he pinned the first badge on his shirt. With this new twist in his travels being careful now became even more of a necessity. Blade reflected for a moment about how careful he'd been in some parts of his life but yet how foolish he could be with cards and how foolish he had often been in relationships, he let the thoughts pass. Spreading out bed roles and finding a suitable place to lie down had become second nature to Blade and in a few minutes he was as satisfied, under the circumstances, as he could be with his present accommodations.

The crack of light sitting on the western horizon gave Blade enough time to build a small fire. He snapped a handful of wood from a dead tree. The tiny tree stood alone, the only one for miles, and looked like it had been planted here by some hapless homesteader who lasted a short while before leaving for greener fields or maybe left for good, dying trying to make a life in a place that didn't want him. To Blade it looked like some kind of shade tree, might have been a nice elm or ash in its earlier days. The smoke had a pleasant aroma and Blade wished he had something to cook, but he didn't. For a moment, he thought about hunting a rabbit and then gave the thought up and decided to rest and sleep instead.

The sun sat on the horizon, the fire softened to a red glow, Medicine stood and rested then walked a small circle eating. Blade dozed off with his head propped against his saddle and one of his green wool blankets pulled up to his chin. Dreams came as soon he was comfortable, the night and hard ground playing with his tired mind.

Nicholas Holmes washed his hands and nodded to Blade as he came through the kitchen door carrying two rabbits and a mallard hen. "Looks like you had some luck this afternoon son."

Blade nodded back toward his dad and then looked over to his mother and said, "Ma can we eat the duck tonight, I sure am hungry for duck, they're starting to fly through again, it really would taste good."

"Mathew, now you got me hungry for duck too, take it out and skin it while I grease the skillet."

"You sure do pander to the boy Virginia."

"I know, he is such a good boy but he worries me, coming up on his sixteenth birthday, he's a lot more man than boy now."

"Don't know why he is a worry to you then, said yourself he's a good boy."

"What worries me is his hunting, fishing and tramping around out in the hills. He's always been one needs to know what's over the next hill or beyond the next bunch of trees or around the bend in the creek. He's a wanderer Nicholas, the older he gets, the more he roams and he'll stray from the farm forever someday, maybe soon. "

"I spect, you're right Virginia, I'll talk with Blade later and see if he has anything special on his mind."

Blade washed up while his mom busied herself dipping the various parts of the duck in fresh milk and rolling each in a mix of flour and cornmeal before dropping them, with a delicious sizzle, into the frying pan. Nicholas Holmes sat in a straight back cherry-wood chair at the table in the southwest corner of the kitchen. He hadn't opened the Bible or any of the history books he was so fond of reading each evening. Instead, he had scooted his chair back away from the table, crossed his legs and looked lost in thought. Blade pulled a chair up to the table across from his father and opened a copy of a Beadles' Dime Novel he had almost finished. "Blade, your sixteenth birthday is coming soon, you are a man now, have you thought much about what you will do with yourself? You going to stick around here and farm, ma's more than a might worried about you and your wandering ways?"

Blade was a little taken back by the question, but he knew his answer. "You know Pa I really love it here, but I want to see what others are doing, I want to see what's out there and I want to see the west and then come back."

"About what your ma and I thought you would say, you know the forty over on the bend in the creek, if it were cleared could be a great farm, a place to put some roots down, and it's yours if you want it."

"Someday pa, but not yet, don't believe I'm ready for roots now, but when I come back, it sure is a great piece of land." Neither believed the words. Blade spoke the words, and his dad heard them, but they were spoken with so little emotion it seemed a certainty he would never come back, or if he did it would be to visit, he would never stay.

Virginia Holmes had been listening to the conversation while she peeled potatoes and sliced onions at the stove. More than once she wiped a tear back into her red hair. When she felt composed enough she turned toward the table and said, "Matthew you take care of yourself and let us know where you are and that you are alright, there will always be a place for our prodigal son at this table and on this land." With that she turned, brushed another damp spot from her face and went back to her work at the stove dropping square chunks of vegetables into a large black frying pan. Potatoes and Duck cooked, the three sat down to eat, ma and pa worried as they ate and Blade ate and daydreamed of the West.

Three weeks later Blade turned sixteen and said his goodbyes while eating birthday cake at the kitchen table. The next morning, a little before four, with no sign of light in the sky and without waking his folks he packed what he thought was needed, saddled his horse and headed west.

The first signs of light were peeking through the darkness in the east. Morning would be here in another hour. Blade hadn't moved, Medicine stood dozing on his feet an arm's length away and the night was quiet. Another hour had passed before the time came to get on the trail. Thirty minutes later horse and rider were a mile away and the campsite had disappeared from sight. Blade figured if he pushed Medicine he could reach Laramie City in four days, but he had no real reason to push very hard. Instead, Blade decided to do some hunting, take his time, maybe a week or more. Blade stayed within view of the Laramie River as he rode. Something haunted him from last night's dreams of home, wasn't sure what or why. Now he turned his thoughts to the future. He smiled when his daydreams turned to Emma Fick and Kansas City.

Chapter 11

Luke Templeton was still mad, as smoldering mad as when he had been hopelessly lost less than a day earlier. He'd made mistakes at Fort Laramie and now he ran away. He could think of only one place to go, the only place he knew in this God forsaken country, Cheyenne. He had to go back toward Cheyenne, maybe a little east of the town itself. Then he would cut the Union Pacific tracks and turn east following the tracks through Nebraska and keep following them all the way to the Atlantic Ocean and then hide out and take up a new profession.

Now he'd ridden most of the night and planned to ride most of this day. Tired, sore, hungry and mad, but he needed to get as much distance as he could from the fort, and the soldiers as quickly as possible. Every bone-jarring mile felt worse than the one before, the prairie all looked the same, nothing but scrub grass and sagebrush. He tried to keep track of the sun as he rode hoping not to ride in circles, but he was not sure if he stayed heading due south as he intended. Maybe they weren't even following, maybe they were, stealing the Calvary saddle had been a dumb thing to do, really dumb. He'd given them enough suspicions asking accusing questions about Blade Holmes, who ended up being a friend of theirs. Stumbling his way through the conversation with Colonel Merriam, struggling to talk while he wiped sweat dripping from his forehead making him look like a guilty man, nothing like he wanted. He fumed and kicked the sweating Brown as he rode, thinking how he'd acted sitting on the stool in Merriam's office. Feeling more like the accused than the Pinkerton detective he wanted Merriam to believe. And worst of all, knowing Merriam saw right through him, saw him for the liar and thug he was, that was what made him nearly lose control today on the dreary Wyoming plains.

Riding the tired brown, now letting it slow to a walk, allowed Templeton plenty of time to reflect on what had gone wrong the past few weeks of his, now turning wretched life. He had been doing alright in Kansas City, stealing a few cows and sheep from local area farmers and then selling them to butcher shops that asked few or no questions. With those little successes going to his head he decided to take it to the big time, get some real money in his pockets, and some left over to put in the bank. Gain respect from the big boys of the city, the bankers and money lenders and other people who mattered. He needed their respect. He often fantasized he was one of them. He wished to be of real importance in the Kansas City social and financial circles. From that point on things swirled out of control.

Robbing the stage office in the middle of the night had been easy, but then, as he did so often, he had to overdo it. He robbed the Haberdashery shop just up the street from the stage office. He robbed it because he could. He'd watched Holmes and the beautiful lady who owned the shop sashay around Kansas City for half a year and somehow in his bewildered mind decided if he killed Holmes he could have his lady friend. Have her because now he'd have fame and money, he would be like Holmes.

How could he have known the lady running the place would be working so late? But why did he shoot her, panic, maybe? He'd panicked over a lady, carrying a bolt of cloth in one hand and a needle and thread in the other. She surprised him robbing the place and he shot her. She was a real looker too. He had watched her from a distance, followed Holmes and her around the city. Now he wished he hadn't killed her, but at such close range and the bullet hit solid, he was sure of it. He'd killed before but never a woman and this woman he liked and wanted. Oh well, Templeton thought as he bounced along the gray sage prairie, there'll be another day and another woman. A smile turned the corners of his mouth for the first time in the past twenty-four hours— lots of women and lots of more days to find them, just as soon as he got rich.

Templeton stopped and dismounted in the middle of the prairie and wished he knew how to find water, water, and food. He plopped down on a patch of dry grass and wished he had the makings for a smoke. Too many mistakes he thought, he had made too many mistakes and

Holmes had gotten in the way, mistakes and Blade Holmes, both problems he could solve.

The getaway from the Kansas City robberies had been total confusion. After shooting the haberdasher lady, his horse ran off and he'd ended up running, walking and stumbling for the better part of a mile before he found another horse to steal. And to get this one he had shot and robbed a Pinkerton man. A Pinkerton man he knew or at least almost knew. This Pinkerton was the working partner of an acquaintance, Roy Tibbs, an old friend gone straight or straight most of the time. Tibbs, like Templeton, had started out as a small-time criminal but somehow managed to worm his way into a lower level job with Pinkerton's Kansas City agency. After he had got through with his training period, the agency reassigned him to Cheyenne. Tibbs had stayed in touch with Templeton and kept his hand in the small time crime scene in Kansas City while simultaneously keeping his hands clean in Cheyenne.

Templeton stole the Pinkerton Detectives badge thinking it might come in handy someday and as a kind of a souvenir. He thought it might be funny someday for one of his few friends to hear this story. The story of how he killed a Pinkerton Detective and stole his horse and he may have been a Pinkerton man looking for him. Funny if it hadn't been him involved and if it did not get worse from here, but it did, now the same thing was happening all over again. He pushed the detective's horse too hard getting out of town, riding all night before boarding a westbound freight thirty miles north of Kansas City. A day later when he took the roan mare off the train in Cheyenne, she limped badly on her left foreleg, lame.

Templeton had friends in Cheyenne, or at least a friend and he went straight to the Pinkerton office to look him up. Early the next evening he killed a Cheyenne gambler for a roll of bills he carried in his pocket. Then he needed to get out of town, all towns, for a while.

Stopping only long enough to complete a business deal with Roy Tibbs and explain to him how he accidentally killed Tibbs's old partner in Kansas City. Templeton left town in less than a quarter of an hour. He galloped north just to get lost for a while, but the horse and the fact he had no food with him needed some attention. Templeton got off the gamblers horse to tighten the cinch. The owner must have loosened it when he tied him in front of the saloon. He pulled the strap through the cinch ring, the dry, cracked leather snapped and the horse took off to parts unknown. Templeton swore under his breath as he walked away from the pile in front of him. A pile of saddlebags and a saddle,

It had taken half an hour before Templeton stole the big brown he now rode. He had left the saddle and saddlebags behind as too heavy to walk and carry. He kept a few items from the gamblers horse including several packages of jerky a small box of matches and a folded paper bag of tobacco and papers.

Templeton started following the man riding the big Appaloosa for the better part of two days to complete his deal with Roy Tibbs, and then to steal his horse. It had been his own dumb luck or as it now looked, bad luck to stop by to see Tibbs before he left town. Now he finds out the guy he is following and hired to kill is some kind of Ned Buntline, Wild West legend. Blade Holmes the same man he considered killing in Kansas City. He thought then about killing him so he could have his life, his woman, and his money and he should have. Templeton shook his head, he didn't like his present situation, didn't like it at all, tired, hungry, angry and lost somewhere near the Platte River in Wyoming or Nebraska slowly moving south toward Cheyenne and the Union Pacific, out of here. Templeton had not thought to ask Tibbs why he wanted Blade Holmes dead, the $500 seemed like a good idea at the time, but now he second-guessed everything about the deal, he was getting out of here, for good.

Colonel Henry Clay Merriam got what he had been waiting for, a return telegraph and it read about as he expected. After the man, Templeton, who claimed to be a Pinkerton man, left the fort Merriam telegraphed: Cheyenne, Bozeman, Laramie City and Deadwood asking questions about a Pinkerton Detective going by the name of Luke Templeton. A return message came from Cheyenne within an hour. A Pinkerton man had been killed in Kansas City three weeks ago and Templeton was being sought for questioning in the matter. A few days ago a body turned up in Cheyenne and authorities there were looking for him as well. Pinkerton's reported they had no men anywhere within a hundred miles of Fort Laramie, yet, and no, no one with the name of Holmes was wanted by the Pinkerton's or any of the local law in or around Cheyenne. The message ended: "Sir if the Holmes you cited is Blade Holmes send him after Templeton and we will have this mess over with." STOP

"Maybe, just maybe, my luck is starting to change," Templeton muttered under his breath, as he watched the ancient looking mountain man making camp.

He couldn't believe his good fortune. He had stumbled upon an old man dressed in skins, like the mountain men of fifty years ago. The old man had food, guns and horses, one to ride and one for packing. Templeton tied the brown and watched for half an hour until he felt sure the man was alone. He was uncomfortable lying in the rough grass with sharp crumbling bits of shale cutting into his arms. After he had all he could take of lying on the hill he mounted and rode from his vantage point down the hillside and into the camp. He started to whistle and act relaxed as he rode in. The old man was putting what looked like speckled egg shells in the steaming coffee pot. "Howdy there in the camp friend, could you see your way to share some coffee with a thirsty traveling man."

The old man looked up, his expression unchanged. Templeton knew the mountain man was not surprised to see him ride into camp. The old man had seen, heard or smelled him or maybe all three. He must have known he had been there all the time, perhaps watching Templeton as much as Templeton watched the old mountain man. The ancient man nodded for him to sit near the fire and the coffee pot. The old man looked to be a fair cook, some kind of fried meat with onions and thick dark coffee, the best meal Templeton had eaten since he rode the train to Cheyenne.

Forty minutes later Templeton rode out of the camp at a trot on an unshod black mare with three white stockings. He now had a saddle bag half full of jerky and a near full canteen of coffee. He ate and drank as he rode, maybe his luck had changed and just in time. He was tired but knew traveling a few more miles would be needed before making camp tonight. Templeton felt like he should be careful, but he wasn't sure why, no one was after him, not yet, and he had given up on the idea of the army tracking him down for a stolen saddle.

When Templeton left the old man's camp, he turned away from the south and a little east he had been traveling and rode straight west toward the peak they called Laramie.

Colonel Merriam decided not to wait. It had been a long time. The Indians were by and large peaceful, travel on the trail had slowed and it had been a long while since he had headed a real patrol. This patrol was on a mission other than the usual show of force reminding people, both good and bad, that the army was in the area. Talk from Washington the last few years had been about closing the fort, maybe this would help keep it going, they would catch this guy, yes they would catch him.

It had become army business now because this man, a man who struck the Colonel as poorly dressed and not well enough spoken to be a Pinkerton man, had come to the fort under false pretense and attempted to con its commanding officer out of information, information about a man who had worked for the army. Under most circumstances that would not be enough to get the military involved, then he stole the saddle. Now there were plenty of wrongs, against the army, to be righted. Templeton seemed to be wanted for something everywhere he'd been the past year and now the Colonel took it upon himself to find him.

Merriam knew he and the men would get but a few miles today, but it would be worth it for him and his little-used troopers.

At noon the day after Templeton left Fort Laramie, Merriam followed with twenty-four men and four pack horses. Merriam stepped on more than a few of his junior officer's toes to lead the two regiments. The usual protocol would put a major at the head of each troop and this small group of two squads Merriam led today would be headed by one of the forts lower-ranking officers. But not today, Merriam had grown tired of sitting on his backside all day and building furniture, to keep from going crazy, every evening in the forts carpenter shop.

Fifty-year-old Colonel Henry Clay Merriam, hero of Antietam, hero of Fredericksburg, decorated for gallantry at Port Hudson and winner of the Medal of Honor in the last battle of the Civil War at Fort Blakely in 1865, saddled his big bay himself. Also not protocol, but today he headed into battle and when he went into battle he liked to do things for himself. Merriam swung astride and smiled, looked over his right shoulder, signaled with white-gloved raised right hand and led the men on something of importance for the first time in many years. The troop left the fort at a gallop.

Chapter 12

Colonel Merriam and the troopers rode hard until the deepening dusk made it a risk for the horses and men to travel any longer over the rough terrain. The army was changing and Merriam thought a bit about his soon to be life as a retired soldier as he watched some of his green soldiers bouncing in the saddle, but they didn't complain when he pushed them hard. The trail had been easy to pick up since yesterday's incoming patrol had met Templeton a half mile from the fort, traveling south, as they came in. The patrol leader reported Templeton seemed to be in a hurry with a sour look on his face like he was mad, saddle sore or both. Odd he thought Templeton made no acknowledgment to the troopers, acting as if he didn't see them even when passing within twenty or so feet of the soldiers.

The Calvary cut the trail where lasts nights incoming troops said they would and the single horse had been moving fast enough to leave a clear trail. The troopers made good time in the few hours they rode and camped much closer to the site of Templeton's latest handiwork than any of them could have imagined.

Vultures circling at sunrise were never a good sign, the Colonel watched them, the men watched them and they followed. The blue coats followed the trail and the trail led to the circling birds. In thirty minutes the small Calvary

Company out of Fort Laramie arrived at the site where the ancient mountain man had camped. He was still there or at least parts of him were. The scene was both unbelievable and disturbing. How could anyone do this? Merriam knew the answer and he also knew who did it.

The youngest of the Calvary, most of them in their late teens or early twenties and Irish or German immigrants stayed mounted but were leaning over their saddles throwing up after looking at the carnage. More experienced men wiped moisture from under their eyes with the backs of their hands or the yellow bandannas around their necks. Longtime soldiers cussed, including two tough veteran soldiers, line sergeants who had seen war. They had fought against each other for the north and south in the Civil War and fought together against Indians in Wyoming and South Dakota shortly after. For most of the last twenty-five years, they told new recruits that they, "had seen it all," and they thought they had, until today.

Today the two spit matched streams of brown tobacco juice and dismounted to inspect the scene of the slaughter. The two old army warriors, their faces now showing even more age than yesterday with deep frowning furrows hiding as much of their emotion as they could. They walked around the body inspecting the remains and then the entire site. Five minutes later the two grisly old veterans stood apart from the troop talking with Colonel Merriam.

Although the conversation was muted, the men were animated waving their arms and pointing as they talked. It was clear the Colonel had great respect for these two men listening and nodding as they described what they thought happened and what they believed needed to be done next.

Throughout the years, soldiers had come and gone from the fort. Most of them had listened to the stories of years past from the old mountain man. Some learned from him, some wanted to laugh with him, but all had enjoyed his stories and to a man they liked him. He told tales of the old days when beaver was king and the mountain men walked in the kingdom of the wild. He'd sat in the warmth of the forts winter wood stoves talking of a time which seemed more fantasy than reality and every year young troopers passed the long Wyoming winter listening with eyes wide and ears hanging on his every word. He'd first come to the west when the only white men in the area were a handful of trappers. No forts, no soldiers, and even the Indians were spaced far apart. He talked of buffalo or buffler, he called them. He talked of wild injins and the way the tribes were before the whites came. According to his stories game in the mountains was so thick you could live like a king on nothing but red meat and, sweet as honey, mountain water. The old mountain man had lived as hard and dangerous a life as possible on this earth and now he was dead, killed by a city raised thug masquerading as whatever suited him.

The old man, John Ryan, had come to this territory, near the end of the trapping boom, in 1838 at the age of fifteen. Others left when beaver hats went out of fashion but he stayed to guide the wagons, hunt for the railroad, and scout for the army and the last few years to shoot wolves and coyotes for area ranchers and herders. He had wintered and supplied at Fort Laramie over all those years and was known to nearly everyone who had been stationed at the fort.

The old man had never put on weight like city people seem to do as they age, instead he stayed about the same size as when he came to this country, small and wiry, sinewy muscles with skin wrinkled and tanned so he looked more like an old Indian than a white man. Now the body had been gnawed on throughout the night by the same animals he had hunted so successfully the past two decades. He had been scalped in a clumsy and unsuccessful attempt to blame Indians, but even when scalping was practiced the victor never scalped from forehead to the back of the head. Scalps were always small and precise from the exact spot on the crown of the head. Merriam and his old Sergeants had witnessed scalped bodies before and this had nothing to do with Indians. A greenhorn like Templeton might have thought there were still tribes of wild, scalping Indians running around all over the west. He was a vicious killer who didn't know anything about the west, a deadly combination. The men tracking him now, as they looked around, understood just how dangerous a man like that could be.

A dead horse, also partially eaten by night predators, lay nearby. The Colonel didn't recognize it, but one of the men did. It was the brown horse Luke Templeton rode into the fort two nights earlier. A young corporal inspected the horse and found a bullet hole in the middle of the forehead. It had been killed for no reason, no reason at all. Templeton could have turned her loose, but instead he killed her. A half hour passed since the small band of troopers arrived and to a man they now realized how important their mission had become. A spotted Indian pony standing on a hillside three hundred yards east of the killing site watched the troopers, the old man's pack animal. The pony was still hobbled and bleeding where he'd pulled one leg loose and ran when the wolves came in the night. Now he was back, waiting, standing on the hillside eating and watching, watching for the old man who would not be back. And nowhere to be found was the beautiful black mare old John Ryan had ridden the past two years.

The men took their time burying the remains of the old mountain man giving him the proper respect he had earned after a lifetime in the mountains. After filling the grave, they stacked moss covered flat rocks on the grave to keep scavenging animals away. A man like John Ryan deserved a decent and proper burial. Most of the men felt he deserved a hero's burial and wished they could do more, a burial befitting of one of the great early men of Wyoming. When the grave, at last, met everyone's approval the men mounted without saying a word and left, moving at a trot. The pack horse, a fine looking animal, was doctored, hobbles removed and turned loose. As they left the valley, a few of the men turned in their saddles to take one last quick look back at the beautiful meadow in the morning light. A beautiful meadow now turned red with the blood of a friend, a meadow where not one of them wanted to return, ever.

Templeton didn't know it, but he had done something right, the troopers were heading from the murder and gravesite riding south and he had detoured to the west. He had a feeling someone might be after him when they found the site of the murder if anyone ever found it. Then again, he thought, maybe nobody even knew the old fool mountain man, maybe no one would care, but somehow he had a feeling he might be wrong. Finally he turned his thoughts to a smile, he was sure he'd done right by heading west after he murdered the old mountain man and killed the horse that got him into this mess in the first place. He laughed when he remembered putting a bullet into the head of the brown horse.

After less than an hour, at a full trot, Merriam pulled the troop to a halt at a small spring. The men were happy to get a chance to stretch and to talk. Merriam asked his captain and the two old sergeants to join him. "Something's bothering me; might just be instinct but I think we're going the wrong way."

The shorter of the two sergeants cut a chunk of greasy black tobacco and tucked it with his forefinger into the corner of his mouth before he started to talk. "I'm getting the same feeling Colonel, unless the guy we're a following is as much of a greenhorn as some of the fellas seem to think he's got to know we spect him to keep heading due south. Naw, think you're right he's turned, I'd bet on it."

Merriam nodded, took off his hat sat down on the ground and motioned for the three men with him to do the same. "I know we can't be sure but, it's just a feeling, he expects us to follow and knows if we find the killing ground we will pick up the pace and not look for his trail. He may be as green as the new grass out here, but in the short time I had the unpleasant experience of talking to him he made me think he might be a city boy, green out here, but not green about everything. We have to believe he can at least think. I'll bet a month's pay he turned west. No one there, cities and civilization to a city boy like him is to the east and south, people, marked roads, and cities, so he went west. Probably not for long, but could be long enough to slip us if we aren't careful. He won't cross the mountains, didn't appear to have the internal makings to make that trip, but he could sure ride some of the thirty miles toward the mountains. He might be scared to go too far, might get lost, no he won't go over a couple of hours, maybe four or five miles, seven or eight at the most."

Merriam's inexperienced captain shook his head, "I don't think so, I believe we keep going south and then if we don't catch up we swing west and see if we can cut his trail."

But the Colonel and the two Sergeants, all more than twenty years older than the young captain won this argument. The Colonel was a hard man and a tough commander, but the men trusted him and respected his war record along with his honesty. With the soldiers remounted he turned the men west and they hoped his years in the field had told him the right direction. To a man, they wanted Templeton. As they left at a lope the Colonel said to no one in particular, "he made fun of my three-legged stool, it took me two months and a lot of sweat to build that stool and he laughed about it. I had the oak for my office table shipped all the way from Ohio. If he had made fun of the roundtable

I built, I would have shot him right where he sat. The half-wit.

Chapter 13

Blade spent the day fishing in one of the small, cold, nameless streams dotting the foothills and the plains near Laramie Peak. Today he enjoyed life and the fact he wasn't in a hurry and would soon have trout for supper to go with the wild onions he found along the stream earlier. Much of the day Blade acted like the little kid again out exploring the countryside away from the Ohio farm he grew up on. He sat barefooted fishing in the clear pools, enjoying the day as much as he enjoyed catching fish. No longer did he feel like anyone still followed him and that gave him a chance to relax and rest, maybe this was who he was, relaxing, living on the bounty of the land. But he knew he was only trying to convince himself it was alright and normal to ride a hundred miles north, within a few miles of Fort Laramie, then turn and head back southwest toward Laramie City.

Two days of rest and relaxation was about all Blade could stand. On the morning of the third day, his belly full and Medicine content and rested he saddled up and rode east and then south. It felt good to have saddlebags with smoked fish, dried rabbit, and wild onion shoots. At least he wouldn't be hungry with nothing but hot water for a meal anytime soon. If Blade had it figured right, he should be able to take his time and still reach Laramie City in less than a week. Once he got there he would, he had no idea what he would do.

Medicine walked along at a slow pace Blade daydreaming loose and lazy in the saddle as they crossed the prairie he remembering back to his Ohio farm again and then to Kansas City. Maybe settling in wouldn't be such a bad idea, it sure had worked for Nicholas and Virginia Holmes. They were as happy as the richest people in America, happy as any of the great kings or queens ruling in Europe or some other far off place. They were happy just to be together working the land, talking with the neighbors, taking pleasure in the meager social life offered by a nearby small town and their church, enjoying life and enjoying every day. Blade shook his head as he wandered along; maybe he needed a life like his parents, quiet and rewarding. But he didn't think so.

Blade never went back to Ohio to live or even for a visit, when he left ten years ago, he felt sure he would never go back to stay. He just couldn't tell ma, it might have broken her heart. Pa, he understood, a man thing, and it was Pa who told him, "a man must do what it is he is put here for," and for Blade that meant the west, wandering from place to place and once in a while, when he had time, maybe a few days of fishing.

Blade had written a few times and his mother had answered. But now it had been, what, six years since he had written. Someday he needed to go home again for a visit, no, it would be a visit to where he grew up—home was here in Wyoming Territory. Someday, someday he would go back for a visit to Ma and Pa's Ohio farm, but not right now and probably not anytime soon.

Kansas City had almost become home, if he had asked, Emma would have said yes, he knew it. Two years older than Blade and if ever there was a combination of grace and beauty, she was it. Stunning to look at and always dressed impeccably. With her auburn hair and flashing green eyes, she was a wonder to behold and she loved Blade and he left her, left her in Kansas City. Maybe they had too much in common. She had grown up on a Missouri River farm and left home at sixteen to be a dressmaker's apprentice, at twenty she opened her own shop and in a few years became a successful business owner in the swift-growing western city.

Medicine shied as a rattlesnake warned them they were in his territory. The furious rattle of the snake always spooked Medicine and made Blade smile, no idea why, he liked their speed and fury. Blade pulled the shoulder knife to kill the snake then changed his mind and slid the knife back into the collar of his coat. Looking around it appeared like all this area may be more suited to rattlesnakes than humans. The rattling shook Blade from his daydream back to today and the prairie he rode through east of

Laramie Peak and seventy miles north of Laramie City. The Peak still had snow on top a sure sign summer was still a ways off. But it felt like spring here in the foothills, the day was warm, the grass was showing spots of green, rattlesnakes were out of their dens and Blade felt like he was in control. In control of everything important and in control of what was here and now on the plains and he hoped in his life. He pushed a heel into Medicine's side and the big stallion responded, happy to pick up the pace.

For no particular reason, Blade reined left and decided to ride east a few hours, even if it was out of the way. There was no real urgency to his life this spring, making it a matter of little difference as to which way he rode today. No real reason to hurry to Laramie City as he had no idea what he would do when he got there wasn't even really sure why he was going there. Luke Templeton had drifted as far from his mind as had his days tangling with Roy Tibbs back in grade school. Funny, they didn't look anything alike, but it still bothered him. Templeton reminded him of the way Tibbs acted back in grade school. Virginia Holmes would have called them two peas in a pod.

He smelled the smoke before he saw it, stopped Medicine on a small rise and reached down for his field glasses. But he didn't need them. He could see the smoke now, little white wisps against the dark blue sky and not more than a quarter mile straight ahead, but he couldn't make out a fire. He trained the glasses on what appeared to be the source of the smoke, what looked to be a small fence post setting alone. Blade held Medicine still and steadied the field glasses, it wasn't a campfire and it wasn't a fencepost it was a stovepipe coming from the ground. Blade dismounted and walked Medicine toward the smoke approaching as slow and quiet as possible in the knee-high sagebrush. Then he heard a baby cry.

He found a Soddy, another hardscrabble sage brush ranching upstart trying to make a, barely scraping by living, running a few cows in the sage and living in a hole bored into a small hillside with sod stacked to form the front, a sod house. Blade walked Medicine around to the front of the sod house tucked into a small south facing hillside. A young woman holding a little baby eyed him with more than a little bit of suspicion. She looked tired and worn but smiled unafraid, the baby started to cry and the young mother rocked back and forth holding the baby tight against here. Blade hadn't spent much time around babies, matter of fact babies were one of the few things he actually feared.

She nodded acknowledgment toward Blade and pulled part of a tattered blanket over the baby's head. She seemed to relax a little and brushed a hand down the side of her worn calico dress, looked down, thought better of it, looked back up and pulled the gray blanket back away from the baby's head. The quick precautions she had just taken and then tried to back off from led Blade to think the two of them were the only ones around. Her mothering instincts had taken over protecting the young one from harm, real or imagined was first on her mind. Blade smiled hoping he had not frightened her and tried to look as unassuming and safe as he could. "Howdy mam," Blade said, trying not to stare at the baby or look her in the eyes.

"Hello, my man's not here right now, we don't have much food in the house, but the well has water and you're welcome to it, you and the horse."

"Thanks, mam, but no thanks, just riding this way and saw the smoke, thought it might be hunters or such camping."

"Don't see many travelers through here, most ride the train over West going up to Casper from Cheyenne and Laramie City. My man works for a rancher over west of here. You likely crossed his land to get here; it's eight miles to the ranch so this little girl only gets to see her Papa every few days."

"And you stay out here by yourself, must get pretty lonesome," Blade answered, trying to make a bit of conversation before riding on.

"That it does, get lonely, only the baby helps lonesome, I'm not alone now, not with the girl. My husband was here for three years, but the last two winters took half our stock. We didn't have enough left to make a go of it so he took the top hand job over at the Long's. I do the best with the cattle as I can when he's not here, me and the girl. Man's home when he can, we're getting by."

"I hope it all works out for you here."

"Oh, I'm sure it will, we started with a few mavericks, built this heard up to a hundred, then the winters, but now we have near two dozen head including the little ones. In the fall, we can add a few mavericks. Might take more time to build back up what with the Stockman's Association, down in Cheyenne claiming all the mavericks on the open, but we'll get by." She smiled, patted the baby and pulled the tattered blanket down to the baby's shoulders.

"I'm sure you will, I best be headin' on, good luck to you and the little girl." Blade tipped his hat, "mam," turned put the toe of his boot in the stirrup and swung up into the saddle, nudged his knee into Medicine, turned and started to ride out from the tiny ranch.

"You might see the army if you head a little more south," the young mother said as he started to kick Medicine into a trot.

Blade stopped and turned back, "the army?"

"Saw about twenty or thirty of them riding off to the south early, I was out gathering eggs," she nodded toward a tiny weathered chicken house where four or five red chickens were scratching about.

"They were moving at a good clip, too far away to notice the two of us standing here watching." With a smile turning the corners of her mouth and the slightest of twinkles in her deep-set eyes, she added. "If you hurry could probably catch up, or if you keep going east, you could miss um entirely if it's your need to."

"No, no need to avoid them, think I'll see why they are this far out. Good day."

Blade nudged Medicine again and they were at once into a smooth trot and headed the way the sod house ranch wife had pointed. Blade thought about his family farm and how much better it had been than the little place he'd just left. Then he reminded himself someone started with little or nothing on his farm also, only it was generations ago, not a few years. Blade tapped his heels against Medicine and let him gallop. Suddenly he felt some urgency to find out what the army was doing.

Two years ago working for the army Blade helped with some trouble up on the Powder with Red Cloud and his bunch, but the Powder River is north and this is south. Lots of cattle out here, people ranching, no Indians, a few outlaws rustling cows, but why the army, why were they out here with a full patrol? Blade let Medicine have his head figuring they both could use a little haste right now. Medicine, now in a full run, ate up the ground. Blade leaned low over the saddle horn felt the wind in his face and reflected on the one woman he couldn't stop thinking about—his thoughts returning to Kansas City.

Blade met Emma at a time when he was most vulnerable. Sure he had reward money in his pocket from bringing in Big Ed Whitten, but he also was hurting from a hole in his left shoulder where a fancy Kansas City Doc had dug out Big Ed's .41 caliber derringer slug. He knew, at the time, it would be several weeks, maybe months before he would be back to his old self. He planned on lying around the city, maybe playing some cards, he even thought for a moment about a trip to Ohio but dismissed it as too taxing for his physical state. Some days it seemed like the Doc did more damage than good, but he said the bullet needed to come out lodged so high and close to the neck and spine. Blade guessed he did an alright job because in a few months it healed and he felt near normal again, except for the back pain when he rode too long or slept on the ground too many nights. Doc said the pain may never go away, "could be nerve damage," he said, bullet up high, pain down low, didn't make sense to Blade but then again he wasn't a doctor.

Now as he rode, the aching pain returned making Blake think he should have stayed in Kansas City. There he would be sleeping in a feather bed and enjoying life. Instead, he was galloping across the Wyoming plains in pursuit of a U.S. Calvary patrol out of Fort Laramie.

Medicine had long since settled into an easy gait that helped with the pain and let the miles and the time pass quickly, he could go on like this for hours. The brisk feel of the air in their faces refreshed them and Blade felt a more urgent need to catch up with Colonel Merriam and his Fort Laramie Troopers. It had been several months since he felt needed, needed for a job. That was not necessarily true but wearing a badge in a small cow town didn't count, not today anyway. Perhaps the Colonel could use a tracker or a gun. Not only use one, maybe he needed one. Why the army rode out here Blade had no idea, could be Indian trouble, but seemed unlikely. No, Blade decided it must be outlaws on the Bozeman Trail or someone infringing on government rights or property.

As he rode, Blade let his eyes and ears cover the empty path ahead and his mind drift back again to Kansas City and Emma Fick owner of Emma's Haberdashery and the love of his life. What did she think of him now? A few months ago they had been quite the big city couple. Her striking beauty left many a cowboy speechless with her flashing green eyes and always dressed to the nines, he standing over six feet with those intense dark eyes and the arresting near white shock of blonde hair. It wasn't just their near perfect looks that made the couple standout. Emma came from a new breed of women, a successful woman and business person. As for

Blade, well Blade might be the last of an old breed, a dying breed, a twenty-six-year-old who had reached near legendary status and he didn't even know it. Blade Holmes might be remembered forever, an expert with horses, guns and knives a lawman and a gunfighter. When needed, he could be everything good or what was bad about the dying breed of American cowboys.

Kansas City social circles were full of gossip of the businesswoman and the dime novel cowboy hero. The couple seemed oblivious to it all. When they were out, they had eyes for each other and no one else. She had no idea how beautiful she was or how much envy women in the city felt when they saw her. Emma walked, lived and worked in a class by herself in a city where women, for the most part, still fulfilled age-old traditional female roles. She was a hero of sorts to women of the city, she had it all. Blade sometimes thought Emma looked so spectacular he felt invisible. When he was with her, he believed others thought of him as some unanimous forty dollar a month cowboy or hundred dollar a month lawmen. Blade felt like some kind of faceless and nameless person, one who no one knew and none cared about, but he was mistaken, badly mistaken. He had no idea that, to the locals, he had already become a legend, more famous and more popular in Kansas City than President Grover Cleveland. The locals who he thought didn't notice him, indeed did but he was so famous no one wanted to look him in the eye and then again Emma was pretty easy to look at.

Together they mistook the town people's standoffish attitudes toward them as uncaring, but in reality they were being accorded the celebrity status the people of the city saw in them. Both men and women stepped back and whispered when they were near instead of greeting them. The everyday doings of the couple were at the center of half the conversations in the city. The two most admired and celebrated people in the fast-growing city; they just didn't know it and would have been embarrassed if they had.

In love and obliviously close to marriage and then he left. She might be sitting and waiting for him right now, she knew of his wandering ways. Or she may have decided he's the biggest scoundrel since John Wilkes Booth or worse yet she might think of him as another Bob Ford who shot local legend Jesse James in the back of the head six years ago.

She had softened him some during his more than half year stay and maybe that was why he left, maybe not. He'd drank more tea than coffee during the stay and few spirited drinks, although he never acquired much of a taste for alcohol and seldom drank anything stronger than beer or the strong coffee he preferred even when he sat and played cards for hours. He'd spent more time on the porch drinking lemonade than setting with a nickel beer in front of him in the neighborhood bar. He talked most days with Emma more than he did in a month on the plains or in the mountains, and he read more.

Blade had always enjoyed reading, somewhat odd for a cowboy of this day, but certainly not unheard of. He packed away a few books in his saddlebags whenever he reached a town large enough to have a general store with a few books for sale. Over the past few years, Blade had sometimes borrowed books from friends at Fort Laramie. At times, of necessity, his reading was limited to his King James Bible, his constant saddle bag companion. But when he could find them, he enjoyed reading dime novels of western heroes, some of the same books he read as a kid in Ohio. In recent years, he developed a taste for some of the great American authors and especially liked Hawthorn. Emma tried to interest him in poetry and together they had attended a twice a month poetry club.

Blade learned to like her favorite, Henry David Thoreau and managed to memorize a few lines from Ralph Waldo Emerson, someone he found both interesting and insightful. Blade never pretended to understand Emerson and his transcendentalism but loved to quote him. "Do not go where the path may lead, go instead where there is no path and leave a trail." Emma thought those words fit Blade entirely.

Blade slowed Medicine to a walk, braced his feet in the stirrups, stood and tried to stretch, leaning backward in an attempt to, once again, ease the ache in his tender back. Taking off his hat, Blade wiped the back of his right arm across his forehead, started to sit back down, changed his mind and hung his hat on the saddle horn. Out of the blue, Blade remembered an Emerson quote he'd memorized for one of the Tuesday evening poetry sessions. He looked toward an ancient buffalo wallow, picked up his hat and made a sweeping Shakespearian actor arm movement, and said, "Finish each day and be done with it. You have done what you could; some blunders and absurdities have crept in; forget them as soon as you can. Tomorrow is a new day; you shall begin it serenely and with too high a spirit to be encumbered with your old nonsense."

Realizing how loud he had been reciting Emerson he patted his big Appaloosa on the neck and said, "Don't worry Medicine I'm not losing my mind, just a little bored I guess, or a little lonesome."

Embarrassed that he was both spouting poetry and talking as loud as he could to his horse Blade looked around, afraid someone might be watching. Nobody was. Like a kid who got the answer wrong, he felt the schoolboy flush of his face, but he didn't care, he let himself smile and kept heading, now south and east. Every time he thought about Emma he felt like this, he knew why, but couldn't accept that much civilization, not yet.

Blade grinned, again thinking of the poetry sessions with Emma then started to laugh, Emerson really knew his stuff, and he knew life. Then he shouted to the skies.

"Always do what you are afraid to do. It is not the length of life, but the depth."

Chapter 14

Luke Templeton rode back south before turning east putting in a long day in the saddle. He would avoid the fort if he got mixed up and came too close, but he felt sure his path now would take him well to the south. Early on he found the North Platte and followed for a while, not along the river, but up along the bluffs where he could see the river valley. "They may have been treating me like I don't know anything and maybe I been makin' a few mistakes, but I know how to lay low and hide, they'll never find me now," Templeton said, under his breath, as he rode along the high ridge.

Growing up in the city he wasn't much of a horseman, and the river far below in the deep canyon kept him well back from the edge. On Three Legs, the old mountain man's horse, he felt unfamiliar and more than a little uneasy riding such a spirited mount. But he was happy to have it and recently took to calling the mare, Lucky; because of the luck he had in getting her with so little work. He smiled thinking back to shooting the old man for his horse and provisions, "he never saw it coming," he said, and that made him throw his head back and laugh.

The ranches were getting farther apart and he saw fewer cattle along the river as he rode. More and more rocks were in his way and the good pasture grass of a few miles back had turned more sagebrush than grass. Finally deciding he'd come far enough he rode down into a small grove of cottonwoods with a warm spring half as big as a Chicago city block. He believed he must be back within a day or so of Fort Laramie and decided to ride due south in the morning at first light. He still was not sure if anyone followed, but because in a wrong move, when he wasn't taking the time to think straight, he'd taken the saddle, he guessed maybe they were. Templeton thought, "I'll show them, lead um in a circle right back home, till right here, because tomorrow I'll ride as straight as I can toward Cheyenne."

He reined hard to a stop, leaned back in the saddle and let a sly grin cross his grimy face, "they're not following me, why would they, not this far, not for a stupid ten dollar saddle, naw, they're not following."

Templeton spit a stream of brown tobacco juice toward the ground some splattering his pant leg and shoe and some hitting the rocky limestone he was riding across. Then he laughed out loud, laughed so hard it started a fit of coughing, "why would they come after me for a stupid army saddle?"

Templeton still trying to recover from the coughing fit dismounted and tied the black mare to a stubby pine tree, not bothering to make sure if there was good grass or any type of graze she could reach. But the entire area, this close to water, looked like it would soon turn lush with spring. The black horse the mountain man named Three Legs, for its three white stockings, grazed on what she could find but still looked spooked as she had since first taken from John Ryan. Templeton didn't trust this horse, no not one bit, but he did admit he looked good riding her.

Building a fire was not one of Templeton's strong points but in a quarter of an hour he had a decent blaze. He poured what coffee was left in the canteen into a cup and set it on the outside of the fire and bit off a tough piece of jerky. It felt nice to have food and coffee again. He threw one of the buffalo robes on the ground and grabbed the red and white Hudson Bay to cover up with, both compliments of the old man. He felt no misgivings, whatsoever, about killing the mountain man, instead believing he may have done people a favor getting rid of someone so old. Even if he would have felt bad about killing the old man it wouldn't have lasted long, he now rode a new horse his saddlebags were well stocked and best of all he felt satisfied, at least for the moment. Killing the old man was worth it.

Templeton slept better than he had for days and felt rested and ready to travel by daylight. The remains of the campfire were still smoldering as he rolled his blankets mounted Three Legs and turned at a walk south and a little east. He twisted and looked back over his shoulder as tiny wisps of smoke from the fire rose with the new sun, kicked a worn out brown oxford into Three Legs and galloped away.

Colonel Merriam and the troops were fed, saddled and moving before the sky saw the first tiny bits of gray morning light. The soldiers followed the North Platte River west and according to his map were only a few miles from a place called Warm Springs. Merriam and many in his troop had been there before, many times. And others, hundreds maybe even thousands, had been there before them, it had been used for the past forty years as a laundry tub for people on the Oregon Trail. Everyone who had ever been in this area of the Platte knew this place. It had water and shelter in a tight group of trees the troop leaders knew the territory well and covered the ground to get there in a hurry.

Three hours after Templeton rode out on Three Legs the men of Merriam's Calvary troop saw smoke near the springs. Remains of a small campfire still smoldered and had started to burn the grass outside the makeshift fire pit. Someone camped here last night and left either carelessly or in a hurry. The troopers stayed long enough for two teenage privates to bury the fire. The tracks leaving the camp were deep, recent and leading south and some east. Merriam pushed the men and horses harder than he wanted, but he could almost smell it now. It brought back memories of Antietam and the war. Not a bloodbath like the war but the adrenalin rush before going to battle. Now it was the thrill of the chase and his fifty plus years felt like twenty all over again.

Hopelessly lost, that's what he was, lost again. Templeton looked into the skies trying to find the sun through the gloom and in minutes the darkness brought on a light mist, the leftover sunlight was too filtered by the overcast to see anything but straight ahead and then for no more than ten or fifteen yards. Templeton never needed directions in the city, but right now he needed the clouds to break so he could find the mountains in the west but it didn't look likely anytime soon. He would need to trust his instincts and hope his horse had some idea of where he wanted to go. For a brief moment, he considered stopping but since he left the river, he had not passed a single tree and without one in sight he was not sure what he should do. With no place looking safe enough to camp staying in the saddle and pushing on seemed the best thing to do.

But not to Merriam and his men who were now close enough to see Luke Templeton, if there had been sufficient sunlight to see him.

Chapter 15

Blade wasn't sure why, but he always knew, must have been some innate ability he figured, he always knew where he was. Not just somewhere close but often the exact location, like a built-in map in his head. He knew he was now sixty, maybe one or two more, miles north of Laramie City and near twenty-five miles east of the mountain called Split Rock. Blade still remembered the full curl bighorn sheep he killed near the top of that mountain several years ago. The pursuit, the kill, and the meat helped him through a tough winter.

For a reason Blade didn't understand, he decided if he wanted to find the Calvary he needed to travel at least another twenty miles east to cut their trail. Blade turned to his left tapped his heels into Medicine and took him to a full run. After three or four minutes, they slowed to a trot. Both horse and rider felt better, they would cut the trail in a few hours.

It was still several hours until sunset, but the midday skies were black as a moonless night if any sunlight filtered through it was scarce, just enough to see, kind of. A light mist turned to light rain. Blade stopped, unrolled his slicker and pulled it over his head and remounted. Not a single reason to stop now, Blade knew where he needed to be and where he wanted to be. Riding the plains with no sign of shelter, continuing on was his best option. Within five minutes the skies opened and large raindrops splattered against Blade and Medicine. He ducked his head into the storm and hoped Medicine would do the same. Even if there had been shelter enough to camp it would have to be within arm's reach, about how far Blade and Medicine could see in a downpour. Medicine walked on across the prairie picking his way through the waist-high sagebrush the pounding rain ruining the silence of the darkness.

Ten minutes later Blade started to slip into one of his occasional hopeless feelings of melancholy. He wasn't lost, but he was miserable and he started questioning many of the things he was doing and began to worry about things out of his control. Only when he was alone, out here and alone, did these feelings come to him, he felt like he should be able to push them away by thinking of better times, maybe the Ohio farm or Emma. But no sooner than his mind started to work free of the melancholy he pulled up Medicine and stopped. An old sheep headers shack or cattle ranch line shack stood within a few feet and Blade almost missed it. The shack sat near a dry ditch cut away over the years by spring runoff, brush around the cabin stood almost small tree height. So high it reached the bottom of the eve on the small cabin and may have obscured the view of the little shack even in good light. Blade walked Medicine in a circle around the shack then tied him on the back side where the slight wind and much of the rain would be blocked by an overhang that might have once covered a small porch. Interesting Blade thought the shack could not be more than twelve by sixteen or twenty feet. Why would anyone put a porch on such a poor home? Someone must have thought this to be the start of something big once, but it had never panned out. Unsaddling took only a minute and Blade carried the saddle, blanket, and all his belongings into the shack.

He pushed aside a piece of tattered canvas serving as the back door and stepped in. Once inside it seemed even smaller than he expected. Trying to look around into black on black darkness Blade waited for his eyes to adjust. After a few seconds, he fumbled through his saddlebags for a match. Striking it against the inside wall a burst of yellow light let Blade make out an empty room with grass and sage pushing through the dirt floor. He dropped his saddle and belongings against the back wall snagged the canvas door on a wooden peg and sat down on the roughhewn threshold of the doorway, his feet on the ground outside the shack. The rain had changed from large drops to more of a mist, he stretched his legs and pulled the slicker off over his head and tossed it inside. Although he seldom carried a watch Blade knew the time, four-thirty or maybe four forty in the afternoon. He didn't need the sun, directions and time always came naturally. Sometimes it was good, sometimes more of a curse.

He would wait until morning to decide which way to go, but as for now the melancholy left with his new found good fortune and he felt better here, sixty miles north of Laramie City and twenty-three east of Split Rock Mountain. Blade ate some of the fish he had smoked, relaxed and spread out the slicker and bedroll in the ancient living room and laid down to rest and think.

Blade hadn't realized how tired he was and didn't think he would be able to sleep when he stretched out on the cabins prairie floor. But now as he started waking up the rain had quit and stars twinkled from horizon to horizon with a soft breeze warming the night. The warm breeze brought along the scent of sage and spring rain reminding Blade why he liked the Wyoming plains so much. With the bright light of the moon, both horse and rider were ready to start a new day, even if it was one-thirty in the morning. Clear eyes could see, maybe, a hundred feet, much better than in the wet darkness of the afternoon rainstorm. By daylight, he could be miles from the shack and miles closer to a reunion with the Fort Laramie soldiers.

A little more than four hours later the first rays of the new day's sun felt good. Blade reined Medicine to a stop dismounted and took several deep breaths. He stretched, took off his hat, laid it crown down, in the bushy sagebrush and started to build a small fire. He made quick work of skinning the pair of sage chickens he had taken moments before. Shooting the chickens hadn't worried Blade, he figured if anyone heard the shots they would come to him, much easier than him finding someone. A temporary spit held the two birds a few inches above the flames the meat sizzled and dripped over the fire as Blade waited and hoped for someone to join him.

In Kansas City, he never ate alone, out here it seemed to be always alone and he never wanted company more than he did right now. Blade started pulling the dark meat free of the bones and eating when they still dripped red, partially cooked, by the time he finished eating the two birds were well done or past well done. He sat on the ground, Indian style, with his legs under him sipping water from his canteen wishing he had coffee and company, but he had neither.

The sparse meal left Blade without the urgency of the past few hours, he was tired and sleepy, his back ached and he needed to rest. It was six forty in the morning or maybe six forty-five and he decided to take a nap. Two hours later with the sun bearing down on his left side Blade and Medicine galloped south. Now in search of – he wasn't sure what.

He rode south and later a little east for two and a half hours. Smoke fingers in the distance were the first positive sign Blade had seen since he found the shack last night. Blade slowed Medicine to a walk, found the high ground where he could most easily be seen and carefully approached the smoke. No guards, now Blake was more than a little worried, this was not going to be the Army he thought it would be or hoped it would be. "Hello the camp," Blade called out.

Seven men looked up from their mid-day meal as Blade rode in. The coffee smelled good and the men looked neither surprised nor worried as he came into their camp.

"Coffee?"

Blade nodded and took a knee near the campfire with the group of men he now realized were not the working ranch cowboys he first suspected, they were either running from the law or they were the law. Blade accepted the coffee, blew the steam away from the top and tightened his fingers around the cup. It felt good after so many hours of holding reins in his hands. Years on the Plains had taught him many lessons and he sat in silence and waited. Blade blew across the top of his cup and took a small swallow of what he found to be surprisingly good coffee, or maybe it was because he hadn't drunk coffee in a few days. The small group sized up the newcomer but like Blade sat and drank coffee without a word. After a time Blade considered long enough, he sat his empty cup on the ground, looked into the face of each man around him then asked. "What you boys doing out here, doesn't seem like you need the exercise, my compliments to the cook, coffee's pretty good, I sure needed it thanks."

A man, older than the rest replied, "we're the law mister, posse, since you and the horse don't look anything a-tal like the man we're after you're welcome in our camp, there will be beans and bacon in a while and you're more than welcome to stay and eat if you're hungry. I'm Sheriff Roy Watson out of Cheyenne." He stood and stuck his right hand out for Blade.

"Blade Holmes sir, glad to meet you."

"Holmes, Blade Holmes, should have known as soon as I saw the horse. He is one magnificent looking animal."

Blade smiled but was puzzled by Sheriff Watson and thought, how would he know of me. "Sir if you don't mind my asking, I've spent precious little time in Cheyenne don't know why you should know me, hope I didn't break too many laws in the few days I spent there."

"Maybe you don't know, there's a new Buntline book out called, Blade Holmes and the Riverboat Capture of Big Ed, quite a story, just finished reading it myself son, you're a book readers legend in these parts."

Blade stretched and took a long drink from his coffee cup, "a story about me, why would anyone want to read a story about me, or for that matter, why would anyone want to write a story about me?"

A young man about Blade's age touched him on the arm and nearly shouted, "why you're famous Mr. Holmes, famous as Jessie and Frank James, no I didn't mean that, famous in a good way, like Wyatt Earp, Bat Masterson or something."

Blade shook his head not believing what he was hearing. He spent the next few minutes talking and meeting all the members of the sheriff's posse. Blade declined the beans and bacon but did take the time to refill his coffee cup for a second and then a third time before setting down beside the sheriff to talk business. "Holmes, we could use your help, we're after a man wanted for murder and a shooting in Kansas City and then a horse thieving and murder in Cheyenne. Worst is, he shot a woman in Kansas City and killed a Pinkerton man in my town. These ol' boys with me are good men, but the guy we're after is a cold-blooded killer, not sure my men will shoot first like they might need to against a killer."

Blade thought for a few moments about telling Sheriff Watson he couldn't help them out, that he needed to catch up with a Calvary troop out of Fort Laramie, to do, he didn't know what. For the first time in two days, it dawned on Blade just how odd it sounded and how odd it really was. A grown man out here chasing around after the army, what for, to see if they could make him feel better by telling him they needed his help. He hadn't thought much about his reasons, but that was about it. He wanted to be needed, easy he thought. The guys in the posse believed him to be a hero of sorts and they wanted his help, they needed him, he now felt better than he had since leaving Kansas City and leaving Emma.

Blade stood and flipped a sprinkle of grounds from his cup, "I'll be glad to help sheriff, I was heading for Laramie City but don't really need to be there anytime soon, who we chasing?"

"Hey boys, Blade Holmes is joinin' up, he's coming along with the posse." The sheriff looked pleased but even more relieved.

"We're after a guy named Luke Templeton but the"

"Luke Templeton," Blade interrupted, "short, chubby, bad city suit, English accent?"

"You know who he is?"

"Followed me once," Blade answered, not wanting to say too much yet, "I slipped away and lost him, never figured him out, didn't know what he was after, he seemed out of place."

"Sounds like the same guy, except this guy was from Kansas or somewhere before he came to Wyoming Territory and didn't have an accent as far as the information Pinkerton's gave us. He likely wanted your gun, your money, your supplies or all of those, could have been anything, who knows? Petty crook, according to the record sheet we got, till a few months ago, then looks like he tried to move up to the big time, started killing people."

"I saw him a few days ago, I was a couple of days out of Cheyenne, North, heading to Fort Laramie and I knew someone was following. I could feel it, and then he showed up. He came up on me after dark, snuck up, or tried to sneak up on me, not a real quiet guy walking at night. I could have killed him, almost did, sounds like maybe I should have. We talked for a while he told me he was a writer and a school teacher from England traveling around writing a book about the American West. Wasn't far from here maybe fifteen miles east and some south?" Blade wasn't used to talking so much and finally stopped, embarrassed when he looked up with the entire posse crowded around the sheriff and him.

"He's a bad one Holmes, stole a horse in Cheyenne after he killed the gambler riding it. Not sure if he lost money to him or just needed the horse to hightail it out of town. We know he went north because he stole Reverend Scroll's buggy horse after the gamblers horse run off on him. Scrolls just had his horse shoed. Left good tracks, the horse had a few years on it, but still a pretty good horse, a big brown, was he riding it when you saw him?"

"Didn't see a horse, must have put it out of sight before he came into my camp, seemed peculiar. What chased him from Kansas up to Wyoming?"

"Robbed a stage station, killed the night man, got away with the days business money and a good saddle horse. He only went a few blocks and robbed a haberdashery shop, shot the lady who owned the place, took a brown suit a derby hat and what money was in the shop change drawer and lit out."

Blade had a lump in his throat and didn't know for sure if he could get sounds to come out when he needed them, he swallowed hard several times, then asked, did you catch the ladies name, the lady from the shop?" His voice cracked, but he had to add, "Did she make it."

"Never heard a name but the report said she gave a full statement on the robbery, so if she died she lived for a while but don't really know what happened, report doesn't say."

Blade took a long deep breath, there was no way he could know, after all there were a half dozen or more haberdashery shops in Kansas City but only one he knew of owned by a woman. Blade tried to look nonchalant as he got up from his seat on the ground, stretched and then wiped the back of his hand under each eye while walking toward the still-smoking remains of the cooking-fire. He poured the last half cup of coffee from the pot and took a long drink, hardly noticing the coffee was as much grounds as liquid. Blade thought for an instant about telling these boys he changed his mind jumping on Medicine and getting to Kansas City as fast as he could. On the way, he would pray Emma was alive and when he got there he would beg her for forgiveness, get married, settle down and be happy if she would have him.

Blade wanted to leave, go right now, but knew he was needed here and had to stay. He turned and said, "Well boys we still got five hours of good light, let's not burn any more of it."

A dark, squat man of about twenty caught Blade's eye then looked at the ground as if he was not sure of what to do next. He looked back up and nodded, walked past Blade and poured a canteen of water on the dying campfire before using the side of his boot to cover the smoking coals. Blade, Sheriff Watson and the rest of the posse were mounted and looking for Luke Templeton in less than ten minutes. Five hours later, losing light with a second evening of misting rain starting to dampen the sage and scrub plains they watched the shape of a lone rider, sky-lining, along a ridge to the west.

Chapter 16

Several hours ago Templeton spied the posse, off in the distance, and avoided them. He'd stopped to rest and walk to relieve the pain in his saddle sore backside. Spotted the posse, a quarter mile away, through a small opening in a sparse stand of aspen and knew he was lucky, but decided instead he had outsmarted them.

Once the posse passed by he mounted and rode out. But he didn't go far. Instead he circled back, followed, staying at a distance trying to figure out which way the Cheyenne posse was going, wondering if they were after him. He doubted they were, wasn't even sure it was a posse. He knew it could be possible, it could be the law and they may be after him, he didn't want to take any chances. Being so unfamiliar with the west and with little or no understanding of how a posse worked when they were searching high rough terrain Templeton made a near fatal mistake. This time, the posse saw him first.

The instant they saw him on the bluff not more than two hundred yards away a clap of thunder changed the misting rain to pelting drops and hail the size of corn kernels. The posse tired from days in the saddle and now spoiling for a fight charged up the hill six guns and rifles pulled with the posse cowboys firing random shots through the storm at Templeton or shadows in the rain. They had waited too long for this and were not about to wait any longer.

This time, he hadn't seen them and he'd not heard them, not until the shots started and the lead whistled through the driving rain all around him. Maybe he'd been a fool riding along the ridge. The hail stung his face he could see the nose of his black mare but nothing beyond. Pouring rain ran down his face and he ran for his life. Today he'd lost the caution of the past few days, caution that served him well in this unfamiliar country. What Templeton didn't know was the posse in their wild unorganized dash up the hill in the blinding rain gave him a chance to escape, a chance he thought he'd lost.

He looked around; panic marking his face then did the only thing he could think of. He forced Three Legs down the back side of the hill, running at a full gallop until the sleek horse shied and tried to stop and turn as they reached a steep-walled ravine near the bottom. Templeton kicked hard attempting to force Three Legs down into the ravine. She wouldn't go, instead bucked hard, one time, depositing Templeton on the seat of his pants in the sagebrush and mud. With more luck than skill, he managed to hold the left-hand rein tight enough to not lose his horse. He climbed back into the saddle and slow-walked the horse in a tight circle around the hill until he was headed in the same direction the posse came from. He rode as silent as he could creeping along the bottom of the ravine his horse had not wanted to jump. Templeton knew it might be his one chance, the rain made it impossible to see more than a few feet and he guessed the men chasing him would take care of their horses first. They would guide them away from the ditch the instant they realized how close they were to danger, avoiding any chance of injury. He guessed right.

Twenty minutes later with the rain not letting up the posse quit the chase. "He vanished, like some kind of a ghost," shouted a kid, who looked no more than eighteen, to anyone in the posse within hearing distance.

Most of the men now regrouped at the bottom of the hill where the mad dash started. The men that were not back yet were either walking their mounts on their way back, riding in circles or lost for the moment. The ones who straggled back carried the discouraged looks of the defeated with them.

"No I think it's the rain, the rain let him disappear," Sheriff Watson hollered out over the sound of the rain pounding the sage and prairie grass. Small rivulets of red-brown water rushed down the side of the hill in dozens of places. Irritated but already resigned to spending more days in the saddle, if the posse would, the sheriff looked around to gather the rest of his men. Blade Holmes rode down the hill, Medicine splashing with every step, toward the discouraged group.

"Holmes, you see any sign of him, you were up the rise before the rest of us got half-way."

"No didn't see a thing," Blade answered, now wishing he could get off his horse and kick himself. It was less than a half hour ago the chase started and it should have ended with the capture of Templeton twenty minutes ago.

Blade was furious but tried to hide it from the men, "I never make mistakes like this," he mumbled as he twisted in the saddle in a futile attempt to ease the low back pain. He twisted as far around as the sore back allowed then slapped his hand down hard on the saddle horn spooking Medicine, who nickered and skipped sideways before settling down.

"What's that Holmes?"

"Nothing Sheriff, nothing at all, just irritated with myself, he was riding the ridge right alongside us and he slipped away."

"Any idea as to how he got away from us?" Watson asked.

"No, no idea, none at all," Holmes said. "We need to head back toward the river see if we can find some trees, some better shelter to make camp. Come back here when we can see better in the morning, should give us some answers if the rain doesn't wash everything away."

An hour later with the rain still pounding down the small group sat in a dark cottonwood thicket near the North Platte River. Several attempts to start a fire in the best shelter available failed and now the men sat in a small circle of silence chilled to the bone. Blade sat off to the side by himself leaning against a tree with his slicker pulled up to his chin, his hat pulled low with water running off in puddles. He sat and he brooded about what could have been, using his memories of the last two hours to beat himself up for being such a fool.

Setting alone and miserable Blade had plenty of time to plan the next few days. An hour slipped by with Blade alternating future plans with condemning himself for the way he acted chasing Templeton in the rain. He'd charged up the hill with a posse of greenhorns and acting like one himself. He knew better and now knew a killer was still loose and his carelessness helped him stay free. Templeton may have murdered the love of his life and might have been trying to kill him a week ago on his way to Fort Laramie.

Medicine could do things most horses could only dream of doing if horses could dream. Blade saw the ragged ditch in plenty of time to stop and go around, but riding the finest horse he had ever seen he'd let him jump, maybe right over the top of Luke Templeton. After jumping the ravine, he charged at top speed on to the west and he would bet the knife in his boot Templeton was heading east at the same time below him in the ravine.

Blade smelled smoke and looked up. So lost in thought he hadn't noticed someone, at last, got a fire going, small but burning brightly. The rain had stopped and now a half moon and a few stars were casting dappled light on the countryside. The breezes of earlier were gone and the smoke from the fire crawled straight up through the trees. Men were moving around and getting ready to cook and eat. Blade was hungry, no wonder he thought, getting late for supper, seven fifteen.

It took time to get a good fire going but soon the damp wood blazed high enough and the men congregated around warming, drying and complaining. The trail food was starting to get old to the members of the posse. Several of the men were married and used to home cooking and a variety of food. Now beans and bacon had to do every day. Blade didn't mind, he'd been eating what he could find and what he caught for a lot of years, these men were used to better. He had been in situations like this before, the posse was ready to go home and so was Sheriff Watson.

Blade never liked talking about his past, even the recent past; he didn't want people to see him as a braggart. When an older rider in the posse asked about the riverboat capture of Big Ed, it was time for Blade to talk about his past; he could not avoid talking this time. He put his plate and coffee cup down and started to tell the story. As he told the tale, Blade hoped the posse could stay together, at least a few more days. If they did, Templeton would be caught and then maybe he could find out why he followed him out of Cheyenne.

"I was working a Missouri riverboat, the *Pride of the Blue*, most days on a short run, Kansas City up to Saint Joe. I worked security in the card rooms, kind of like a sheriff in a gambling hall but on a boat, a real big boat, some days I spent more time playing cards than doing any real security. I tried to let luck make a living for me and I was doing alright. Well, kind of alright, for me. I was on my second week on the river and I'd made the day trip five or six times by then. Staying in Kansas City, on the days I didn't work or playing cards with a free ride on the *Pride of the Blue*, I was sitting at a table in the main hall playing draw poker with whoever cared to set down and join in."

"Big guy with kind of a flat nose and a scar on his cheek sat down, wasn't much of a player, I could see it right away. After a few hands, he lost most of the hundred or so dollars he'd laid down to start. Wasn't long and he started arguing and complaining about everything and everyone at the table. The more he talked the worse he played and the more I thought I'd seen this guy before, yet I was pretty sure I didn't know him. Then it struck me where I'd seen him, or rather his face, on a poster. I'd given up a deputy job in Missouri, not a month before, and remembered seeing a poster of this guy. The picture was perfect, it was Big Ed, but I wasn't in any hurry to turn him in. Not while my cards were running sort of good. Wasn't even sure if I wanted to turn him in at all since it would blow my cover and ruin my chances of any more free rides and riverboat games."

"Then old Big Ed, I'm not sure what brought it on but it was like he cracked, like a buggy whip, one pop and he went crazy. He pushed his chair back leaped to his feet and started accusing everyone at the table of cheating him out of his money. I knew it was just frustration talking. Mad at losing, no one at his table including me, played well enough to cheat. The four of us sat there, me, a hardware salesman from back east, a mortician from Omaha and Big Ed, no one cheated him, he just played bad poker. He made a quick reach across his chest to the inside of his jacket pocket. He wore one of those shiny big city jackets, fit too tight on him. I knew right away his hand was grabbing for a derringer. He was kind of slow with the coat too small on him. I threw my collar knife and stuck his hand to his chest. He wasn't pulling a little pocket gun like I thought, he was pulling a forty-five, much too big for a jacket gun, it just kind of fell on the floor.

Anyway, Big Ed just stood there staring at me then at the blade stuck through his hand and into his chest. Then he kind of toppled over like a sawed through tree you give one last push to tip it down, except he didn't need a push he just went down. Then I saw the derringer on the ground and felt the pain in my shoulder, he had shot me then grabbed for his bigger gun, must have had the .41 derringer in his hand for a while before he shot me. Anyway, it wasn't much, all healed up now; he wasn't too good of a shot, even up close. That's it not a great story, not really."

"How'd you keep from killing him?"

"Knife caught him in the loose skin between his thumb and trigger finger pinned his hand right to his breastbone, wasn't even hurt too bad."

"How can ya throw a knife like that, I can't even stick my knife in the ground every time playing mumblety-peg?" Blade couldn't help smiling at the teenager after he asked the question.

"Well, the knives I have are balanced, not simple pocket knives or skinning knives like you buy in a general store and I practiced some as a kid, maybe there was a little luck involved too." Blade had no idea why he said it was luck because he was that good, but for some reason he got embarrassed when he talked about how good he was at anything. No matter what people said about him and no matter how big the stories became they should not have embarrassed him, he was that good.

The men sat around talking and drinking coffee for another hour, Blade loosened up some and told a few stories about life growing up in Ohio. One by one the men took their, now dry, blankets from the branches near the fire, made their open-air beds and went to sleep. Blade took a while longer, leaning back against the tree sheltering his bedroll, needing some time to think. He sat for more than an hour under the tree looking around the camp making out the images in the tree-filtered moonlight. At last Blade was ready. He lay down and pulled the army blanket up over his chest. In less than a quarter of an hour he fell asleep with his mouth curled into the slightest hint of a smile, he knew where Luke Templeton was headed.

Chapter 17

It had been almost a month since Blade Holmes left. Every day she prayed it would not be forever. Emma Fick gave a quick tug to the bottom of the shade and let it roll up keeping the slightest bit of pressure on it so it would not go too high. She pulled back the beige curtain and looked out as the early morning light streamed into her upstairs bedroom. Emma enjoyed this morning like she did all mornings, the early sun felt warm and renewing. Turning away from the window she glanced at the mantle clock on the bureau, ten minutes after six. Funny, she thought, Blade would have known the time without looking, she missed him so much even thoughts about his ability to always know the time of day brought tears to her eyes. Despite the morning sun, she felt a chill and pulled her robe tight at the neck.

Emma dressed and walked the few steps to her tiny kitchen trying to work up a smile. She really didn't feel like making breakfast, settled on a biscuit from a bowl on her sideboard. After taking one small bite, she reached for the jar on the counter and covered it with chokecherry jam. Two bites later she sat down on the floor and started to cry. It made her feel like a school girl, crying over a broken romance. Oh, how she wished he would come back. Maybe she'd pushed him too hard, maybe tried too hard to civilize or citified him, there must have been a reason he left. Emma hoped more than anything in life that their relationship was not over, she was not ready to give up on Blade, not yet. She would wait, didn't matter how long it took, she would wait.

Emma stood straightening her dress, dabbed under her eyes with a napkin and forced herself to go to work. She only needed to go downstairs but still didn't feel like being there. Once downstairs she went straight to the workroom instead of putting the open sign in the front door and unlocking like every other day. Working on men's suits was her primary business but never her favorite part of the job, making wedding dresses, which was supposed to be a secondary part of the business, she liked best. But she needed to make a living and men's clothes paid the bills and made the money in her flourishing business. Before making the white buckskin jacket for Blade, she'd found no particular pleasure in making men's clothes. Then Blade Holmes walked in off the street and took her breath away.

That first meeting was a disaster, now looking back it seemed more like a pleasant fantasy than the nightmare it was. She had trouble talking with him, and measuring him, worst of all she couldn't stop thinking about Blade from the minute he left. He'd asked if she could make the jacket out of white buckskin and she immediately said she'd do it. Before Blade came into her life, Emma turned down any and all work with leather. It was too tough, hard to work with and much too barbaric and old-fashioned for her taste. But for Blade it was a different story, how she loved making him that buckskin jacket.

A loud tap, tap, tap at the front door snapped Emma from her daydream.

She rushed to the front room and opened the door for customers. Emma made it through another day much like all the days the past few weeks. She sat working or chatting with customers looking up every time the leather strap of sleigh bells on the door jingled in a new customer. Each time wishing, wishing the next time the door opened it would be him, standing there wearing the white buckskin jacket.

Emma tried to keep from falling apart. She continued attending the poetry readings at the library, the ones she enjoyed so much and drug Blade to twice a week for several months. Her friends were split between telling her he would come back and telling her to forget about him, he wasn't coming back. Nothing worked; she wanted him to come back and could think of nothing else because nothing else mattered in her life.

One of her friends dropped off a copy of, *Blade Holmes Catches Big Ed on the River*; she laughed and tossed it on her work table. Couldn't believe some hack writer, back east, made up a story about Blade and his arrest and the bringing in of Big Ed Monday. He had told her the story and she had asked enough questions she felt like she knew as much about the arrest of Big Ed as Blade did. As soon as the shop was closed and locked up for the day she took the book upstairs and read it cover to cover, and then read it again. She stayed up most of the night, spending hours laughing, crying, praying and reading. When she opened a few minutes before eight in the morning with red swollen eyes Emma looked as if she was feeling the effects of the two or three hours of sleep that finally came in the early hours of the morning.

Last night she remembered everything about their relationship and everything about him. Where they went together, conversations they had and words they'd spoken about the future and a life they would share someday. This morning she felt ready to burst from the memories. Emma could see him walking, hear him talking and feel the touch of his hand on her back as they walked. She remembered holding his hand, the two of them laughing together, talking, eating late dinners and going to church and poetry readings. She remembered his smile and the twinkle in those piercing dark eyes.

She also remembered the way people turned to look when they walked through the streets of Kansas City. Most of all she remembered the first kiss and after months of dating, sleeping with Blade, every memory hurt.

Keep a stiff upper lip she told others when times were bad, and now friends were telling her. She could not, could not keep a stiff upper lip, instead thinking of him made her lips quiver and she cried, cried more than she ever had, she couldn't help it. Work helped and she was thankful for it.

Matthew Holmes come home, come home Blade she prayed every night.

Chapter 18

The shots were so close together it sounded like more than one gun, two maybe three. Three shots came before most of the men were aware of the day. A few were moving about, some were still in their bedrolls, one attended to a loose shoe on his horse, but none was ready for this. The early morning shots rang through the bluffs guarding the river turning the quiet of dawn into a deafening series of echoing gunshots. Oliver Stevens lay on the ground near the coffee pot with two ever-widening blood stains leaking through his shirt. No one dared move toward Stevens for fear of being shot themselves. Instead, the men crept deeper into the trees hiding from the shooters. It would not have helped if they could have reached Stevens immediately. Two slugs, one low in his shoulder and one in the middle of his back had already taken his life.

When the three shots came the men dove, dashed or crawled for cover trying to save themselves and none saw where the shots came from. Except Blade, he saw them, two riders on the rise coming up beside a slight bend in the river. Both men were astride smallish looking dark horses small enough to be Indian ponies. Even From his two hundred yard vantage point he was sure neither of the shooters looked anything like Luke Templeton.

A five-minute wait followed by three minutes of confusion had passed before the sheriff and Blade convinced the men to finish up here and follow. The shooters already had a ten-minute head start and waiting a few more minutes would make it safer and give them a chance to make the proper preparations the sheriff explained. Blade was beginning to like this sheriff; he knew his job and would not risk another man's life when he did not need to.

Oliver Stevens was an unknown, not one among the men knew him and none of the men had noticed before they left Cheyenne when Sheriff Watson took him aside and spoke to him alone. They watched the sheriff ask for a name and nothing else before swearing him in for the Templeton posse. Like all territorial posses, this one was made up of whoever volunteered, no questions asked. Last night the men sat up late drinking coffee, smoking cigarettes, making small talk and telling stories, Stevens laughed and smiled with them but didn't join in much. He seemed to be enjoying the evening but never told a story. He did give an occasional nod of the head to something another of the riders said. Thinking back Blade couldn't remember him saying a single word. At the time it didn't seem out of place, now it did. Why did he join the posse, for protection, maybe he was running himself, or maybe he was a drifter looking for some excitement in a new west, a west changing too fast for his middle-aged tastes? Blade didn't think Stevens fit any of those possibilities but for some reason he needed to know.

The men took turns digging a grave on a small sandy loam bank near the river. The digging should have been easy, but the soil, saturated from two days of heavy rain made each shovelful twice the weight it should have been. The men breathed hard and sweat soaked their shirts even as they took turns at the job no one wanted. The grave digging took more than an hour before it was three feet deep and wide enough for a proper burial. Two men, one holding the dead man by the hands and the other his feet lowered the body, minus his Navy Colt, into the ground. They made quick work of refilling the hole then stood and looked at each other to see if anyone knew anything to say. After an uncomfortable moment of silence, the men turned walked the fifty or so feet back into camp and started readying themselves and their horses for the day. Riding away two men at the tail end of the posse promised each other they would come back someday and put a marker on the grave of this brave man, but, deep down they knew they wouldn't.

The rain softened Prairie made the trail easy to find and easy to follow. The tracks could be seen for thirty yards along the hillside where the two horses were spurred into an instant run and had thrown bits of grass and wet dirt the ponies pushing hard for instant speed. Blade and the sheriff fell back and let the eager posse follow the soft tracks. Blade waited until the sheriff looked over at him then asked, "Sheriff, did you happen to notice the clothes Stevens had on?"

"You mean the gray hat and light colored vest, same as me?"

Blade rode another fifty yards before saying, "Could have been you they were after."

"Possible, could have been me he was after."

"You have any new enemy's sheriff or old ones mean enough to take a shot at you?"

"Nothing out of the ordinary, someone's always mad at the law, not often mad enough to kill though." They continued riding in silence, listening as the posse argued about which way the tracks were leading.

"Blade"

"Yeah, sheriff."

"You'd just woke up this morning when the shots came, saw you unwrapping yourself from your green blanket, could have been you they were after—soon as you got out of the blanket and pulled on your white jacket."

"Thought about it, you know what's bothering me the most about this whole thing sheriff?"

"Yeah Blade, I know, how'd they find us?"

Blade and the sheriff rode on in silence for several minutes before Blade turned to the sheriff, "they were following us, sheriff,, we were looking for Templeton and they were looking for us, following us, never heard of outlaws following the posse."

Sheriff Watson pulled his hat down another inch on his forehead, nodded and bit off a chew from a plug of tobacco not looking at Blade or saying a word.

The men slowed their horses to a walk then slowed even more and after a few more yards stopped. Two of the younger members of the posse got down on their hands and knees searching the prairie and disagreeing over which way the trail led. Blade rode to the front of the pack leaned over Medicine's side for one or two seconds and pointed the posse back east, toward the river.

Blade fell to the rear of the pack again and slowing down to make more distance from the others. He didn't know what he was doing, oh sure he knew how to track and he could track these murders with his eyes closed, they would catch up with them. No, it was what he was doing, a few days ago he rode along in a melancholy mood not caring where he went or what he was doing, not caring much about anything, except for thoughts of Emma. Now he rode with an untrained posse chasing after three killers, leading men in a life or death situation and all he could think about he finally mumbled, "I was riding to Laramie City for no particular reason only looking for some bright saloon lights and a game of cards."

Blade shook his head, took off his hat, wiped his brow and attempted to clear the dust from the hat with a quick snap of his wrist. Hearing Blade's soft words Medicine picked the pace up on his own catching up with the rest of the group.

Blade found the pair of horses easy to track even in places the rest of the posse couldn't see any sign. Now following a short distance behind Blade and the sheriff the men were talking, just above a whisper about Blade, asking each other how any man could track across this country. The more they followed, the more they believed all the stories they'd been told about this man. The men were tired, they had skipped the usual noontime meal and Blade knew it was a few minutes until four o'clock in the afternoon when a tired sheriff, a man about twice Blade's age, suggested they stop. "Maybe best if we do rest up and start again in the morning," Blade said, as he led the posse down near the river to a campsite. The site was not unlike the night before, but this time they took the time to find an area of downed and tangled limbs making sure the camp could not be seen from the river bluffs.

The men needed this break, the dollar a day posse wages and food weren't enough for the saddle sores and aching bones the men were feeling. And tonight they would eat the last of the beans and bacon. By noon tomorrow the posse would either go out of business or ride somewhere to re-supply. In the last few days Blade had traveled west, south, and east and now south again, they were close to Chug Creek and maybe a place to get supplies. But right now Blade tried to concentrate on the two killers from this morning and Luke Templeton, what could the connection be, or was there a connection?

The camp quieted tonight, the killing of Oliver Stevens sobered the youthful personalities of the men and the sheriff needed rest and sleep. All were ready to go home. But they still had a job to do. Blade took his second cup of coffee over near the sheriff sat on a log and drained half a cup in one long swallow, "Sheriff we'll catch up with those two tomorrow, maybe late but it'll be tomorrow."

Watson turned his tired eyes toward Blade and said, "Why do you think tomorrow, seems pretty quick?"

"They're riding double, got a lame horse."

Watson now looked surprised, "You can see riding double and a lame horse in their tracks?"

"I've been tracking animals since I was a button of a kid growing up in Ohio, always came easy to me. They're double alright."

By this point in the conversation the men had all moved and were standing or sitting close enough to hear. Their spirits were lifted listening to Blade explain how he knew one of the shooters had a lame horse but were keeping it with them and riding the other double. Blade explained he believed they were leading the horse to trade and the one place close-by to trade horses would be Chugwater station.

The men once again felt like they were doing something of importance and within minutes the mood changed from one of apprehension to one of eagerness. Again they questioned Blade and now the sheriff about their adventures and they stayed up for an hour past sunset before spreading bedrolls and nodding off, one by one, to restless sleep.

Benny Market and Jackson Beckworth sat in their cold camp discussing the day. They were tired and hungry, camped back from the river in an arroyo hidden by the sage, still two or three days out of Cheyenne. The two talked in low tones as they sat shivering in the breeze. They were sure they'd killed the Pinkerton Detective following Templeton, but now they both worried about the rest of the posse. "They're good. I never thought it would come to this, been followed a dozen times and never needed over a few hours to give any of um the slip," Beckworth said.

"If that worthless horse hadn't gone lame, we would be gone from this place by now and a day from a hotel in Cheyenne, and good places to eat," Market answered.

"Way I see it we got two choices, head over to Hi Kelly's place and see if we can get another horse, or circle back and take one from the posse," Beckworth said.

"Don't like either one," Market answered, "Hi might not have much stock left since the stage line quit last year and even if he does might be stage pullin' horse's stead of riding horses."

"We got to do something, they're following us like a dog sniffing down a rabbit hole, backtracking, riding in water, circling, nothin' worked. We can't sit here starving and freezing forever."

"I know, I know," Market said irritated, he stood and started pacing back and forth, "can't believe it either, when we circled and they cut across on us. If they wouldn't a stopped, we might have had to shoot it out with them and I don't like our odds shooting it out with that many guys."

"I wanna know who the cowboy on the big Appaloosa is, every time he gets off his horse and looks for sign they come straight after us, if I find out Templeton knew anything about the guy I'll kill him. I might kill him anyway soon as we collect the rest of our money." Beckworth added.

Benny Market stood and tried to slap some life into his cold arms before he said, five hundred lousy dollars is not enough for all the trouble it's been getting the Pinkerton guy. And Templeton still owes us four hundred of it, shoulda made him pay it all up front."

"It was your idea," Beckworth said, "to go to work for that dandy, told you he would get us in trouble, knew it right off when he asked us to hang around the sheriff's office and wait and see if someone tried to follow him. We had nothin' but pure dumb luck when we seen the Pinkerton come in on the train rent a horse and join the posse, kind of gave it away. Both of us knew right away he was the guy Templeton was scared about."

An hour after dawn Blade Holmes, Sheriff Watson and the Cheyenne posse gave up the tracks and went on a direct line for Hi Kelly's Chugwater station. Market and Beckworth left for Kelly's an hour before.

The sun was straight overhead when Beckworth and Market rode into Hi Kelly's ranch four miles north of Chugwater station. Kelly laughed when he came out of his cabin and saw the two riding double leading Beckworth's horse. "Looks like I can help you boys out if it's a horse you're looking for." Ten minutes later Luke Templeton's two murdering employees left Hi Kelly's place with two fresh horses on a dead run.

"One-fifteen, maybe one-twenty, we made good time," Blade thought, as the posse rode up to the hitching rack in front of the ranch house. Kelly came out of the ramshackle barn north of the house carrying a bucket in one hand and a rifle in the other as the riders dismounted and started to tie up. "This place seems to be turning into a real city, second visitors in the last hour or so."

"Two guys, two brown horses, one lame, they get here before us?" Blade asked.

"Horse with a bad shoe, bruised foot, she'll be alright in a couple of weeks, twice the horse of the one I traded them, and I charged full price plus the trade. Got to make a go of it somehow since the stage quit," Hi Kelly said, as he set the bucket down with a half dozen brown eggs covering the bottom.

"What can I do for you today sheriff, I take it with this many men deputized you mean some real business out here somewhere." Kelly then looked from the sheriff over to Blade and said "I don't think I've had the pleasure of meeting you, but I do believe I am in the presence of Mr. Blade Holmes."

The last few days it seemed like everyone knew something about him and Blade felt a little-taken back by Hi Kelly immediately recognizing him. "Pleased to meet you, Mr. Kelly," Blade said climbing down from Medicine. He pulled the glove from his right hand with his teeth and stuck out his hand to Hi Kelly, "I'm Blade Holmes."

"Sheriff Watson stepped toward Kelly and said, "We're in need of provisions, may be a few more days before we finish our business out here. Beans, bacon, hardtack, peaches, if you got um, maybe some tobacco and flour, can't think of what else right off, can you help us out?"

"I can, but we'll have to ride on down to the station. Give me a few minutes to toss a saddle on and I'll be along."

Five minutes later the men headed south toward Chugwater Station, a stage stop of importance for many years, but now with the Cheyenne-Deadwood stage out of business it was just another remote general store, soon to be out of business. As they rode from the ranch, the men veered around a fenced area with a handful of stone markers, a family cemetery. The place where relatives of Hi Kelly's Sioux wife were buried, Blade had read stories about Sioux raiding party's who'd terrorized this area a decade ago. Too many good people on both sides died, Blade thought, these markers were the last reminders of those good people, probably part of something they didn't want or understand.

Must be a lonesome life Blade reflected as he rode letting the loneliness and feelings of melancholy creep back into his mind. It took Blade a few minutes to remember what he was doing out here. He felt like he needed to be back in the city and the bright lights, playing cards and having fun, but what he wanted most of all was to be in Kansas City with Emma. But not today and maybe not any day soon, someday and soon, he hoped.

Re-supplied, the men were talking among themselves unsure of what to do next. A balding middle-aged man who reminded Blade of a shop owner back home asked, "Sheriff, where do we go now, go after Templeton or the two guys who just ran from here?"

The sheriff looked at Blade and then turned back and looked over the rest of his weary posse. "I think there's only one thing we can do, get the guys who killed one of our own, we're about two hours behind them and it looks like they're heading toward Cheyenne. Boys, I think we can catch um, let's ride."

Blade thought that to be an interesting choice as he nudged Medicine into a gallop. Supplies for a week and we're a day and a half out of Cheyenne, don't believe the sheriff thinks this is going to be easy as he's pretending.

Chapter 19

They were close enough to Cheyenne to see the dim glow of the city's new gas lights against the black on black of the moonless night. The distance lights were of no help this far from town. The darkness of the night made traveling another two or three hours to get to the city impossible. The posse had made good progress riding hard following a clear trail all afternoon and into early evening. Making camp tonight they all knew the two men they were following, the killers of Oliver Stevens, were far enough ahead of them to already be near Cheyenne. Or maybe they were already in the bright night lights of Cheyenne. The posse could do nothing but look on from a distance. The killers would enjoy the company of friends if they had any, a good meal, and a soft bed tonight. As for the posse, they would spend another night on the high plains and in the morning make a decision.

The disappointment of not catching up with the murders lasted only a short time the men rested and filled their bellies with strong coffee, biscuits, and jerky gravy. The conversation around a blazing campfire turned lighter as the men knew they would be home by noon tomorrow and done with the posse, most of them forever. They sat near the huge fire swapping stories, laughing, joking and telling tall tales. Blade chose to set near enough to hear but far enough back to stay out of the conversation. He busied himself cleaning his Colt revolver. His bad run of luck with the cards cost him everything he owned except for the clothes on his back, his Colt, rifle, horse, saddle, bedroll and the two throwing blades but right now he felt like he didn't need anything else.

He finished cleaning the six-gun and then starting spinning the pistol, first one way then in reverse each time letting the pistol slide into the holster. After a couple of minutes, he switched and began drawing pointing and spinning the .45, this time parallel to the ground and once again ending with a nearly invisible placement back into his holster. Blade repeated the process a dozen times before he noticed the quiet. He looked up and everyone, including the sheriff, was looking at him, watching him. Embarrassed Blade sat down and tried to act like none of them had been watching, then fidgeted and decided to start gathering more firewood.

"Mr. Holmes," a kid who looked about sixteen said, "where'd you ever learn to draw and spin the guns, the stories about you are true aren't they, about you being the best, maybe the best there's ever been, where'd you learn it?"

Blade didn't want to answer but knew he needed to, "Not sure, guess I always could, far back as I can remember anyway," Blade replied, walking toward the fire to empty his small armload of firewood.

"Mr. Holmes is your gun a regular ol' Army Colt?" The kid asked as he stood beside Blade at the fire.

"One of Samuel Colt's best, regular single action Army Colt .45, started making this one fifteen years ago, 1873, it's a lot better than the .44 cap and ball 1860 I carried when I came out west from Ohio. I have smoothed the action some and worked the spring over; keep it and the inside of the holster polished and slick. Not that I want to draw on someone, but if I have to, I want to be as fast as possible."

"Mr. Holmes did you ever draw on anyone, like in the books?" The same young man asked. Blade nodded toward the young man not feeling much like talking anymore, he'd said about as much as he wanted for the time being. He filled his tin cup half full of coffee walked over and picked up his saddle and bedroll and moved farther into the shadows before tossing down his makeshift bed. He sipped the hot coffee and thought about his Colt, the posse, tomorrow, and the rest of his life.

For all of his ten years out west, Blade had been careful about where he camped. He'd camped when he could, where the water runs away from him always on the outside curve of a stream never the inside. Greenhorns camped where it was easiest to get to the water. He camped back away in cover. Blade found campsites near something solid enough to stop a bullet and always away from the light of the moon, stars, and campfire.

Long ago Blade learned someone standing near the fire had a tough time seeing him if he stayed backed off into the shadows. He liked the darker areas because it was easy to see from the shadows into the light. Blade could always spot those not used to being out here on the high plains living off the land. They would be camped right beside the fire, even on a warm night. He thought about warning this group to move back, but he didn't think they were in any danger, not tonight. Blade looked around at the exhausted bunch of greenhorn lawmen and doubted any of them would be too eager to volunteer for a dollar a day and food posse again. He watched the men one by one settling in for the night and listened as the men grew quieter and the sounds of the night took over. The breeze rustling the sage and the sounds of early spring birds and crickets seemed right tonight. Blade liked the night sounds, missed them in the city, right now he wasn't sure what it was he thought he liked so much about the city, then he remembered Emma.

Blade wanted immediate sleep but was bothered tonight by the death of Oliver Stevens. He couldn't remember the two exchanging any words in the short time they rode together, so his death, although unfortunate, was not riding his conscious hard.

No, it was not that they were friends he'd only learned his last name after he was killed. It was the why bothering him tonight. He hated it when things did not seem to fit neatly in place. The man appeared to know what he was doing and yet someone followed him and this posse out on the prairie and killed him, why? The shooters they trailed toward Cheyenne killed the man they wanted, Blade felt sure of that. Stephens was the man they were after, but why him, what was special about him, what made him a target?

Blade picked him out as soon as he joined the posse, didn't look anything like the rest of the posse members; they were kids, businessmen, and ranch hands. But not Stephens, he carried an excellent gun and looked like he knew how to use it, but he rode an old horse with a rental brand from a Cheyenne livery stable. Yet he knew what he was doing; he wasn't a local helping out his community, doing public service, out helping a posse catch a wanted man. No, he must have been some kind of a lawman. U.S Marshal or maybe Pinkerton even military was a possibility. Blade laid back on his saddle and thought again about the past few days, trying to make order from something and then from everything.

Thoughts of his brief conversations about his trip out here from Ohio returned to his mind. Childhood memories of good times crept into his mind and he gave up his thoughts of Oliver

Stevens and why he was killed. For a moment lying on the ground under the stars, Blade thought maybe he should have stayed in Ohio. He would have become a good farmer by now, married, kids. Blade pulled the green wool blanket up to his chin. The chill had come back in the air tonight. Ten minutes later Blade woke up thinking about Ohio and Kansas City, Oliver Stevens, Templeton and his upbringing on his parents Ohio farm. He shivered more from the melancholy that sometimes visited him than the cold and worried about why. Blade chased in and out of sleep for the next two hours before reaching a deep but fretful sleep.

Sheriff Watson had another blazing fire going an hour before dawn; Blade suspected its size was being used as an alarm clock for the men. Watson waited to approach Blade until he saw him sitting up rubbing his eyes and stretching. He walked over and kneeled beside him sipping steaming coffee from a battered, rusty cup. Blade smiled up at Watson watching the fire reflecting off his bald head. The sheriff, hurting and stiff, had a hard time kneeling, his gray eyes looked tired and old. "Blade I have a favor to ask of you."

"Sure sheriff, whatever you need."

"I can't go on, too tired. I want you to go after Templeton with as many of these men who'll go. I need to get back home, I can do a better job there of tracking the guys who killed Stevens.

There's something about Stevens I didn't tell you, he didn't want anyone to know, he worked as a detective out of Kansas City, Pinkerton man. He thought it best to ride along like any other cowboy, don't think he pulled it off on you, but I think the shooters got the man they wanted. Not sure why they wanted him dead but maybe when I get back to the office, I can send off a few wires maybe sort this stuff out." He took a long moment before continuing, "I'm not sure I can keep up anymore."

Blade listened to what the sheriff had to say, and then both men sat quietly watching the others as they started to wake and move around the camp. "I'll do it, but I need to go it alone. These men are all good men, but I can't afford any mistakes, these boys are pretty raw."

"I thought that might be your answer and I'm sure these fellas will be glad to be let go in town. I need to deputize you proper, not just part of the posse. Part of my duties as County Sheriff and Assistant Justice of the Peace allows me to swear you in as a Deputy U.S Marshal for thirty days. All I have to do is wire Washington and let them know. I expect a month should be long enough, being a marshal allows you to travel where ever you need to go. Regular marshal pay, eighty a month plus rewards if there are any and I expect there will be. Load up with what supplies you need I'll split the rest up with the boys as a bonus. Good luck!"

The sun-splattered its first bits of golden light over the horizon as Wyoming Territorial Deputy Marshal Blade Holmes rode out of camp, this time going back, to the north. The circle was about to complete itself.

Chapter 20

Blade had no idea where to begin; maybe he would go all the way back to Fort Laramie. For now riding at his pace and making his own decisions suited Blade fine.

He knew he was no dime novel western hero or at least not like the ones he'd read about as a kid. But the perception he was, held by so many others, so many more than Blade could ever guess, told him the job ahead of him may be harder than anyone believed. It might be impossible. Blade needed to be careful and he needed to be good, people expected it. It wasn't because he wanted or needed to be a dime novel hero. No, it was more, at last Blade started to realize who and what he was. In the past, he'd often rode aimlessly but today he knew he was the hunter riding with the awareness of the hunted. He rode north.

Sometimes he didn't like to admit it but today Blade knew he was in his element. Sure he thought about the city, bright lights and a good game of poker but days like today were what made the melancholy go away, this and thinking about Emma in Kansas City. Blade let his mind wander, but only for a few minutes, he remembered his first hunts as a kid in Ohio. But those hunts were for ducks and rabbits and, as a teenager deer. His mind snapped back on task, today he hunted again, hunted Luke Templeton. He was not worried any longer about the two shooters who had taken the life of the Pinkerton agent with the posse. They were in Cheyenne and could be dealt with later, or maybe they would be jailed by the time he reached town.

Like all trackers and hunters Blade tried to put his mind into Templeton's. "He wanted you," Blake blurted out, "he wanted you, big fella," he repeated, as he patted his big stallion on the neck, "why didn't I think of that before, he needed a horse, why not the best?"

"He didn't want me to see his horse. He needed mine, and while he was at it, my weapons and provisions. He may have been after me but what he most needed was a horse— doubt a greenhorn like him could have stayed astride of you big fella," Blade said, patting Medicine on the neck again and letting him have his head for a few minutes.

Blade smiled remembering he had been out of food and about out of luck when Templeton walked into his camp a week ago. How fortunes do change in a short time, Blade thought, as he rode. He now wore a badge, had a job and a purpose, and saddlebags full of provisions. He remembered his mom telling him, maybe too many times, "the good Lord helps those who help themselves."

He wasn't sure he'd helped himself enough to get the Lord's help, but then again maybe this was what he was supposed to be doing. Maybe Blade Holmes was put on this earth to ride the high sagebrush prairie, working, looking, hunting and happy. He knew his mother would agree. But she might not approve of his quarry.

Following a limestone ridge for a little over an hour Blade rode Medicine down to a small stream, dismounted and sat with his back against a moss-covered rock outcropping. He didn't need the rest, but he needed the time. Lots of things were running through his mind and he didn't want to ride without all of his concentration on the task at hand. After fifteen minutes, Blade walked Medicine downstream a quarter of a mile until he found what he looked for. A deep cut in the bank created from centuries of snowmelt and rainwater runoff, hidden from all sides but the river. Blade tied Medicine to a snow broken limb of a juniper tree, walked a few steps and laid down on the sand. A tangled mass of roots and smooth river rocks protruded from the crumbling cut near the river bank made him almost invisible. After readjusting several times, he ground an elbow through the crust of the sand, propped up his head, at last got comfortable and started to relax. He didn't need to nap, not yet, but he needed a safe place to figure things out.

The only thing Blade knew about Luke Templeton's destination was what Sheriff Watson and the posse believed. The man headed for Fort Laramie when he left Cheyenne several days ago. The posse rode all the way to the fort only to learn he had been there and left. Now things were starting to make sense to Blade. Templeton reached the fort before the posse leaving before Watson and his men arrived. Blade wished now he would have, at least, stopped in at the fort and said hello to Colonel Merriam. Things might be easier now.

After an hour of relaxing and thinking Blade's mind cleared and the answer came to him. He'd given too much credit to Templeton. Trying too hard to figure out what he was doing when in all likelihood he was making it up as he went along. There was the answer Blade had been looking for.

Now he believed the troopers he'd watched from a half mile distance by the dreary mother in the sod ranch house had to have been chasing Templeton. But how did the troopers know Templeton was a killer, didn't matter, could have been as simple as a wire out of Cheyenne or maybe they were after him for some other reason? But they were after Templeton, couldn't be anyone else. He along with the army and the posse were all after the same man, so where has he been hiding, where is he now?

Blade knew, he's running, because he can't go back to Cheyenne or back north near the comfort of the fort.

The wind started to freshen, might be a storm coming in, Blade sat up and looked around. The trees, down here in the river bottom, were beginning to look more and more like they'd been touched by spring, green leaves unfolding all-round. More cover, Blade thought, easier to hide, if he's smart enough.

The more he relaxed and contemplated the more his mind started to wander. The sun began to disappear behind gathering blue, black thunderheads as Blade climbed back in the saddle. The long rest made it too early to stop for the day. He rode twenty minutes crossed the river and continued riding up river two or three miles, crossed again and rode back down stopping an hour later in the same place he'd left the hour before. Blade camped and spent a fitful night tossing and turning and dreaming of Kansas City and of things yet to happen.

Back in the saddle with the top of the sun peeking over the eastern horizon and the moon still high in the sky Blade and Medicine left at a trot. The river in front of them sparkled like a glass ribbon and the crisp morning air cleared Blade's mind to think about the day. The plan was simple. Ride a four-day circle, west for a day, then south for a day and east for a day then back north. Not much of a plan, but at least a plan. Then, well then, Blade would go to Cheyenne visit Sheriff Watson, tell him he was sorry but a hundred thousand square miles of Wyoming territory was too much. One fitful night of sleep and the central part of Blade's plan had changed, now it was to give up after a few days. Kansas City would be the next stop. Unless Templeton made a big mistake and let

Blade find him during the four-day circle. But today, today Blade rode north.

Templeton might be a novice out here but maybe not so much in other areas. He was a killer, out of his element, but still a killer. Blade reminded himself, once again, to be careful. City people ride in buggies, hire coaches, ride trains or walk when it isn't too much of a bother. Blade knew about life in the city, he had been a city dweller not so long ago, but it wasn't what he was thinking of now. Now, he thought about Templeton and what he might want or need when he was in trouble. He needed city things when you are out of your element; you search for your element. He needs the only part of the city he can find out here on the plains, he needs a ride, one he thinks is better than a horse, he needs the railroad. Blade knew where Templeton was heading, to catch a train, that's how he would run to get away in the city, run for a coach or a train, and it's how he would look to run now.

No reason to change his plans, Blade would ride the four-day circle he planned only not as far west as he first thought, too far from the railroad. Templeton could be anywhere, but he would not go west of the tracks, Blade was sure of that. In the last three or four days the posse, Calvary and maybe others were pushing him, he would be zigzagging and backtracking, countless times if he were smart, to avoid being seen or tracked if possible. Or maybe he's already gone, Blade thought, already in the middle of Nebraska or Utah, on the train and far from here.

But Templeton wasn't safe on a train in the middle of Nebraska, Utah or anywhere else. At present he sat roasting a chicken, over a sage wood fire, in the doorway of a sod ranch house two days ride north and west of where Blade and Medicine traveled under darkening midday skies.

Luke Templeton seemed uninterested in the body of a young woman lying bled out in a pool of crusting and blackening blood not twenty yards from the Soddy where he sat. Chicken fat dripped on the burning wood causing fingers of flame to reach near the top of the doorway. Templeton licked his lips at the smell and sounds of the roasting chicken. He pulled the stick with the chicken away from the fire, touched it with his index finger then licked the grease from the finger. He smiled and then laughed out loud.

Chapter 21

Today with at least some semblance of a plan Blade felt good as he tapped his heel and Medicine responded wanting to run, but Blade held him back. Six-fifteen in the morning when he headed out of camp and Blade didn't want to push Medicine hard early. It might be a long day. Medicine won the first battle of the day and Blade let him move at a lope instead of the walk he wanted. They had covered two or three miles of ground before he reined Medicine back to a walk. Using the combination of walking and loping the big Appaloosa could keep going with little stress all day long. By noon much of the bright blue of early morning disappeared and the sun now peaked in and out of low-hanging grey-blue clouds. Blade reined to a stop near a sweeping bend in the river to make a noon-day camp. After building a small fire, he made a pot of coffee, ate a piece of hardtack and several pieces of jerky. It felt good to have provisions again. Tonight he thought he might make a mess of biscuits and enjoy overeating for the first time since he left Kansas.

Blade rode the rest of the day following the river northwest. He didn't need to look for tracks anymore and traveled much faster moving another ten miles before he made his camp and sat down to cook and to overeat. To go with the biscuits Blade had been thinking about for the past three hours he opened two cans of beans and carved a dozen thick slices of bacon. Together it should be enough to fill his stomach for the first time since he left Cheyenne.

At seven-forty in the morning a rested Blade rode out of camp in pursuit of a killer who a week ago tried to convince Blade he was an English school teacher writing about the American West. Now riding away from the river with the warmth of the sun on his back Blade felt comfortable. The terrain started to change as he rode through the hours, the flat river lands gave way to more and more soft rolling hills and the sandy, grassy areas turned to rocks and sagebrush. Like yesterday Blade kept his eyes up looking for a man on horseback not down looking for tracks. He knew he'd taken a calculated gamble trying to get inside Templeton's head and figure out where he was going. But his gut feeling still felt right, he knew where Templeton headed.

Every hour or whenever he came to high ground, Blade stopped and used his field glasses to scan a complete circle, starting and ending looking down his back trail. Ten years in the west, the self-taught hunting skills from his youth and time he spent in the mountains and with Colonel Merriam had served him well the past years. Now he found himself in a position to need all the skills he knew. No longer did Blade think about riding back to Cheyenne and giving up. Now he wanted to catch up with Templeton, he wanted him bad. A decade of living in the

West helped Blade learn caution and developed his innate survival skills. Out here on the plains his skills had got him out of some tight squeezes, he didn't want to be caught off guard, today Blade wanted to make sure he was ready, for what, it could be anything.

Riding throughout the day, stopping only for rest and water Medicine and eat a small piece of jerky at a tiny bubbling stream around noon, Blade made good time. He poured out his canteen before refilling it with the running water, took a long drink then filled it to the top again and decided he wasn't ready for a meal yet, but maybe it was time for a break. Medicine spent two happy hours grazing on the prairie scrub grass and the greener shoots near the water then drank his fill from the stream. Rested they were ready to leave and continue the search for their squat, brown-suited prey. Blade swung up into the saddle and horse and rider continued west. The remainder of the day proved to be uneventful. Blade built a small camp on the backside of a rolling hill and fell asleep thinking of the lady and her baby in the sod house.

Throughout the night, Blade tossed and turned dreaming good dreams and bad. By five in the morning, the camp was cold and forty minutes behind him. Blade still rode west, not south as he planned. Maybe the dreams were too real, maybe something else, but Blade headed for the sod ranch house another four or five hours west.

As he rode, some of the old self-doubts came back. Why wasn't he following his own plan? The plan seemed to be a good idea; after all he made it. Today East, the third day of the circle and he should be going South. But, then again, he should have been riding south yesterday. Guess my plans have changed, he thought. Blade smiled, tipped his hat to no one, taped Medicine with his heels and he loped along with Blade trying to convince his mind he was doing the right thing.

He thought about his skills and about the talents others attributed to him and hoped today his instincts were right. He took off his hat, ran the back of his hand across his brow and let the breeze blow through his hair. He hoped the breeze would clear the doubts, but again the creeping melancholy came.

Call it intuition; call it his lawman nature. For some reason he felt he needed to see the young mother in the sod house again. He needed to know she was safe. Blade's instincts when playing poker were about as bad as instincts could be, but not out here, not about something like this. He knew it was right to go back, right to check on her, about what he did not know. He only knew he needed to backtrack to the Soddy.

Blade agonized over why he was going back as he rode and at last felt sure he needed to forget about going to the sod house. He decided instead to turn south, his original plan, but he couldn't. He rode on.

Chapter 22

Templeton knew he'd pushed the three-year-old horse too hard after he killed the tired looking woman outside her sod house yesterday, Three Legs was tired. He decided to stop for a rest and to eat. There hadn't been much food in the sod house but he had found flour, salt, coffee, a few eggs, and some dried roots and berries, along with a small package of bacon. Those provisions fit well with what he took from the old mountain man. For now he felt fixed to make a run for the train. "Gotta be safe around here, haven't seen a man since I left the fort," he mumbled.

He took his time securing the horse with a ground stake all the time talking to himself, in an incoherent part speech part rasping whisper, about getting back home to Chicago. Feeling so stiff and sore made the idea of taking a break a good one, a break away from the saddle. Templeton wished he had a bigger more comfortable saddle than the worn thin mountain man's saddle. Thinking back, maybe he should have kept the Calvary saddle. It was newer, a little wider and more comfortable. He had put the stolen saddle on the old brown, in a hurry. He chuckled, remembering back to the day he'd branded that worthless horse and then a few days later shooting it. Deserved it, he thought.

Thinking it should be safe enough here, Templeton sat down on a clump of grass and tried to relax. "No one is following and the woman told me her man only came home on Sundays," he thought. "Three more days till Sunday, or is it two more days, doesn't matter I'll be on the train and out of this country before he can get within two days ride of me," Templeton said, then looked around to see if anyone heard. He bent forward and unlaced his shoes, pulled them off and leaned back to doze a little and plan his escape from the Wyoming sagebrush plains.

Two hours later Luke Templeton, a petty thief, turned murder and fake Pinkerton man built a small fire and tossed on a few dry chips, cow or possibly Buffalo, and watched the flames grow and pop. He didn't worry about the likelihood of someone seeing the fire or the smoke, not here, not today. He cooked bacon and stirred some flour into the grease to make gravy. After eating the skillet of food, he remembered the coffee. Without a pot, he wiped out his skillet and made a skillet full of coffee. Despite the grease, it tasted passable and Templeton's appetite was temporarily satisfied.

With his stomach full he rearranged his saddle and blankets against some small sage and reclined to rest and smoke. The fixings he found in the old man's belongings had been a bonus, he grinned as he rolled the cigarette and spent the next five minutes smoking, his mind blank. Templeton rolled another smoke lifted a piece of dry sage wood and touched it to the hot embers smoldering in the fringes of the fire, he fired the tobacco, inhaled deeply of the strong tobacco and blew smoke back into the fire. For a moment he considered trying to start this entire worthless sage prairie on fire, it would be fun to see. Then he thought the better of it and wished the old man or the girl would have had some whiskey, he could really use a drink. Templeton laughed thinking about the two murders then made another skillet of coffee.

The tobacco and coffee relaxed him allowing him a chance to daydream for the first time in several days.

Chicago wasn't bad, not bad at all. Templeton liked growing up in the city, lots of chances and lots of things to do. But there were things he did not miss, like his family with their constant nagging at him for not working in the packing business like his dad, his uncles, and his brothers. No, he didn't miss them or the Chicago Police; they were always hounding him for something. Most of the time, it seemed like, the law picked him up for little things they imagined or for nothing at all. He outsmarted them when he robbed someone or burgled a business so they made up reasons to come after him. He'd been in and out of trouble much of his life from the age of seven until he left Chicago. He managed to stay one step or part of a step ahead of the law, at least some of the time. When, at last, he skipped town he was out on bail with seven days of freedom before heading to the Illinois State Penitentiary. Thoughts of life locked up in the pen made it most important for him to leave town. Templeton's early years were spent doing too many things he failed to think all the way through. He was impulsive but not a fool, he left at the first chance in a borrowed buggy leaving it at the train station where he caught a train for Denver five or six days to the West. Two years ago it had been, but it seemed longer right now, a lot longer.

Templeton sat and thought about how much he hated camping; hated riding, hated cooking and most of all hated being chased which meant, right now everything he was doing he hated. He pushed his scuffed brown oxford shoes away from his blankets, tossed his derby hat between them and scooted closer to the fire. Leaning back on his saddle he tried to get comfortable moving his back around on the saddle and blankets until he found something close to comfort. He needed to get to the train and tomorrow he would start out east and then ride southeast until he caught the tracks near the little start-up town of Pine Bluffs thirty or so miles east of Cheyenne. Maybe three days, four at the most. He had been there once and it seemed safe, cattle being loaded on boxcars, not many passengers getting on or off, safer than going into Cheyenne again.

The sun started to disappear in the west giving the tall sage an eerie gold color. A slight breeze blew in his face intensifying the smell of sage and dirt. Templeton thought about the smells he missed, smells from the city, bakeries, packing plants, smelters and people, lots of people. He broke branches from a half-dead sagebrush and tossed two somewhat dry limbs on the fire and listened as the fire popped the moisture from the wood. The thick smoke billowed into his face moving him back a few feet and off to the side. The popping sage reminded him of distant gunshots and made him wonder about the pair of out of luck, worthless cowboys he'd hired in Cheyenne to cover his back.

He gave those saddle tramps a hundred dollars, about everything he had. They were supposed to hang around the sheriff's office and make sure no one getting off the train from Kansas City through Denver asked about him. It had taken a ten dollar gold piece to get a list of incoming travelers from the agent. There were only seven names on the list and even those two worthless Cowboys should have been able to pick them out. Templeton doubted anyone was still following, but he wondered if the hiring did any good. Deep inside he felt it, someone following him, a lot like Chicago and Kansas City, someone always followed.

The army might be after him and maybe a posse from Cheyenne, he trusted if there were any Pinkerton's they were taken care of by the two cowboys still waiting for another four hundred dollars they would never see.

Templeton almost forgot about someone else, but now those thoughts came back, Blade Holmes on the big Appaloosa, he could have used the money for that job, but he didn't matter, he ran away in the night.   Templeton drank from his canteen and rolled another smoke. "The guy thinks he's some kind of storybook hero, must have been scared to death of me, running away like he did," Templeton said to the fire and smoke.

At least he's one person out here in the middle of this dreadful Prairie who's not after me, Templeton thought. Then in a thick British accent he said, "at least one person out here who's not after me."

Templeton believed his backtracking and circling would take care of anyone following. It might have been a waste of three days, but he still thought it had been worth the effort. His trail was safe, by now the old man was taken care of by the wolves, coyotes and magpies. The woman yesterday would follow the same fate as the mountain man. Left to the elements long before anyone found the body, maybe even before her ol' man finds her when he gets home Sunday night. Anyone following would be tired and ready to go back to their soft beds and families by now. The rain of the past few days obscured any marks he'd left. He was safe. Yes, in the morning he would try to ride a straight line to Pine Bluffs and get out of here, for now, no one could find him. Then he shivered.

Always a man of few or no regrets Templeton felt satisfied with his past week and what he accomplished during that time. He had food, tobacco and a horse with a saddle. The horse and saddle would fetch a good price in Pine Bluffs, enough to get a ticket out of town. Remembering and fanaticizing as he struggled to fall asleep he thought he should have had some fun with the woman before he killed her. Instead, he asked for water and shot her when she turned to point him to the well. Now he wasn't sure why he was so quick to kill her but it made no difference to him and he was certain to her. Her life would have been nothing but hard, a bunch of scrawny kids and an early grave anyway.

The old mountain man, he needed to die, too old and trying to live in the past. The old fool was still dressed like civilization had never found him. Yes, food a horse and a chance to ride the train east, it had been a pretty good week. A pretty good week after all, a smile arched his mouth, he closed his eyes and fell asleep.

Chapter 23

Blade took a deep breath reached down and rolled the stiff body over in an attempt to make sense of the senseless. The baby girl was there underneath her, suffocated. Blade dropped to the ground next to the body of the young mother from the sod house. He sat for more than an hour thinking, thinking about everything. But what he thought about the most and needed to know, was why? When Blade felt like he understood, or at least had a semblance of an answer, he got up and moved toward the small shed that stood opposite the chicken house.

The sandy loam was soft and easy to dig, thirty minutes and Blade had what he felt was a proper grave completed, three feet deep, twenty or so inches wide and a little more than five feet long. The new grave in the corner of her vegetable garden seemed right for a young mother and her daughter who liked spending time outside. It was a cool day, but Blade was soaked in sweat, not from the work, but from anger, anger at not being here when the poor girl needed him. But maybe it wasn't anger, it seemed more an enormous disappointment, his real anger was directed at Templeton.

The garden showed promise with several short rows of green plants poking through the brown earth. In a few weeks, if taken care of and with a little rain, it would be a fitting resting place. He laid the young mother in the grave with the baby in her arms, walked in the house picked up her Bible from a roughhewn cedar table by the bed and returned to the grave. Blade knelt and with great care he placed the small black Bible on her arm near the baby's head. He covered the bodies with an almost completed red and brown patchwork quilt he found on the kitchen table beside a pincushion, a pair of scissors and several lengths of unbleached thread on small wooden spools. In less than five minutes, he filled the grave with the sandy soil and walked away.

Yesterday, Blade thought, as he put the shovel back where he found it beside the slab door of the sod covered tool shed doubling as a root cellar. He killed her yesterday. Not many things could get to Blade Holmes. He'd been called tough as the leather on an old boot, he had seen things he hoped most people would never see, he had experienced things that would crumble the strongest of men, but today things were different. Today his soul had been shaken. When he walked up to the bodies of the woman and her child he remembered how she looked the day they met when he'd walked around to the front of the Soddy. She looked afraid, but yet secure. It was a look and a feel Blade wished he could emulate right now.

The time had come to find Templeton. If he caught a train Blade would follow him, if he could, for as long as it took, he would find him. But instead of leaving he sat down and leaned against the banked sod of the root cellar and thought of Kansas City.

Blade had heard stories of men killing their wives or of women killing their husbands and lovers killing each other, but he still couldn't recall a case of someone killing for fun. And a woman and a child, it made no sense, Templeton was a madman, he had to be. And Blade now knew, for sure, this was the case, Templeton killed her for fun, he killed her because he could, no other reason. All of the murders he could remember were city crimes, crimes of passion, hidden inside the four walls of a house or a hotel room. Some were crimes for the gain of money, not murders out here on the plains, not out in the open. Blade felt like the melancholy might overtake him again, but it didn't, he was sad and he was angry, but that was all. He had ridden hard and worked hard today, but he felt somehow physically refreshed.

He found Templeton's tracks immediately, they were not hard to find. He rode hard until the last light of the setting sun made it difficult to follow. Templeton had made an attempt to cover his tracks but only for the first hundred yards or so. He must have felt safe by then and gave up on any semblance of covering up and rode away. The tracks were of an unshod horse, but not an Indian pony. Blade knew that Indians would never kill in the manner of the scene like this one behind.

Leaving a simple note behind hadn't seemed like enough but the trail would have been too cold if Blade used up a day or more to find the young woman's husband and tell him the terrible news in person. It had taken as long to write the note as it took to dig the grave. Blade wrote three different drafts before settling on. "I found your wife and baby shot to death. I buried them in the garden with the Bible and the quilt. I am tracking the killer." After thinking for a good minute, he signed it, "Deputy United States Marshal - Mathew Holmes, Cheyenne, Wyoming Territory."

Two hours later with the sun fading into the crevices of Laramie Peak Blade pulled a ragged piece of a worn yellow bandanna from his saddlebag and tied it to a bushy piece of sage and looked for a place to spend the night. Inches from the bush with the yellow marker was a single track of an unshod horse, outlined in the bare gray soil of the high plains. Only a few years ago most high plains horse tracks were unshod, now they were rare and when found were likely from the last of a few wild horses. But this unshod horse was alone, something that would be rare among free-roaming, wild horses. Blade felt sure the tracks he followed were the tracks of the killer. They were easy to follow, but something still troubled Blade. The tracks were going in a straight line heading southeast toward Cheyenne or maybe a little east of Cheyenne. Would a murder make it this easy? Why a straight line Blade thought, he believed he would find out in due time.

He felt like he was getting closer but not close enough to search in the dark. Blade led Medicine down into a small wash where he could build an unseen fire a quarter mile from the yellow marker. The wind gusted hard out of the south, might be another storm coming in, the smoke, if any, would blow down his back trail. Blade took his time picking up chunks of dead sage wood and building the small fire, spent another hour cooking then sat down and relaxed as he ate. Sleep did not come easy but when it came, Blade slept for several hours. Five twenty, maybe five twenty-five, Blade believed as he rolled from his blankets, took a long drink from his canteen and lead Medicine down to an ancient Buffalo wallow to drink from what remained of the wallow pond left over from a nearly dry spring.

Blade stretched some life back into his body as he walked Medicine back to the yellow marker. He took a minute to untie the strip of yellow cloth from the sagebrush, then pointed straight southeast and rode at a gallop for twenty minutes before slowing to a walk then stopped, dismounted and smelled the air.

Walking Medicine up a small rise to the east he smelled the air again then took out his field glasses and searched east and south, then almost as an afterthought he turned and looked down his back trail. He knew no one was following, if they were, he would feel it. No one was following but being careful was a big part of Blade Holmes's nature whether he was on the plains or in the city. But right now he did not have time to think about the city, Emma or the city but it was hard.

Blade understood he had God-given gifts, abilities others did not. John Ryan told him his senses were the sharpest he'd ever seen. He did have good, maybe even great eyesight. His hearing was as sharp as any man anywhere and he could sense things, perhaps his biggest gift. Blade laughed and shook his head as if saying no to an unseen visitor. He wasn't sure about his sense of taste, especially when he was eating so much of his own cooking. But it was his sense of smell he was relying on today; sometimes he was not sure about that either. When he was growing up, he could smell his mom's apple cobbler from half a mile away in any of their fields. But those days were long past from a different time and place, ten years past. Now he tested his sense of smell again, he stood beside Medicine breathing deeply one more time. The breeze carried the faint scent of bacon.

Edging down and around a succession of small brush covered sandy hills that might have been dunes in some earlier time, Blade and Medicine found the deep wash they now walked along. Within ten minutes, he could hear people talking. Blade stopped and listened, too many people to be Templeton, even if he had friends. Blade swung up on Medicine, who bounded up and out of the wash. The two rode at a trot toward the voices.

In the morning light of a rather large campfire, he could see many men and horses. Calvary, troopers from Fort Laramie, "they must be following this same trail," Blade whispered in the breeze. Riding the last quarter of a mile into the trooper's camp Blade smelled the morning coffee, bacon, and biscuits.

Colonel Merriam was the first to meet him when he rode into camp. "Blade Holmes if you aren't a site for sore eyes, I'm happy you're here, hope you're here to work, we could use a scout."

"Templeton, Colonel?"

"Somehow I had a feeling you'd know what was going on. But afraid you might not know the half of it," the Colonel replied.

"We may need some time to exchange information Colonel, believe I may have some news for you too."

Merriam led Blade to a place to sit near the fire. "Breakfast Blade," asked Merriam as the two sat down.

"Sure Colonel, could use someone else's cooking for a change, haven't had biscuits or good army coffee for a while and I been smelling' yours, along with the bacon for the better part of half an hour."

The corporal of the mess brought a tin plate piled high with biscuits, bacon, and beans. Blade had not realized how little he had eaten over the past few days or how well the Army was feeding these days, he cleaned his plate in a matter of a few minutes. Two cups of coffee later and Blade was ready to talk. Merriam had spent the last few minutes sitting, smoking his pipe, without saying a word, waiting for Blade to finish. From the look of his face, Blade could tell the Colonel wanted him to hurry up. But as an officer he sat in respectful silence and even allowed himself a slight grin watching Blade devour the army breakfast.

As soon as Blade sopped the last of the juice from his plate Merriam said, "He killed John Ryan."

Blade was stunned by the news. Then overcome with sadness, John Ryan his mentor, friend, and father figure, dead. He put his plate on the ground and looked at Merriam. He had not expected anything like this and it brought dozens of questions to his mind. John Ryan was as close to Blade as anyone had ever been, for a while as close as his own father. Blade had thought some about Ryan the past few days as he was tracking Templeton remembering the lessons on the mountain. Most everything he knew about survival and the mountains and for that matter life, he learned from John Ryan. "Why, why would anyone want to kill him, an old trapper, he never hurt anyone in his whole life," Blade said.

"We'll find him, Colonel. We'll get him, John Ryan taught me how to trap and track and manage my life all in one long winter. But more than anything he taught me how to stay alive. I spent five and a half months with him up in the mountains when I was nineteen. I owe more to that man than to anyone on earth. Things he taught me have saved my life half a dozen times since and I never even gave it a second thought, not until now. People keep telling me I have some kind of special senses and maybe I do, thanks to John Ryan."

Merriam stood up and started to pace back and forth, it was a full minute before he looked at Blade and answered, "looked like he was killed for his horse and supplies, nothing else, never even took his rifle or pack horse."

"Is that why you're following him, because he killed John Ryan, Templeton killed him?"

"Not what started us following him, the second day out, morning, when we found Ryan's body. We were after Templeton for a lot less, but now it's murder too. He came to the fort, looking for you, seemed real odd everything about him, like he was trying too hard. Had a Pinkerton badge and tried to act official, but the whole thing smelled like a skunk in the henhouse, didn't seem to make any connections. Had on a sloppy fitting brown suit, looked like he'd been in it for days like he didn't have a change. Don't believe Mr. Pinkerton would allow his men to look so bad. Part of the time he sounded normal, like some of my troopers from the city but twice he said something with kind of an English accent, odd. He tried to tell me you stole his horse, described your horse, Medicine, the same one you been riding since I first met you and then he said you were wanted in Cheyenne. But what, in fact, made me mad was he poked fun at my three-legged oak stool, you've seen it, took me six weeks to build it and he made fun of it."

"Templeton was looking for me," Blade interrupted, "I only met him once, about killed him, then talked with him for a spell and decided his company wasn't for me and I left."

The Colonel listened then took a final drink from his tin cup and flicked the grounds from the cup with a snap of his arm. "I sent some wires as soon as he was gone; by the way he stole a saddle before he left, got a wire back from Cheyenne. He's wanted in Kansas, Missouri, Illinois and now, here," Merriam said.

"I met up with a posse out of Cheyenne they told me about Kansas City and what happened in Cheyenne. Do you know anything about what happened in Kansas City? I think it may have involved a woman I know there. Colonel, the lady he shot in Kansas City might be Emma, the lady I intend to marry as soon as I can get back there." Despite the harsh circumstances of the conversation, Blade still flushed after saying he was going to marry Emma. He thought maybe it would be best if he asked her before he started telling others.

"There are a lot of people, a lot of women in Kansas City you may be jumping to some conclusions and worrying about something you don't need to worry about Blade, but we do need your help. I don't want you riding after him alone and getting yourself in trouble."

"I won't let anything happen to me Colonel, I forgot to mention I was deputized as a U.S. Marshal before the posse went back to Cheyenne, so I'm legal and I'll be careful."

"Let's refill these empty cups and see what we can tell each other about Templeton before you ride out," Merriam said, then grabbed Blade's cup and walked toward the fire.

The two spent the next three-quarters of an hour talking about what they knew of Luke Templeton and speculating about how and where he might be headed. When Blade told the Colonel about the lady and child murdered by Templeton, Merriman turned red with anger and nearly ended the conversation before Blade finished his tale. As they discussed the rest of what they knew about Templeton, the troopers enjoyed the extra free time, drinking coffee, swapping stories and relaxing before starting what could be a long day. Near the end of their conservation, Merriam noticed the men creeping closer when he looked up a few minutes later most of them were within a few feet of where they sat. Like the men of the posse they sat transfixed on every word, Blade spoke as he outlined what he believed was going through Templeton's mind and what they needed to do to catch up with him.

The coffee, bacon, beans and biscuits were gone, the fire was doused and Colonel Merriam the troopers and Deputy Marshal Blade Holmes rode at a trot from the camp. They traveled southeast. They rode with a purpose.

Chapter 24

Templeton felt like he might drop from the saddle. He was tired and needed to stop. Two days of hard riding, southeast as near as he could figure, and he still could not see railroad tracks anywhere in the distance. The past few hours he'd stopped to listen a half dozen times and was yet to hear a single train whistle. Resting up for a day would help, he still had plenty of food and another day of rest for his horse wouldn't hurt. He now rode through rolling foothills much greener than two days back and with much less sagebrush. Sizable stands of pine and aspen stood in the high country to the west, a long way off now, fifteen or twenty miles, Templeton thought. Here in the hills he rode past two or three open patches of cleared land with small, rough-hewn homesteader cabins surrounded by gardens and farm ground.

Camping and hiding for a day of rest should be no problem, no one was looking for him anyway, not as near as he could figure and not this far south. There were plenty of cows where he rode now, farm and ranch country, which convinced him he must be getting close to the railroad. He thought for a moment about killing a cow for some fresh beef but decided the sound of a gunshot might bring unwelcome cowboys or farmers his way. He edged his horse down into a canyon leading to a small stream, not more than two feet across. The water was clear with a lone cottonwood standing nearby. It seemed like a good place to spend a day. Looking up through the throat of the canyon he could see the far off trees on the mountainsides and better yet he could watch if anyone came toward his hiding place.

The air freshened. Looked like there could be a storm brewing in the west. He liked this place, shelter, he could see a long way and it didn't seem like anyone could see him from any direction until they were nearly on top of his camp.

Templeton slept through the night and late into the morning under damp overcast skies. He drank from the small stream went back to his bedroll got his canteen, filled it and went back and sat down, he was in no hurry. Setting around felt good and he waited until the obscured sun passed overhead before starting breakfast. Taking his time making coffee and eating made him feel even more rested than he thought possible. Setting under the lone cottonwood he moved twice trying to stay in the shade of the small tree with the sun breaking free of the early afternoon cloud cover. After another hour of dodging the sun boredom or frustration set in, Templeton decided it might be time to move on. He spent as much time swearing as he did saddling Three Legs, the young mare was still jumpy with Templeton in command. When he rode out, the sun was over his right shoulder a few hours before dark. Templeton crested the hill in front of his hidden campsite and turned to look back at the rolling hills behind him.

He saw the men, and they saw him. Panic set in, Templeton kicked Three Legs as hard as he could with the heels of his worn out oxford shoes and Three Legs kicked back. Templeton was off before he knew what happened and Three Legs was running straight at the troopers.

Merriam raised his hand and stopped his troopers. There was no use in taking chances when taking chances was not needed. They were now after a man on foot and they were on horseback. Blade was impatient to spur Medicine into a run for Templeton but with this many men, one man commanding was enough and Blade would not try to upstage the Colonel. Merriam waved part of his troop around to the west and some to the east. Merriam, Blade and a small contingent of soldiers continued to ride in a straight line toward the spot where Three Legs dismounted Templeton.

A train whistles shrill cry startled the men on horseback. It came from an area not more than a half-mile away. When Templeton heard the whistle, he was in the process of stumbling to the bottom of a small but steep hill. He knew the sound of a train whistle when he heard one. This wasn't Chicago, but it was a train. He headed straight as he could toward the sound of the whistle and the railroad, his thoughts were jumbled but cleared and he drew his pistols. He wasn't sure if he could shoot straight with either gun, one he took from the Pinkerton and the other he took from John Ryan. He knew he could stop and kill some of the troopers if they got close enough, but he couldn't kill them all. So he ran. His goal was to get out of here; he needed to keep moving, moving toward the train. He believed he could make it.

Templeton stumbled upon a dark wash running straight toward the tracks. He scrambled down the steep side to the bottom and ran toward the sound of the train, his heart hammered, his chest burned and his short legs chopped along the sandy bottom of the ravine. Snorting, coughing and spitting he didn't worry about making noise as he ran. After two hundred yards his lungs felt like he had swallowed burning embers, he blocked the pain by remembering back to the past few days.

A lot of things he could have done different, he thought, as he stumbled and fell into the soft sand and scrub brush. He was up and running, unhurt, but his feet felt like they had turned to stone and the weight of dragging his feet along became almost unbearable. He staggered around a near square corner where the wash ran under a wooden trestle supporting the tracks above. The steep sides kept Templeton hidden from the troops for two or three minutes and now the tracks and a slow-moving train, a way out of here were right on top of him. He stood under the wooden trestle, hands on knees trying to find another breath. The sound of the train creeping along the tracks above refreshed him.

After a moment's hesitation, he climbed the wooden support beams stretched across the massive log pilings holding the weight of the tracks, like steps up the trestle he went up hand over foot. The rough timbers tore at the skin on his hands and fingers, his worn shoes slipped as he climbed. One step from the top he lost his grip fell and somehow caught himself one rung lower on the trestle. He re-griped took the last two steps again and reached the top. Now on the tracks Templeton grabbed a ladder running up the side of what looked to be an empty passenger car. The train was rolling and gaining speed, Templeton was lucky to catch the third of the four-car train. A minute later the train was a quarter mile down the track moving west with Templeton still attached. He clung to the south side of the train car and wished he could see through the car to the other side, see if the Calvary was close or not. But he couldn't, the first window was four feet away and Templeton was afraid if he tried to move he would fall. He was safe for the moment, without a horse, but safe.

It took another fifteen minutes to pull his hurting and out of shape body along the rolling car to a doorway twenty feet away. Twice he tried to squeeze through windows but it didn't take long to realize his body would never fit. Templeton held onto the wooden sills of the passenger car windows terrified of falling under the moving train. Inch by inch he reached from one window to the next gasping for burning breathes every second of the way. His feet slipping and grabbing at the small bolted ledge along the bottom of the car. He alternated between holding on with one hand and wiping sweat with the other. Taking a deep breath when he reached the door he jerked it open and collapsed inside the empty passenger car. Falling into the first wooden bench inside the car he reached forward, with both arms, to the backrest in front of him and lowered his head trying to put out the fire in his lungs and slow his racing heart. After two full minutes still breathing hard and now with a pounding headache Templeton reached in his pocket and found one six-gun, he checked his holster, the other was still there. He was inside the train, a train traveling west, the wrong way. His horse was gone, but at least he was still armed and safe, at least for now.

As soon as the train stopped he would get off, Cheyenne was growing, a few thousand people, big enough to hide him. The train was rolling, now three or four miles from where he boarded. Templeton knew he'd escaped, at least for a while, He laid down on one of the passenger benches and promptly fell asleep.

When he woke up, the train had reached the outskirts of town, but it wasn't Cheyenne, the sign said Laramie City. Templeton was so mad he wanted to run to the front of the train and shoot the engineer. He moved through the car to the next, it was also empty. Then he turned, went back to the car he'd made his personal sleeping car for the past four hours, and took a seat by the door. This might work out after all. Everyone would be searching for him in Cheyenne and after a few days they would give up, and he would be home free. Laramie City was a stroke of luck, good luck, ol' Luke Templeton was going to get away, at last, he thought.

After circling for an hour then riding back and forth, up and around the hills valleys and washes Blade and Merriam knew he was on the train, the train heading west. They had pushed their horses hard today; they were lathered and tired, too worn out to go any further. The small army made no attempt to find a more suitable campsite, instead settled on a camp near the tracks to wait for morning or another train. Cheyenne was twenty-five miles, Blade thought, flat most of the way, a ride he could make in less than a day, easy.

The sound of a bugle blowing reveille broke the early morning silence at precisely 5:30 in the morning. Blade Holmes was already gone. With Holmes gone Merriam spent time covering the area one last time, but fifteen minutes after the search started it ended. A young private came back at a trot leading Three Legs behind. The horse was still saddled, but a bit skitterish from spending a rider-less night wandering in the hills.

Merriam was surprised the horse had not run farther but then mentioned to the first sergeant, it had been a quiet night with no trains. The silence likely settled the horse down some. Merriam now had a decision to make, turn the troops north and take them home or ride west to Cheyenne and Laramie City. There were troops stationed near both cities and his Fort Laramie patrol may or may not have been within their jurisdiction.

Colonel Henry Clay Merriam, hero of the Civil War and now riding on what could be the last great adventure in his career, raised his hand and waved his men west, toward Cheyenne, Laramie City and the Mountains. A return to the fort would have to wait.

Blade pushed hard, from three in the morning riding across sagebrush and scrub grass flats, up and down small rolling hills never getting more than a few yards from the tracks. In Cheyenne, earlier than expected, Blade rode up to the front of the new red train depot, the first brick building in Cheyenne. He tied Medicine to the rail in front of the station looked north up the dusty main street of Cheyenne and remembered being there in better times a few days earlier. The depot was ornate, its red brick in stark contrast to the shiny white painted wood trim. Cheyenne is doing well, Blade thought, sure to make its mark someday. But right now Blade was more interested in trains and the station agent than he was in the future of Cheyenne.

Blade turned the knob and pushed open the heavy depot door. The station agent stood in front of a large slate board with a piece of chalk, writing a new schedule for the week on the wall-mounted blackboard. "Excuse me," Blade said as he opened the door and stepped in, "I need information."

The depot agent, a thin, bald man who looked near sixty, turned and answered, "If I have it young man, if I have it, what information you need?"

"I'd like to know about a train last night, came in from the east."

"That's not too tough, even for an old man like me," the agent answered, wiping his eyeglasses on his shirt and returning them to his pointy nose then squinted at Blade as if in deep thought. "One train yesterday, the Laramie City Express, only through train we got, don't stop, fuels at Pine Bluffs Crossing then goes straight through to Laramie City. It's a work train most of the time, this one was taking some passenger cars to store in Laramie, don't believe there were any riders; it was on a short run. We call it the express because it goes right on through; it isn't much, never more than three or four cars."

Blade was starting to get a little impatient and cut in. "It doesn't stop, does it slow down?"

"No its top speed when it goes through, doesn't slow a bit, last fall an old timer was driving a freight wagon across the tracks and."

Blade was out the door and mounted before he finished the sentence. Templeton might have jumped from the train moving four or five miles an hour but Blade didn't think he got off, not going at top speed, the guy would have killed himself if he tried. Tapping Medicine with his boot the two galloped through Cheyenne.

Not sure how much further he could go today, he had to try, and the terrain made for comfortable riding. He stuck to his earlier routine, staying close to the tracks. But not as close as before, now he rode the south side a quarter mile off the right- of- way. Two hours later horse and rider were going strong, but the ground was changing, and traveling was about to get difficult. Two hours of daylight remained and the rolling hills had given way to bigger and now steeper hills covered in crumbling limestone with rocks strewn about making riding tricky at best and dangerous at worst.

When they reached the foothills, moss rock, cactus, buckbrush and rock outcroppings became the norm and Blade and Medicine had to slow, picking their way through the rough country in the fading light. The hills were getting steeper and tougher to deal with. Blade knew he could not make many more miles today. He would need to rest Medicine then ride down the steep trail into Laramie City at first light. In recent years, Laramie settled down from the crazy railroad town it was a few years back and Blade was sure he had a chance to find Templeton in the small, more relaxed city, it had become.

Blade rode now through increasingly large boulders, enormous round rocks that looked like they were strewn here by the hand of God himself. "The place of the Earth-Born Rocks," the Arapaho called it, and it was spectacular.

Blade had been here before, once. But now as the sun set its final rays of the day into these magnificent boulders splashing gold and red and framed by the dark green pines, he was struck by the unbelievable beauty of the place. Vedauwoo, the locals called it, Blade preferred the place of the Earth-Born Rocks. He couldn't hold back the smile as he thought about his situation. He was tired, as tired as he had ever been, he was hungry, he was following a murder, his life was in danger and here he sat, hat off, leg crossed over the saddle admiring the beauty that surrounded him.

Blade struck a match on the side of a basket sized bolder temporarily serving as a table. Cupping the match in his hands and touched the flame to a mixture of brown pine needles and small sticks, tiny flames quickly grew to seven or eight inches in the still air. A few larger sticks and the fire grew to several feet with tall skinny arms of red-yellow flames reaching up, then disappearing into the night air. He didn't need a fire this big, but Blade liked it and smiled when he needed to take a step back from the intensity of the heat. Images of the growing flames bounced from the giant granite boulder a dozen feet away, a boulder that looked to Blade to be bigger than the Cattlemen's Club in Cheyenne. After making coffee Blade slid the pot to the edge of the fire sat down and chewed on a piece of jerky, relaxed, and let his mind wander.

By the time the coffee started to boil Blade's daydreams had taken him back home to the farm in Ohio. He'd walked with Emma in Kansas City and trapped and hunted the Laramie Range with John Ryan. Pouring coffee into his tin cup snapped Blade back to the present and he began to think about tomorrow, he thought about Laramie City and he thought about Templeton.

Blade sat the cup aside, stood, stretched, drew his gun aimed and slipped it back into the holster. He repeated, and then continued over and over for the next forty minutes. Satisfied he put the Army Colt away, securing the hammer with a leather thong attached to the back of his holster. Almost as an afterthought, he smiled and patted the side of the holster. Blade tossed another chunk of pine on the fire, drained the coffee from his cup, and set it down near the fire. He clapped twice, like a man chasing dust from his hands, then spun in a half circle letting a knife fly from behind his shoulder and watched the handle vibrate in a pine fifteen paces away. Blade dropped to the ground, rolled pulled the knife from his boot and stuck it two inches from the first. Good enough, Blade thought, as he dusted off, pulled the knives from the trunk of the Lodge Pole Pine walked back to the fire and poured a second cup of coffee.

Funny, he always told people he could shoot and throw the knives, always. Said it was second nature, but that wasn't the case, not at all. He never thought about it much, but he'd spent hours and hours almost every day growing up. Hours and hours drawing the Colt, throwing the knives and something he didn't often mention, shooting the big rifle he carried in a scabbard on Medicine's side. And he still practiced, not every day, like when he was a kid, but almost. Practicing had become part of him, the guns the knives the man.

Blade was good and despite what he told others he knew he was good, but even he had no idea how good. He was the best, with guns, knives and the rifle, maybe the best ever. Blade did not know it but, Templeton was not good, not good at all and Deputy Marshal Blade Holmes was less than a day away.

Tonight as he stretched out and pulled the green wool blanket up to his chin Blade needed more, more than guns and knives and now the legend, he wasn't sure what. But he'd not felt this way in Kansas City. Sleep came, after a time, and when it arrived it was restless and haunted. An hour later Blade was awake but refused to open his eyes, instead choosing to keep them closed tight hoping to fall asleep again, but it wasn't working.

Like he had every night since he heard about the shooting in Kansas City Blade wondered if Emma was dead or alive, he needed her to be alive, he prayed she was alive. Sometimes he rationalized, thinking Kansas City had many haberdasheries and he might be overreacting. Chances are it was not Emma's shop, chances were she was fine. But he knew different, believed it had to be her and he prayed daily she was alive. He was not sure he could live with himself if his worst thoughts were true. The thoughts haunted him, thoughts of running off without saying a word and then letting her die during a robbery.

Lying awake in the dark and thinking often made for a long night and the morning sun was a long way off. But tonight Blade's head cleared as he rested, his thoughts sorted out and his future fell into place. The light breeze shifted and brought the smell of pine and wood smoke back to him the sky twinkled with thousands of stars and Blade remembered other times and other places.

His mind led him to a place that surprised him, he knew where Templeton was going, he knew why he had come into his camp last week, and he knew why he killed the old mountain man and the young mother. Blade knew one more thing; he knew he would catch Templeton. Blade rolled on his side and fell into a deep, restful, and dreamless sleep. Emma was alright. He knew that too.

A few minutes before seven with the sun dancing in and out of a clouded eastern sky, Blade Holmes full of coffee, biscuits and memories of promises kept and promises un-kept saddled his rested horse and rode toward Laramie City. The sun felt good on his back and Blade smiled because today would be a special day.

Riding made thinking easy and Blade thought of what he came to understand last night lying among the oversized rocks of Vedauwoo. Maybe the spirits of that mysterious rocky place were active, as active as they were millions of years ago when the giant boulders were strewn over the mountainside between Cheyenne and Laramie City. Somehow, he wasn't sure how, things had become clear last night, maybe more clear than anything in his somewhat mixed up life.

Blade was positive Templeton knew nothing about him; which meant he was hired to follow, maybe to kill him, or maybe he needed a better horse. But if all he needed was a horse he could have found dozens of good mounts in Cheyenne. No, Templeton was hired to kill him. He didn't know and had never heard of Templeton, so he had to have been hired. The fake British school teacher killed John Ryan for a horse and maybe for food, no other reason. If he'd taken the time to sit a while with him, the old trapper would have traded him the pack horse and as much food as he stole, maybe given it to him. That's the kind of man he was, but Templeton never knew men like him. He grew up a city boy, must have been a hard case since he was only a button of a kid. He killed the young mother and the baby because he could. Mean or crazy, he could kill for pleasure or sheer nastiness. Blade expected Templeton was a little of each. Killed her because he saw her as less than him and because she was unprotected, he killed her for fun.

Templeton's straight line of the last two days was a direct path to the railroad. He didn't want to go back to Cheyenne he was heading to the railroad station at Pine Bluffs or close to Pine Bluffs. He was at least smart enough to know that a tiny hamlet like Pine Bluffs was safer than going back to Cheyenne. In Pine Bluffs, he could sell the horse, buy a ticket and in one day be two hundred miles away from Wyoming. He didn't want to go to Laramie or Cheyenne, he wanted to go east, but he hopped the westbound because it gave him a chance. Templeton was trapped; he just didn't know it yet. Blade tapped his heels to Medicine and he responded breaking into a trot.

A few things still bothered Blade, first, why did Templeton keep the badge after he killed the Pinkerton man? If he were caught with the badge, it would be all the evidence needed to hang him. Blade pushed the thought around in his mind and then thought of the other problem he had yet to solve. Who were the two men the posse followed to Kelly's station on Chugwater Creek, neither was Templeton, he would have been miles away at that point, and Hi Kelly's description of the men did not fit Templeton. They had shot Oliver Stevens from long range and ran, were the three somehow tied together? Blade scratched his head, he didn't think so, but maybe, just maybe, they were connected. It bothered him when there were too many loose ends. He thought again of Kansas City and Emma, and how sure he felt she must be alright. But leaving the way he did was eating at him again. He needed to get this over quick and go home, home to Kansas City.

Riding down the steep grade Blade could see the streets and buildings of Laramie City for the past half hour and now was relieved to be on the mostly flat ground. In another hour, Blade would be in downtown Laramie City hunting down some answers. In less time than he believed it would take he stood near the center of town tying Medicine to a newly placed log rail.

The small city looked good; it had been a while since Blade had been here. Stepping up on a substantial boardwalk, that appeared to be only a few days old, Blade stopped for a moment and looked across and then up and down the street admiring the new buildings. Looked like the city would be a fine one, growing and building, people coming in every week, seemed like a railroad could do that, make a town from nothing in a few short years.

Blade walked a few steps, opened a door and strode into the sheriff's office. Sheriff Roy Watson sat in the chair with his feet on the desk. "Hello Blade, what kept you?"

Blade shook his head, "what are you doing' in Laramie, thought you headed home to Cheyenne?"

"I did, even rested up a little, rode the train over here to ask around some about Templeton. But what was bothering me," Blade interrupted before he had a chance to finish the sentence.

"The other two guys, the shooters."

The sheriff stood and walked toward the front window, put his boot on the ledge and said, "Yeah seemed like too many loose ends and too many unconnected connections, so I grabbed the train, day before yesterday, over the pass to look around some."

Watson drug one leg as he walked back to the chair behind the battered pine desk and sat down. He motioned for Blade to pull a chair up beside the desk. Blade spent the next few minutes filling the sheriff in on his search for Templeton, the murder of his friend John Ryan and the poor young woman and her baby at the sod house. He filled him in on the Calvary and Templeton's narrow escape and his flight toward Laramie on the train. After five minutes, a considerable speech for Blade, he looked around like he expected someone to come through the office door and asked, "Where's Sheriff Holloway or is he not in office anymore?"

"Oh, he's still in office," Watson said, "out making rounds I suppose, haven't seen him yet today myself, his coffee is cold and terrible. I'll make a fresh pot, by the time we finish it up he should be back, not so much town for his rounds to take too long. "

Blade scooted his chair close to the wall, leaned back and stretched his legs out putting his feet up on the desk. He took off his hat laid it beside the chair leg on the floor. He needed the rest and decided a cup of coffee or two, and resting with his feet up would do him some good. Blade and the sheriff made small talk waiting for the coffee to boil. The coffee was strong and good, Blade could not remember the last time he drank real Arbuckle's, on the trail it was always the same, cheap coffee beans cut with chicory. The conversation turned from Templeton to Sheriff Holloway and back to Templeton. The conversation and the coffee relaxed Blade, his eyelids drooped.

An hour had passed before Blade realized, still in a half-conscious state, that he had been asleep. He drug his feet from the desk tipped the chair forward and let it bounce hard against the uneven plank floor. He could feel the time, almost three o'clock, he was alone and hungry. Blade got up and stretched trying to roll the kinks from his back. He bent side to side, grimaced then bent low down over his knees. He straightened with a groan, stretched his arms overhead and put his palms flat on the shiplap ceiling of the office. Lots of places still hurt, but he did feel a little better. Slipping the Colt from his holster he checked to assure himself it was ready. He touched the two knives he'd carried for ten years then opened the door to the bright lights of a downtown Laramie City afternoon. He wasn't sure if he wanted to find Sheriff Watson or go get something to eat. He decided on food and looked up the street toward the Laramie Cafe.

"Blade, Blade, hold up!"

Blade turned as Sheriff Watson ran up on him from the opposite direction Blade had turned. Watson's face was drained of color, and he was gasping for breath. He didn't need to tell Blade anything, Blade knew it was bad. "It's Sherriff Holloway Blade; he's dead, dead in the livery stable along with the old man who ran the place. Gunshot through the head, both of um, killed while they sat there playing checkers."

Blade followed Watson to the stable wondering if there could be a logical reason for the two dead checker players. Or would he find two more murders for senseless reasons? He saw nothing he did not understand. Templeton, it had to be him, but why, it all looked the same as last time at the Soddy, no reason at all. Blade thought about John Ryan, he'd been killed for a horse, did he do it again? Templeton jumped the train to Laramie, now he needed a horse. Blade knew he couldn't wait; he had to find Templeton's tracks and then find him, find him in a hurry.

Templeton had seemed so unfamiliar with the area Blade assumed he would travel what he did know, the railroad tracks. Blade rode Medicine at a gallop out of town to the east, the sun would soon die and a few hours at best would be all the daylight. Blade took to the high ground along the tracks. He tied Medicine to a scrub juniper took his field glasses from the saddle bag and spent the next half hour surveying everything he could see. Looking up the trail then north and south and finally down his back trail thinking maybe Templeton didn't get out of town as quickly as he thought. He found no sign of him or anyone else. No one traveled the road at this time of the day including the murder

Luke Templeton. The sun still peeked half above the Medicine Bow Mountains when Blade rode back into town to wait for morning and the eastbound train. The rest and nap in the sheriff's office had cleared his mind. The ride back to town gave him the time needed to think. He'd needed the rest, and the time, and felt grateful for both. Now he had a plan in place, this time he would catch Luke Templeton.

Chapter 25

Emma Fick kept herself busy in the haberdashery shop, a dozen new orders were stacked on her work desk, and she thought, at times, about hiring help. Business was great, but her life, her life right now didn't seem to be going well. Most days she was able to block thoughts of Blade with work and with the customers. But in the evening it was impossible, and when she slept her dreams were full of what had once been but seemed like nothing but a young girl's fantasy now. But she wasn't a young girl, she was a woman on her own, a respected business owner, and oh how she missed him. She hadn't given up hope, she knew Blade was in love with her and she believed he would come back and she would wait for him. How long did she have to wait, another week, another month, a year? Emma didn't want to wait, not another second, but she knew she must. Blade would come back, someday, she knew it.

Leaving the shop often turned into a nightmare-like experience. Everywhere she went people asked her about Blade, "how's Blade, what you hear from Blade, when's ol' Blade comin' back, you and Blade getting hitched up when he comes back, what's he up to these days?" It drove her crazy because each time they asked she wanted to cry.

She didn't know the answers to their questions, none of them, she wished she did.

Blade had become bigger than life, a modern-day hero, a dime novel cowboy hero. Some knew him, some didn't, but everyone asked. Word about town was another book about Blade's adventures was soon coming out, and when it did she would be asked even more about him. She wasn't sure she could take it, didn't know if she was taking it very well know. Emma usually smiled and nodded when asked about Blade and when forced to answer it was more often than not a polite, "yes." or "I'm not sure."

Emma passed the time in the evenings doing what she did best, sewing. She was working on a new jacket for Blade, not really a jacket, it was longer, more coat than a jacket, and it would be a great coat, her best work ever. This coat would be a Norfolk style, favored by the most modern of sport hunters and shooters, but longer and made of Buckskin instead of wool plaid. While sewing she told herself over and over, "if that man is going to be some kind of a fairy tale to people, I want him, at least, to look like a storybook hero."

She wasn't sure she felt comfortable with Blade Holmes being a dime novel hero, in the last three months of their relationship she had taken to calling him by his given name, Mathew, instead of Blade. Mathew, she liked it, and when she called him Mathew he liked how it sounded too.

Emma sat sewing now, and thinking, it was half-past ten, more than an hour after her usual time to turn in, but time didn't seem to matter when she thought about Blade.

Stitching together part of the collar her thoughts turned to Luke Templeton and that awful day. She'd been working late, much like tonight, sitting and sewing. She was not working on any particular item, instead trying to finish several small projects, catching up. When the man burst into her shop she had been in the middle of stocking bolts of cloth from the storeroom, Blade's room, to the new shelves he had built for her under the front counter. Keeping the most popular bolts of cloth in the front helped customers make up their minds and she preferred keeping people away from Blade's old room. His room she thought, it shouldn't be made into a shrine, but she couldn't bear to let anyone else in there, not after Blade, not yet anyway.

The front door had not been locked when Templeton burst in, she had placed the embroidered CLOSED sign in the window, but she had not yet locked the door. He had shot without saying a word. All she remembered was a flash outlining a squat, hatless man in a dirty gray work shirt. When she fell, her head hit the back counter and that was her memory of the worst night of her life. Not much but it's all there was. The bullet hit the green bolt of cloth she carried, "All nine of the old cat's lives," the Pinkerton man had told her. "Looks like you used all your lives up on one forty-five slug in that pile of green cloth."

Emma tried to explain she'd held a bolt, not a pile of cloth, then realized how silly it all sounded and gave up. Now shuddering, she thought about how close she may have been to never seeing Blade or anyone else again.

The Pinkerton man may have been right, luck or as she preferred to think, the hand of the Lord was with her then and she prayed it was with Blade now. Her luck on the night Templeton shot her was carrying a box of thread in one hand and a Derby hat in the other. To save an extra trip she'd crossed the huge bolt of green cloth from her right hand across her chest to her left shoulder, the kind of balancing act she often used to save a few extra trips. The bullet hit the bolt of cloth dead center; the impact toppled her against the back counter. Either Templeton thought she was dead, didn't care, or he didn't take the time to check. But whatever the case, she was happy that she must have appeared to be dead.

Emma never found the Derby hat she carried that night, it was meant to be part of the new front room display, and the brown show suit was also missing. Emma still could not understand why she was shot for a brown suit and a Derby Hat, but it sure seemed to be what the robbery was about, that and the little bit of change she kept in a drawer under the front counter.

Emma kept the bolt of green cloth, the one with the bullet hole, in the back room, Blade's room. The bullet went a little more than halfway through, the sheriff said it was a light load; she was not sure what he meant by light load but assumed she was alive because of it. The egg-sized bump on the back of her head hurt for more than a week. She realized now that hitting her head on the counter after being jolted by the bullet may have saved her life. Maybe the week of headaches was worth it and now that the pain was gone, only the memory remained. With the thoughts of Templeton shooting her fading Emma walked to the front of the store, shook the door handle and checked the lock bolt again, it was secure.

Occasionally when brooding over the missing Blade, she fantasized, believing if he had been there Templeton would never have left the store. Emma was not particularly in favor of violence to solve matters, but when robbery and violence were involved it may have been needed. In her daydreams, Blade wounded Templeton with a knife or sometimes a gun then pushed him through the front door of the shop and hauled him to the sheriff's office by his coat collar. Sometimes she envisioned cheering crowds as Blade drug the stumbling Templeton by the scruff of his neck down the street. It made her laugh and embarrassed her when she thought of Blade dragging a wounded Templeton through the streets of Kansas City toward the police station.

She missed him more than anyone or anything she had missed in her life, but she knew when she fell in love he might go again. She worried from the day he moved his things into the storeroom, worried she would check his room some morning and find it a storeroom again. Falling in love had not been easy, or at least knowing she was in love was not easy. Thinking back she knew now she had been in love since the first day he walked through the front door. For so many years she had put business first, then he came into her life and everything changed. Love at first sight, she never believed in it, not until Blade came into her shop one day. A day that now seemed like so long ago, too long.

She wanted him to come back, to come home, but the way he left still bothered her, he just left, without a word, left. Maybe it was too much for him, too much city, too much civilization, "too much me," she said aloud.

He had changed some in the time they were together; he read more and played poker less. Matter of fact, she couldn't remember him playing at all the last few weeks he stayed. He loved to play poker but admitted to her several times he was not good at it. Not as good as he sometimes thought or as good as he wished. Maybe the poetry readings, the handyman jobs along with going to church socials and the evening walks were more than he would ever be able to take. He was educated, smart and dashing, but maybe it was his wild streak, something she never admitted that made him even more attractive to her. The lawman, mountain man and plainsmen in him might never be civilized.

Sometimes she thought he might be more like those crazy spring thunderstorms. They showed up in Kansas City every April or May, here one day and then, as if by magic, wiped away. While they were here the storms put on a big show, a big change came and then it all went away. She imagined lighting and rain and the wind then the calm and somehow she pictured Blade in his white jacket with the holstered forty-five and the throwing blades he was nicknamed for. At first she found the knives a little disconcerting but not now, now they brought a smile and warm memories. Time passed so slowly when he was away, it had been weeks and still not a word, but somehow she knew he would be back, she knew as sure as the spring storms would come again. But she didn't know when.

Chapter 26

Blade loaded Medicine into the livestock car and settled him down fifteen minutes before the eight o'clock eastbound was scheduled to leave the Laramie City Station. Medicine had ridden on trains before, but it still bothered Blade when he had to put the big stallion in a railroad car. Blade didn't like hemming him in, maybe it was because he felt the same way. Medicine had the front half of the drafty car all to himself and a great looking pair of matched gray draft horses occupied the rear.

Blade was meticulous moving straw around in the stall trying to get it the way he wanted it before the train started to roll. He checked the hay and the grain twice and made sure Medicine had a good drink before he settled into the freight car. Once Medicine started to relax Blade lifted a pitchfork from a rack on the wall and tossed a pile of new straw from the center of the car to the corner near Medicine. Blade built a kind of half seat, half bed in the straw using his saddle, blanket, and bedroll. He plopped down in the straw and leaned into the corner of the car, not bad, he'd been in worse places, as a matter of fact over the entire last week every place he rested or slept had been worse, much worse. Blade's ticket was for the next car forward, one of two passenger cars on the train, but today he wanted quiet and he needed to think. Being here with Medicine suited his mood and felt like a better place for concentrating on what might come next.

Should be about eight Blade thought and his thought was rewarded when the engine belched and the train jerked to life. The eight o'clock, Laramie City to Cheyenne, right on time. It took Blade two and a half days of the hardest riding he'd ever done to get to Laramie from Pine Bluffs. Now he was backtracking and the train would take him to Pine Bluffs in half a day.

Templeton had been trying to get to the tracks and catch a train for the past few days. Blade was sure he would try to catch the train again. When he tried, Blade wanted to be there waiting. He rearranged his blankets and saddle so he could stretch out. Moved from setting to a kind of between sitting and lying down position. With the straw piled under him Blade started to relax. He was more tired than he realized and decided he had nothing else to do so might as well close his eyes and rest up for later. Blade pictured Templeton, cold, hungry, tired and trying his best to get somewhere, any place where no one was following him, trying to buy a train ticket out of Wyoming. He slid his hat lower to shade the flickering light from the slatted door and promptly fell asleep. The sound of the iron wheels rumbling over the steel tracks, singing the railroad song, seemed to be exactly what he needed.

Blade sneezed, then sneezed again, bringing back memories of waking up as a kid sneezing and wheezing when the corn started to pollinate on the Ohio farm. He laid his hat aside readjusted his saddle turned pillow and fell asleep again. He awoke in a few minutes his head clear, adjusted his position and started to daydream.

The fantasy carried him back to the Ohio farm when he was fourteen and growing restless. Unlike most of the dreams of his childhood, this one did not involve school, his childhood friends, mom, or working on the family farm. Instead, his mind pictured his dad carrying a rifle, a big rifle in a cloth case and he and Blade were walking and talking. The pair walked slow and talked fast, moving down their smooth dirt lane then crossing through the corn to target shoot into a big hill south of the cornfield. "Blade I've tried to level with you about everything, but there're a few things you don't know, some things I don't like to talk about. I never told you much about my time in the war, but you're fourteen now and it's time."

He spent the next quarter of an hour talking about his days as a Union Soldier and the battles he lived through. He spoke of the horrors of war and said more than once, that was the reason he liked farming because it was quiet, peaceful and rewarding. By the time, he stopped with the stories of war, they sat down together on a hillside overlooking the farm. The former

Sergeant Holmes of the Union Army turned to Blade and said, "Son you're as good with a gun as anyone I've ever seen, including all the Union sharpshooters I fought with. Let's see what you can do with this."

Blade had never seen the gun before, the gun his dad now drew from the long wool wrap. Blade knew guns and he had always wanted to shoot one of these. It was an 1874 model 45/70 Sharps with double set triggers. It looked new and Blade found out later his dad had ordered it to give to Blade when he felt the time was right, and to one more time, relive his days as a Union Army sharpshooter. Blade didn't know it at the time, but that day would be the only time his dad would ever talk about the war, and the last time he would ever shoot with his son. He never offered anything else of his life as a Union soldier and Blade never asked.

Blade walked across the flat and then halfway up the hill. If he'd counted the paces correctly the targets were set, as close as he could figure, at four hundred yards. Blade nailed two four-inch white paper disks to the bark of an ancient Oak. With a short stub of a pencil he drew a one-inch circle in the center of each. He stuck one target for his dad about six feet high and set his three feet below.

When Blade got back, his father sat smiling leaning on an elbow smoking his pipe. He held the rifle out to his son, "you go first, take your time, I got a box of twelve cartridges here, six apiece, shoot straight if you plan to whip me."

Father and son took twenty minutes to shoot the twelve bullets, talking, telling stories and laughing, speculating on where each slug was hitting. When they were done, the two took their time getting to the target tree, neither wanting their time together to end.

Blade's lower target had six round holes, none closer than an inch to the border, three in the one-inch center circle. His father's target had two distinct holes near the edge of the paper; three other holes were lower in the tree, between the targets, two were about five or six inches low and one a foot low, they didn't find where the other slug hit. Blade used his knife to work the lead from the tree putting each flattened slug into his jacket pocket.

They walked down the hill to the small creek where they sat and talked for over an hour, watching the rippling water roll past. Blade had not heard his dad talk this much at one sitting in his entire life. The sun was starting to show signs of setting as the two continued talking and started the walk back to the farmhouse. The discussion was light and centered on shooting, the farm, and government, then they talked about life. After that day things went pretty much back to normal for the family in particular between Blade and his father, they never again spoke of the things they talked about that day shooting the big rifle.

The train wheels squealed as they ground the two freight and two passenger cars to a stop. The shrill sound of metal sliding on metal brought Blade to the present. Without looking Blade knew the train had reached Cheyenne, time to take on wood and water after the tough trip up and over the mountains between Laramie City and Cheyenne.

Twenty-five minutes later the train jerked to a start, Blade leaned back in the corner closed his eyes and revisited the Ohio farm. Again he rested, but did not sleep propped in the corner he daydreamed seemingly unaware of the train bouncing and swaying along. It rolled now on nearly flat land at a speed double or more from before the stop. But the additional speed paid a price in bumps and side to side shimmies. Despite the uncertainty of his position in the corner of the car, his mind recalled the day he left home, a day after his sixteenth birthday. His thoughts cleared, he remembered the story, and the scenes came to him like pictures in a book.

Dressed in a homemade wool shirt and pants that were not new but not yet old, Blade saddled the strawberry roan mare he'd bought with earnings from the neighbors and prepared to ride from the farm. A minute before he left mom handed him several days' worth of biscuits, some fruit and dried meat and a small leather pouch. She kissed him on the forehead and on the cheek, held him for a moment, and then pushed him a step back keeping her hands on his shoulders. Looking into his penetrating eyes, she asked him to write. Keeping him at arm's length she took a really good look at him, like a mother looking at her newborn or a mother watching her only child leave home. Wiping a streaking tear from her face mom wished him well and walked toward the house.

Blade swung up into the worn saddle on the roan and waited, watching his dad walk toward him. He shook his father's offered hand and watched his face turn from a grin to a tired smile, one he reserved for the most special occasions. Dad patted the saddle scabbard holding the 45/70 Sharps as the smile returned to his weathered face. He'd given the big rifle to Blade on his birthday the day before. He handed him two boxes of shells, then turned and walked toward the barn as Blade rode off. It was the last time he had seen his parents. He wrote a few times at first, but now years had passed since his last letter home. Sometimes in a moment of nostalgia he thought he might go back and see his folks, but he knew he never would.

Blade was getting anxious and paced back and forth on the loose straw covering of the boxcar floor waiting for the train to reach Pine Bluffs. It was two-thirty and in another hour or so he would be off the train and Medicine would be able to stretch his legs. Blade pulled the Sharps from the saddle scabbard held it out and stared at it for a few seconds then slid it back into place and thought maybe he should go home for a visit someday.

Finding a good place to eat was not hard in Pine Bluffs. It was a tiny railroad town with one cafe, owned and operated by the Union Pacific Railroad. Blade ordered fried chicken with potatoes and gravy and hot buttery biscuits because that was what they were serving today, he had plenty of time. Blade thought for a moment about getting a room for the night then decided to get out of town and find a campsite instead. The campsite he chose was up on the rather large bluff to the south of the city, a bluff the lady in the cafe said the town was named after. It seemed more like a small mountain than a bluff as he negotiated the hillside through a large clear-cut area he assumed the railroad cut for ties.

He wanted a campsite with at least a little protection, seemed like the railroad had cut almost anything big enough for posts or ties. But in the last few years more trees had sprouted from the red dirt and shale and some of the older trees, cut several feet off the ground, had new growth and the bluff looked like it might someday be green again.

More than half-way up he turned Medicine into a small stand of short pines where he could see the tracks to the west. He turned back toward the clear-cut, rode in a large fifteen-minute circle and made camp in the small pines.

The site struck Blade as unusual, once this hill had been a small forest, but now it was a hillside full of stumps and it took time to find a grove of small trees like the one Blade tied Medicine in now. He built a small fire under a rock outcropping with an excellent view of the tracks to the west and the town to the north. The trees were tall enough to hide him but not thick enough to break the view. He put the coffee pot on, made up a bed and sat down to think, and to wait. It would be at least another day, maybe more, before Blade and Templeton would meet—again.

Chapter 27

Luke Templeton sat on scrub grass and crumbling shale beside a lone juniper high up on the side of a windblown hill southwest of Laramie striking match after match trying to start a fire. Disgusted he threw down his last failed match, kicked the wood out of the way and cussed everyone following him under his breath. He needed to catch a train. He was tired of horses, tired of riding and tired of being chased. All he needed was a chance to get out of Wyoming and back to civilization. Templeton looked at his horse, it needed more rest, he'd pushed too hard up the hill and now the horse would need time, maybe an hour, maybe more, to rest, another delay. Not knowing much about horses was starting to be a pain and something that might get him caught some day. This latest of his string of stolen horses didn't look as good now as it did in town, now she looked old and Templeton wondered if the gray could make it to Pine Bluffs, even with a full day of rest.

Templeton chewed a long stem of dry grass and attempted to get comfortable while trying to come up with a plan. He was tired of stumbling around and making mistakes at every turn, he needed a plan. First he would skirt back around Laramie City, then ride a wide birth of Cheyenne and on into Pine Bluffs. Once in Pine Bluffs no one would know him and he was sure it would be safe to buy a ticket to get him as far east as fast as possible. It might take another horse, a good one, or a train ticket to get out of here. But he was afraid of trying to board a train in Laramie City or Cheyenne, too risky, but it sure would ride easier.

The best plan would seem to be, east on horseback, he needed to get to Pine Bluffs. He'd been in tight spots before, more than he cared to remember, but he didn't like this one. He needed to get home; back to Chicago where he grew up, there he could escape because he knew where to hide. Alone on this barren hillside, where he could look for miles without seeing a building, animal or person, he felt crowded, hemmed in and trapped.

Templeton was exhausted, as tired as the horse he had stolen from the livery stable in Laramie City. But being tired was but one of his worries, right now it seemed like everyone was chasing him maybe even Benny Market and Jackson Beckworth the two shiftless thugs he'd stiffed for four hundred dollars. When he hired the two in Cheyenne and gave them a hundred bucks with four hundred more to come, he asked the two out of work gun hands to look out for him and take care of any Pinkerton's or law following. He'd been scared at the time and felt the need for some gun protection after the disaster he created in Kansas City. But he doubted the two bums had done anything to earn the money, so maybe, at least, they were not following him.

He was starting to think he should have forgotten about Blade Holmes and his horse and saved his money to buy a ticket east. If it weren't for Holmes, none of this would have happened. Everything he thought about was a few days in the past and Templeton was a realist and now he needed to go east, get all the way up through the hills and rocks to Cheyenne. To the place, he wanted to go two days ago, Pine Bluffs. He was angry, he'd wasted two full days, and two days he could have used to get out of here.

Templeton still hoped to reach the small town and the train in two or three days but understood now it would be impossible. He was beginning to have second thoughts; maybe he was too predictable. Maybe they will be waiting up ahead somewhere. He realized as he put his elbow on the ground and leaned back against a small stand of bunch grass that riding southwest from Laramie City was the only unpredictable thing he had done in the past three days. He'd lost them. The more he thought, the more he wished he would have taken some time and picked up some food, he needed something to eat, but what he most wanted was a smoke. He had to get back to town after it turns dark he decided. Templeton sat uncomfortable on the hard ground and thought about his predicament for another hour. He ached everywhere and had sat and thought so long he was now confused to the point he started muttering. "Maybe I should head west over the mountains, go to California, get out of here for good, do something no one expects," but only the wind and sagebrush were listening as he sat trying to sort things out.

Templeton camped on the windblown hillside. If sleeping and freezing on the barren hillside could be called camping. He woke every ten or fifteen minutes, finally giving up on sleep as the first breaking rays of dawn lit the eastern sky. He got up hungry, sore, exhausted and feeling like he was picking up a cold. He was tired of sleeping on the ground, he was hungry and without a blanket he felt like he would never be warm again. If he could just be in a town, it could not be worse. His only problem in town would be a lack of money. But money was easy to come up with in town. He shivered then smiled, thought about the girl with the baby and the old mountain man, the smile turned to a laugh.

Running the past few days was becoming all too familiar and Templeton was sick of it. After the hungry, cold, and near sleepless night, but now with a rested horse, he decided to take his chances and go to town for a few hours or a few days at most. But not in Laramie City, no it would be Cheyenne for a few days, no more. He needed to be in town.

Templeton rode slow, it took two and a half days and the burglary of a farmhouse southeast of Laramie to make it, but he could see

Cheyenne at last. In the late afternoon, Luke Templeton rode into Cheyenne and sold the unbranded gray horse from the livery in Laramie City. The sale fetched enough to buy a new set of work clothes and pay for a room in the cheapest hotel he could find. The hotel was so close to the railroad tracks the building shook every time a train rolled in or out of Cheyenne. Templeton looked around at his six-bit a day room, a rusted metal frame bed, a small table and a window overlooking the tracks, nothing else. He had stayed in worse, but he had also stayed in better, but this would do for now. He could steal another horse when he needed one. Decided he might hang out near one of the local cowboy bars to see if he could roll a drunk or two for some eating money. He lay down on the bed, took a deep breath crossed his arms over his chest and fell asleep, a crooked smile painting his face.

An hour and a half nap and he was some better, but still tired. Now he felt more hungry than tired. He left the hotel by the back door and walked down the darkening alley lit only by a full sky of stars and a sliver of moon. Later he enjoying a tough steak, biscuits and gravy complements of a railroader he hit over the head in the alley, the cheap cigars the railroader carried were a bonus. After eating, he strolled over to the nearest bar, deciding it should be safe enough in this rough part of town. Sitting in the corner with his back to a window he smoked two cigars and sipped a few flat beers. Two hours later he decided to go back to the room and sleep. After last night, with little or no sleep and the nap worn away, Templeton could go no more, he needed sleep.

The next morning he was rested and ready to go, but he still didn't know which way. He knew of no reason to go west or north, leaving south to Colorado or east to Nebraska as his options. Still short of money Templeton decided to look around during the day and find a way to collect some cash before heading south, it would be south to Denver.

He waited for the sun to set and the dark to overtake the city before taking up his spot near the Cheyenne Club. The city had some of its new street lights in front of the building and the Social Cub had lights of its own all along the sixty-foot front porch. Templeton had lived in the city and all big cities were lit up at night. He knew people thought street lights protected them, but they didn't, street lights and porch lights lit up small areas, everything else sat in shadows. Templeton knew shadows. He'd spent most of his life moving in and out of night shadows. He loved street lights, made the unsafe feel safe. His plan was simple, catch an opening, find a shadow and hit one of the rich cowboys going in. He knew they would have more money going in than coming out.

Hit um, take the money and run. Get back to his hotel room, sleep; steal a horse in the morning, cross the tracks and head south keeping the mountains to his right side. The plan was so good he wanted to tell someone, but standing in the shadow of a short pine he did not believe that would be a good idea. It didn't take him long.

Templeton crept up behind a well-dressed cowboy as he swung down from the saddle. It was over before either one knew what happened. He hit the cowboy with a broken handle from a spike driver he found earlier near the tracks, catching him on the side of the head. He dropped beside his horse. In a few seconds, the man was relieved of his wallet, pocket gun, cowboy hat and a small packet of cigars. Templeton disappeared in the shadows. He tossed the ax handle under a nearby porch and walked away faster than someone out for a summer night stroll but not fast enough to draw attention to himself.

After walking three blocks, and trying not to look around too much, he ducked down a dark street, one the city had not yet graced with street lights. Chancing a look back as he moved into a block of solid shadows he could see the man, now far in the distance. He was sitting up, Templeton couldn't tell which way he faced, but he sat in the dirt near his horse but no one else. Templeton felt a warm rush, his heart pounding he'd pulled it off, home free again he thought. Sleep would come easy tonight. And the rest would feel even better if the wallet had a twenty or maybe a fifty, he would sleep soundly.

It was all Templeton could do to keep from running. He wanted to get back to the room, check the wallet and smoke one of his new cigars. Every time he robbed someone it was like getting a present. He never got gifts growing up but the adrenaline rush he got when he robbed someone made up for his lacking childhood. He nodded to the desk clerk as he strolled in, hands in his pockets, and walked the stairs to his eight by ten room. He loved feeling like he did now it almost made up for the failings of the last week. He felt better than he had for several days, always got this feeling when he got away with something. Templeton felt the enormous smile on his face, opened the door to his room and propped the rooms single chair under the doorknob.

With heart racing and the mind speeding along almost faster than his thinking skills, he managed to light a candle and crack open the window before sitting down on the edge of the bed. Taking a deep breath, he opened the wallet and counted the money, four fifties, six twenties a ten and seven ones, over three hundred dollars. How anyone could be this lucky, he thought or was he this good, he believed he might be, might be that good. Templeton slid the creaking window up as far as it would go, took off his boots, sat back down on the bed and stretched his legs until his feet rested comfortably on the window sill. Another oversized smile tried to fit his face when he lit the cigar, looks expensive he thought, and then he blew a stream of yellow-blue smoke and watched it curl out the window and rise, mingling with the darkness.

Templeton thought for a moment about tomorrow morning. He would eat a good breakfast then buy a horse or maybe a horse and buggy; he was saddle sore and tired of riding. Then he would ask about trails south and decide what to do. Money in his pocket would make some decisions easy and others more difficult. Templeton patted his new gun then dropped it trying to spin it on his finger. An excellent little pocket Navy revolver customized with a pearl handle, he liked it. Not too big and not tiny like a lot of pocket guns, "might have to pick up some extra cartridges for it tomorrow," Templeton said, loud enough for someone in the room to hear if anyone had been in the room with him. He blew more smoke from a very fine cigar out the open hotel window; things were starting to go his way.

The morning sun poured through the window, Templeton rolled over and slept in, didn't matter; he was not in a big hurry, not anymore. For some reason money in his pocket made him feel safe. Must have been close to nine, might even be ten or eleven, he had no idea. At long last he dressed and left the ramshackle hotel and headed for the cafe across the street. Time for a big breakfast, some good food, before leaving Cheyenne, this time for good, for a moment after he sat down he felt like all eyes were on him, he wasn't sure why. A stubby middle age man, wiping his hands on his pants took his order for steak with fried potatoes and scrambled eggs. Templeton looked around the room. No one was looking at him, not really; he relaxed and enjoyed the food. He couldn't believe how hungry he was, devouring the pound of beef, a large pile of fried potatoes with four eggs and downing it all with three cups of good thick black coffee, all in ten minutes. Now he was satisfied and ready to leave town.

Templeton strolled the few blocks to the livery taking his time looking in shop windows and tipping his hat to several ladies as he walked. The women looked away from him and walked rapidly looking back over their shoulders making sure he didn't follow. Templeton fumed thinking, "if they knew how much money I have in my pocket they wouldn't be so quick to run away. I could buy um all if I wanted, and they'd be happy to have the money and me." He tipped his hat to two kids, started to spit on the road, thought better of it and turned and spit on the window of the boot shop he was passing. He laughed, turned and looked back down the boardwalk, the ladies were gone.

The livery stable had three or four good horses for sale; a small bunch of old nags to rent, and a near new buggy, also for rent. Templeton faked a smile then lied he would be back in a few days and asked about renting a horse to visit a sick friend in Colorado. The stable hand asked if he might be interested in the buggy since he must have luggage to take and Templeton jumped at the chance. He rented the buggy and horse for a week figuring he could sell both in Denver and make a nice profit over the fourteen dollars he paid to use the outfit for a week. Templeton paid the bill, careful not to show too much money, and trotted the horse away from the livery stable.

What the heck, Templeton thought. He stopped the buggy, tied the horse to the rail and walked into Godfrey's Dry Goods to spend some of the money he'd earned last night in front of the Cattleman's Club. He made small talk with the clerk, telling her he'd decided to do some sightseeing and hunting in the area. He'd spent but little time in his life shopping; he usually waited until no one watched and took what he needed. The whole process of shopping lasted longer than expected but in the end he bought two pair of work pants and two blue work shirts. He added a new pair of long johns, socks and a pretty nice pair of work boots. Before leaving he purchased a beaver felt hat, not a cowboy hat but more of a hat worn by the bankers he'd watched in Chicago and Kansas City, the rich guys. He loved the hat, it looked something like the one he had taken in Kansas City and lost a few days ago. For a moment he remembered shooting the lady for the hat and suit in Kansas City, he grinned and the thought left him as fast as it had come.

Templeton paid for his goods, walked toward the door, turned to see the clerk helping an old lady with some green ribbon, no one was watching. He stopped and slipped the lid from a jar and grabbed a hand full of peppermint sticks, stuffed them in his shirt as he reached the door and left. Old habits die hard and he really liked peppermint.

Loading the buggy took but a few seconds, a minute at most. Templeton climbed up on the wooden seat, flipped the reins, trotted toward the corner, and made a left toward Colorado. About a hundred miles, Templeton thought, a hundred miles and then there will be a train to catch, a train east, east as far as it goes, east to the ocean if he wanted.

About a mile out of town Templeton reined the horse to a stop and changed into the new work clothes. Wearing the same clothes for too long never really bothered him. But he wanted to look respectable; after all he owned a very nice horse and buggy, for sale in about a hundred more miles. He started to fold his dirty clothes then thought better of it, wadded them tight and tossed the bundle toward the tall sage. He could always get new clothes, might get another brown suit. Maybe someday after everything cooled off he would go back to Kansas City and have whoever was running the shop where he killed the pretty lady make one for him. Maybe the pretty girl survived being shot, probably not. Would be fun to go back and take another suit from her, he thought, then laughed out loud to the point where he started coughing as he pictured himself shooting her again. Too bad about the lady but she needed to die because she surprised him, but still too bad. Then he smiled his yellow crooked tooth smile and snapped the buggy whip savagely across the horse's rump.

It was already mid-afternoon and the gray-black clouds in the west hovered below the tops of the distant mountains. The dark sky gathered and looked ready to open up. Templeton watched dozens of lightning bolts flashing in the foothills. The wind freshened, blowing up clouds of red dust from the worn dirt road. The buggy horse snorted and tried to run. Rain would reach in minutes and Templeton made another quick decision, tomorrow was a better day than today. He didn't think about it for even a few seconds, slowing the buggy and making a sweeping left-hand turn, lashing the back of the horse as hard as he could he headed north, back to Cheyenne.

Templeton was soaked, his shirt plastered, like paint, to his back, by the time he crossed the tracks south of town. The rain now came down in steady pounding sheets. The horse spooked every two or three minutes as a new clap of thunder rattled the skies. He guided the buggy more to the center of town than where he stayed last night and found a small, but what looked like a brand new building, the Arthur Hotel. He tied the storm skittish horse to a tree at the edge of the long boardwalk and porch that fronted the hotel.

In typical Wyoming fashion, by the time Templeton was inside the hotel, the rain had stopped. Minutes later the skies were no longer dark with the sun only minutes away from peaking between the still rain loaded clouds. "Tonight's all," Templeton told the desk clerk when he asked.

Chapter 28

Three days and Luke Templeton did not show. Blade had been frustrated this morning, but by late afternoon he was mad. He guessed wrong and may have let a murder go because of it. His frustration boiled over, Blade could feel his face burning and his mouth roll into an angry smirk he seldom showed. It was a look his mind reserved for times like this, and these times had not often come hopeless times. Even the few times he'd been embarrassed or fooled he fought off the anger, but not this, not right now. In his life he could remember being mad, really mad, on two or three occasions, but never had he felt as disappointed and as mad, mad at himself, as he felt right now.

Blade let out a desperate chuckle, a near hopeless laugh, and then said as if someone stood beside him on the hillside, "some dime novel hero. This will make a terrific book, *Murderer Outsmarts Blade Holmes and Gets Away Laughing*, what a story." For a moment, he closed his eyes so tight it made his head hurt then he thought about Emma wondering if she would be mad and disappointed in him.

It took a few minutes but the anger passed, replaced by the melancholy that sometimes followed him. A melancholy today freezing him in this time and place, sticking him here on this hillside like the pine and juniper stumps surrounding him. For now Blade thought of only bad things, troubling things, everything he thought he had done wrong the past few days. Now the anger returned and he started to blame himself for everything, "Why did I ever leave Kansas City, why couldn't I save the woman and her baby in the sod house, how'd I let John Ryan die, why'd that old mountain man have to die?" Blade swiped at the tears streaking down his face questioning why he was even here, here on this hillside and here on this earth.

Everything seemed to get worse before getting better. Blade stood over a cold fire pit hollering at the top of his voice, "why did I leave Cheyenne, why did I leave Emma alone, why?" And at last in a whisper, "why did I ever leave the farm, it was a beautiful place, should have stayed and none of this would have happened, none of it." But talking to the trees and rocks didn't make him feel much better.

Blade walked over and sat down in the small pines letting his mind tumble through the past three days. He had checked the train schedule in Cheyenne when the train stopped to take on two freight cars. Three eastbound trains and he had checked all of them. Not from the hillside, he had boarded each of them and walked through and then back through. No Templeton, he had done everything possible, he'd guessed wrong.

Blade gathered a few sticks and started to build a fire, time to wait it out and stay another night. Then he turned grabbed his saddle from the ground, packed up his gear, saddled Medicine and rode out. Wrong, he might be wrong again, but he didn't think so, not this time. There could only be one answer, Templeton felt safe, he didn't think he needed to hurry. He was still in town, Cheyenne or Laramie City.

Blade eased Medicine down the slope. So where would a safe feeling murder be right now? Blade reached the flats at the bottom of the hill and kicked Medicine gently letting him have his head. The big Appaloosa broke like a racehorse throwing chunks of grass and dirt as he dug down trying to reach racing speed. He seemed as anxious as Blade to be off the side of the hill and on the road to Cheyenne. Blade had to rein Medicine in some, but let him continue faster than they needed to go. Medicine kept to a stiff-legged trot, it felt good with the wind in his face again and the steady movement of the great horse under him. Blade had a smile on his face now, and rode west, riding with a purpose.

Once again Blade rode along only a few yards of the railroad right-of-way. This close to the tracks the ground had been leveled and cleared of brush and trees, faster travel than across the open range. Cheyenne was a good day's ride in the best of conditions. For Blade, it would be a ride into the setting sun surrounded by distance rain clouds highlighted by lightning flashing near the center. Looked like a long, dark and wet ride, but if things went well, he could make Cheyenne sometime in the morning.

Nine-fifteen, no later than nine-twenty, Blade opened the door and walked into the city of Cheyenne sheriff's office. Sheriff Watson sat at his desk drinking coffee from an ancient looking tin cup, reading through the day's mail. "Must mean you didn't find him," Watson said, without looking up.

"No, not yet, but I have an idea he might be here, right under our noses."

"Tell me what ya got, I'm ready to go after him, never thought it would be here in town, how'd you come to that, you sure or are ya guessin'?"

"Not sure, just a gut feeling, I been wrong before, but not this time, he's here alright," Blade pressed his lips tight and shrugged his shoulders, "somewhere."

Sheriff Watson pushed the mail to the back of his desk, drained his coffee cup and stood up, "where ya wanna start? You got a plan, I'll help out, anything you need, I can round up a few men if you think we'll need um."

Blade considered the sheriff's comment for a moment and then answered. "The two of us are all we'll need, here's what I think we need to do. Now that it's too late for breakfast, we can sit here for a while, then when it is closer to noon take a look at some of the eating places in town, we'll concentrate from mid-town to the tracks, can't see Templeton comfortable anywhere else."

When the battered clock on the sheriff's desk showed eleven-fifteen, the pair headed toward mid-town and the favorite dinner-time stops for locals. While they walked the three blocks to their first stop Blade asked about any recent robberies, burglaries or break-ins around town. "Not regular stuff, something new, different than usual, maybe more violent or something that seemed too odd, maybe cruel?"

Never thought about Templeton being in town, not once, can't believe I missed it, the sheriff said. "Seems like some kind of epidemic the past two days. Railroader hit over the head walking home from work, robbed of two dollars and four bits, all he had on him. Then, last night, a guy named Remple got hit from behind, same as the railroader, cracked over the head with a gun or a rock, piece of firewood, something hard. The guy got robbed while tying his horse in front of the club. Didn't talk much when he came around, wouldn't say how much he lost but I expect he might have had a roll, he's a regular up in the card rooms we lawman aren't supposed to know anything about. I'm friends with one of the local big wheels, cattle buyer, plays some pool or cards over there quite a bit. Told me if a guy didn't have two or three hundred you needn't even set down at the tables upstairs. Around here it's always been people getting robbed at gunpoint or drunks being rolled, not many times people get clubbed unconscious and robbed, not till the last couple a days."

They walked the next half block without speaking before Blade said, "Sounds like something he could do. Surprised he didn't kill them, but in town he must have been smart enough not to use his gun, didn't know if he could think things through that well, anything else?"

"Oh, there're always a few smaller things, things go on around here, the routine stuff in a cattle and railroad town that hasn't grown up yet. But the bigger things like the two fellas who were assaulted and robbed, not too many of those, not anymore. I think you're right, sounds like they could be the work of the same guy, someone like Templeton. The papers I got on him mentioned stuff like this. Note from Kansas said he's dangerous and might do about anything, the Pinkerton there called him a thug, city thug, I think they said. Once a two-bit thug, always a two-bit thug, and now a killer too, thought he might be long shed of this place by now, I'd about forgot all about him."

"Blade"

"Yeah sheriff."

"For a lot of reasons I hope you're wrong, I don't want him here in my town, but if he is, and we can catch him, might help out the whole territory if he was caught or dead, where you wanna' start?"

Blade pulled open the door of the Mid-Town Eatery with the sheriff following. This one didn't take long, four people sitting at one table, two couples eating an early dinner. The lawmen turned and walked across the street. Sheriff Watson mentioned they might still be a little early. He and Blade took seats near the front window and ordered coffee. This place, Bill's, had a few more customers but none with any resemblance to Luke Templeton. After ten minutes and two empty coffee cups, they walked south toward the tracks.

The sheriff and Blade, with two uneventful Cheyenne cafes behind them, were making small talk and smiling when they stepped through the door of the Railway Diner. The roar of the forty-five was deafening in the close quarters of the little diner. A black powder cloud filled the room, guns flashed again, in a matter of two or three seconds it ended.

Sheriff Watson lay bleeding on the floor and two cowboys one in front of Blade and one to his left were also down. The cowboy in front of Blade lay agonizing; writhing on the floor with one of Blade's long-handled knife's buried in his shoulder. His partner was on his back, unmoving with a bullet hole centered in his chest, blood oozing on the plank floor from under his body. A group of twenty or twenty-five diners sat in motionless silence, stunned at what they had witnessed.

Blade Holmes holstered his six-gun, stepped over to the man, now unconscious, with the knife buried in his shoulder. He placed a boot on the man's shoulder, inches from the knife and pulled it free. Watson was setting up holding his blood-soaked upper arm and waved Blade it was alright to go after Templeton or whoever was responsible for trying to kill them. Blade wiped the knife across the wounded man's pant leg, shoved it behind his collar and left. Someone else could clean up the mess. He had things to do.

Chapter 29

The door squeaked a shrill greeting as Blade stepped into Dr. Andrew's office at seven the next morning. He felt responsible for the sheriff's condition and wanted to make sure he was recovering before he left town to find Templeton. Blade had no medical training, but he didn't need any to see the sheriff was going to be fine. When Blade walked in the old lawman sat leaning back in a wooden chair near the window with his feet propped up on the sill reading a newspaper and drinking coffee. His arm was in a sling but other than that, the man didn't look much different than he did yesterday. Watson smiled when Blade walked in, folded his newspaper back to the front page reaching out with his good arm he handed it to Blade.

The headline said everything that needed to be said. "Sheriff Watson Injured, Drifter Wounded another Killed—Blade Holmes saves the day." Blade tossed the paper back to the sheriff and shook his head. He hadn't saved the day and didn't care what the newspapers said. The stories lead paragraph said he saved twenty-three people who were eating at the time. But Blade and the sheriff knew the real story, they walked right into an ambush, he didn't save anyone, he was reacting to the situation, nothing more.

People from the cafe shooting were busy spreading the legend of Blade Holmes; one man reported time stopped when Blade went into action. Said everything was so fast there was no way time advanced, said his watch quit ticking, that he'd never seen anything like it. Watch hadn't run since. Others talked about how fast and how deadly he had been. The newspaper didn't help, reporting, "Blade made a rattlesnake seem old and slow the way he released the knife and so accurately fired the one slug from his Colt." Seemed like everyone in town was claiming they were eating in the cafe when Blade went into action.

Blade walked with Sheriff Watson back to his office. Surprisingly the sheriff moved along without a hitch, looked to Blade like he would be good as new pretty soon. Blade knew it was not his fault, but the way things had been going he was having a tough time not blaming himself for the sheriff getting shot. One more reason Blade needed to get on the trail, find Templeton and bring him back. For an hour or so last night, Blade had about made up his mind he would shoot him when he caught up, get it over with, now he knew he couldn't. Late yesterday he decided to play some cards, relax. He watched a game for a few minutes, laughed for thinking about playing when he could be relaxing, went up the street to the hotel and fell asleep.

The sheriff allowed Blade to open the office door for him, they walked inside and found Benny Market stretched out, but wide awake, on his jailhouse bunk. He had a sour look on his face and winced when he saw Blade as if he expected another knife coming at him. One question and he didn't take long to tell his story. Both he and the dead man, Jason Beckworth, were paid by Luke Templeton to protect his backside. When questioned about the murder of Oliver Stevens, Market claimed to know nothing about it, but both Blade and the sheriff thought otherwise. "So just who were you protecting Templeton from, who was he afraid of?"

Market shook his head started to say he didn't know anything and then admitted it was Oliver Stevens they followed out of Cheyenne. "But I didn't shoot anybody, never fired a single shot, never planned too, just needed money, it was Beckworth that shot him, Beckworth, not me."

Neither Blade nor the sheriff was buying what Market said, but they would worry about him another time. Or let a judge and jury figure him out.

Blade shook his head, turned away from the jail cell, took his hat off and walked toward the front of the office. He ran his fingers through his hair, blew out a long slow breath, put his hat back on, then tipped it back, put his foot up on the sill and looked out the front window toward the street.

Funny how things work out Blade thought, Market and Beckworth were after Templeton along with the Army, the posse, the Pinkerton

Detective Agency and Blade. Market and Beckworth drew because they thought Blade and Sheriff Watson were looking for them when they stepped into the cafe. That single fact was what led the two lawmen to believe Market and Beckworth were connected to the murder of Oliver Stevens. Now Market was in jail and Beckworth was dead, all because Templeton stiffed them for four hundred of the five hundred dollars he promised. Had he paid upfront they likely would be a long way from here and riding hard. But you can't tell about a pair of owl hoots like them, might have stuck around for fun to spend their money.

Blade and Watson stood talking near the front window of the office while Blade readied his bedroll and packed his saddlebags getting ready to continue his pursuit of Templeton. Watson walked over to his desk and pulled out a new poster and a letterhead from his office. "Got this new poster with a bunch of them came in this morning, $2000 for Templeton, I filled out the order for the money, all you need to do is sign it when you get back, expect to see you in the morning, or the day after, if you ever get out of here and get after him."

Blade had already delayed his departure more than he wanted with the extra day, now it was time to go to work. Blade shook the sheriff's hand and bid him good day reminding him to, "rest up," before he opened the door to leave it was pushed open from the outside.

A Western Union delivery man handed Blade a telegram marked Urgent.

-Hold Market and Beckworth for authorities from Fort Laramie-STOP-
- Both wanted as U.S. Army deserters-STOP-
-Regards
-Lt. Col. H. C. Merriam
-Fort Laramie

Blade shook his head, army deserters hanging around, looking to make a buck, and Templeton found them. He doubted Merriam would be too upset when he found out one of the deserters was already dead. There was also a note from Pinkerton's district chief, said he was on his way to talk with Blade, but that conversation would have to wait. Blade walked to the livery, saddled Medicine and left town at a gallop.

It took Blade less than an hour to trace Templeton's actions from last night. He found where Templeton signed his name for a rental horse and buggy. The bottom of the page entry in the rental log was signed by, L. Pinkerton, clever Blade thought, no imagination at all, could have signed Brown, Jones, Waring, anything, but he signed it Pinkerton. "This guy should be easy to find but somehow he keeps getting away," Blade said to no one at all in the empty livery.

Riding across the railroad tracks and along the rutted road out past the city limit sign marking the southern boundary of Cheyenne Blade found tracks, dozens of them, too many, way too many. Buggies coming and going every day, he hoped as he rode on South Templeton's buggy tracks would be easier to pick out. He had to have followed the main road with the buggy, but why did he take a buggy. Buggies were slow, hard to hide and much less manageable than a horse. Maybe he was tired of riding, being the greenhorn he was. Riding along Blade wasn't sure he needed tracks; he knew where Templeton and his buggy were heading, Denver and then the train. Nowhere else he could go. Not if he was going south.

Blade tapped Medicine with the heel of his boot and the big horse responded with a quicker pace falling into the stiff-legged trot he favored. The road was well worn and soft. The trip to Denver would not take long. But it could be slow going with a buggy and horse on the soft road, time to make up some miles. Blade daydreamed as Medicine ate up the distance; he figured eight or ten miles to the hour. Two hours passed when a relaxed Blade heard the shot at the same moment he saw the sun glittering from the rifle barrel on the hillside.

"You alright son, can you hear me, ya okay?"

Blade opened one eye, the one with the least amount of road dirt in it. Through the clouds of a clearing mind, he saw a scarecrow like old man, dressed in a rumpled black suit. Blade blinked again to make sure the scarecrow was really a man and not part of a dream.

Blade propped up on one elbow before answering, "Maybe, looks like I'm all here, something shook me out of a pretty good daydream and it appears my horse deposited me in the middle of this road, believe I'm alright, don't see any blood, feel a little sore. Where's Medicine?"

"Don't appear you'll be needin' any medicine son, think you otta make it, look good enough to me, here let me help you up." The old-timer reached down with a weathered hand and Blade took it.

"No, no, my horse, my horse's name is Medicine." Blade tugged on the old man's arm almost pulling him down beside him, but with a little effort he stood with a long groan.

"There's a big paloosa standing back there by the trail, expect he might be yours."

Blade shaded his eyes and could see Medicine standing about a hundred yards back down the trail. He stood there looking up the road as if to say, "What do you want me to do now?"

Blade brushed the dust from his arms, looked around for his hat and allowed the old man to brush off his back, either removing more dust or checking him for injuries. He bent at the waist dusted off his pant legs and decided he looked pretty good. Except for a small tear in his right pant leg, he could find nothing out of the ordinary and then he noticed it. He had been shot. Looked like the bullet hit his Colt, Blade pulled his six-gun and the outside facing of the grip was shattered. The bullet hit the grip ripped through part of the holster and tore a small hole in his pant leg. No blood.

Templeton

He'd been bushwhacked and had been lucky, he really did not know how lucky. Blade never suspected he could have caught up with Templeton, not this fast. Tomorrow, he had intended to be careful, tomorrow, get off the road, ride slow and catch up. But today he had been foolish and should have known better. Blade thanked the old gentlemen standing quietly beside him and asked if he had seen the shooting. "No, never heard anything either, must have been a while before I came along. Likely knocked yourself out when you came off your horse."

"If you're feeling up to it I believe I'll take my leave and head on down the road, need to get to Cheyenne. Ya know you look some like the Holmes fella everyone's been talking about. Drawings of him on the front of some books I have seen around these days, I even read one of them myself. Town folk say he's supposed to be in these parts, but me, I think he is one of them, made up, book heroes. Not sure anyone could be as good as he is in the books. Made him up to sell more books, that's what I think, don't spect he's real. Well, I'm off, Cheyenne, Cheyenne afore dark."

With the talking over the frail old man in the black suit put both hands under his left leg and lifted a tired looking black boot into the stirrup. He pulled hard on the saddle horn, and with effort was able to mount the sway back gray. Blade didn't know if he should have helped him up into the saddle or not, he decided not to help, but he cringed as he watched him take the better part of a minute to get mounted. The old man wiggled a bit then settled in the saddle and reached his hand down to Blade. Taking the hand Blade again started to thank the old-timer for coming along and helping him, but he was cut off in mid-sentence. "By the way I'm Parson Christie, Joshua Christie and looks to me like you should be thankin' the good Lord, luck only rides with God son, believe he's been looking out for you today."

Blade continued to shake the parson's hand, "thanks, I'm Blade Holmes, I appreciate your help and the help of your upstairs boss too."

The old minister smiled a warm country preacher smile, tipped his hat and rode away, his broken down horse walking at an old horse pace. He rode but a few steps before he stopped and turned, the best he could in the saddle, looked back over his shoulder and hollered,

"Knew it was you, knew it right along, good luck son."

He rode a few more steps and then, almost as an afterthought, he stopped the old gray, this time turning the horse around in the middle of the narrow road and looked at Blade from thirty yards. "I'll let the boss upstairs know you appreciated his help, hope you let him know yourself. Yes, sir, I'll let him know Blade Holmes, I'll let him know you appreciated the help."

Sermon over, Parson Joshua Christie headed for a pulpit in Cheyenne.

Chapter 30

Blade and Medicine caught up with each other in the next minute. Blade spent some time checking out his big mount, calming and talking to him. Everything seemed fine and Blade blew out a sigh of relief. He looked to the sky, not the horizon but straight up, he smiled, nodded his head thinking about what the old parson said to him. He walked Medicine, still a bit skittish, up a small knoll about a hundred yards ahead and on the west side of the road. It took Blade only five minutes to find the place where Templeton fired. Many footprints and two brass casings made Blade wonder if he'd found this site too easy, and then he wondered about the second shell casing. Templeton shot twice, not once, must have shot again when I fell or fired again after I was already on the ground, Blade mused, as he squatted on his haunches and plucked a long stem of grass and working it between his front teeth.

Too sore, too tired and too many things to think about, Blade decided to stay for a while and rest. He unsaddled Medicine and turned him loose to graze, figuring if he didn't run off after the shots he wouldn't go far now. Blade sat down on a small grassed-over mound of dirt, one day, long ago, it might have been piled outside a badger den, but the badger was long gone with only a small indention in the grass showing the former front door of the den. He hung his hat from a broken branch of a little sage and thought, moved a bit to find some reasonable comfort and thought about Templeton and thought about the badger, long since gone.

Blade wondered if his life in Kansas City would return to what it once was. Or like the badger be forgotten, forgotten forever. The longer he sat and thought the more his mind cleared. Blade was sore and frustrated, but his mind was doing alright. The sun started to close shop for the day, ducking behind a grassy hill to the west, when Blade stood and stretched, saddled Medicine and headed south. This time he would make no mistakes, this time he would let Templeton make the mistakes. Blade hoped he wouldn't be forced to kill him, despite all the thoughts he had a few days back about doing just that. Killing was never easy, even when he wore a badge allowing it. There were answers he needed first. Blade stood in the stirrups and looked west and south if it had to be, Templeton's life would end tomorrow out here on the Wyoming plains if it had to be.

This time both rider and horse stayed off the main road, choosing a path a quarter mile or more away. Part of the time Blade rode east of the road, sometimes west. The sun was setting and Blade knew he still had miles to go, he wished he knew how many.

It was his lucky day when Templeton did not take the time to check and see if he'd killed his target. Or maybe he had been too sure of himself, or the preacher came on the scene and spooked him away. The old preacher may have been right; maybe someone was looking out after him, Blade thought. Blade's mind raced ahead as he crossed the empty trail again and rode up a small ridge dotted with junipers.

If Templeton thought he'd killed his quarry, he may stop early, make camp and relax. Blade continued running ideas through his already overloaded mind. Maybe Templeton doubled back to Cheyenne; maybe it wasn't Templeton who shot him. Maybe, maybe, Blade closed his eyes in an attempt to let his mind clear, took off his hat and brushed his hair back but he couldn't clear his cluttered thoughts. He thought first of Kansas City, now of Templeton and then the old Parson, maybe he had come along just in time to save his life, what did he say his name was, Joshua Christie? Blade reined Medicine to a halt, put his arms above his head and stretched, took in a deep breath of the sage-tinged air, wishing it would calm him. He took one more deep breath. He wasn't sure fresh sage air could soothe a man's soul.

Riding in the dark was never easy, but tonight, tonight it was almost too much for Blade. His back ached, his left shoulder throbbed where he'd fallen on it, and now he could feel the pressure of his right ankle swelling in his boot. This ride was harder than any night ride he had attempted in the past. Riding slow and easy he continued to cross from east to west. At four thirty in the morning, or close to four forty, Blade saw the fire, a long way off, but unmistakably a campfire. Riding within a quarter mile he tied Medicine in a small ravine to a twisted root stretching down and out of the banks sheer side from up above. Blade walked carefully keeping the fire in his sight as he approached taking one slow, quiet step at a time. Keeping to the small washes and with much tall sage to break up his image, Blade was invisible.

Chapter 31

By all measures Luke Templeton looked like a contented man, snoring softly, wrapped in blankets he laid in a deep dreaming sleep a pace away from the fire. His dreams were filled with thoughts of what a great day today had been. A beautiful day, starting with a slow buggy ride, and ending with a big meal and well-deserved rest. In between the big guy who had been hazing him, for what seemed forever, was now dead, dead on the road a half day back. With his belly full of biscuits, boiled eggs, and half a bottle of whiskey Templeton now slept dreaming like a baby, a crooked smile on his face. The campfire puffed and blazed a bit with thick pieces of pine now heating, and spitting last bits of moisture, causing flames and sparks to reach into the night air. Something stirred him to a semi-awake state, then he woke, and the smile of his dreams turned to a shocked frown of reality when he felt the knife at his throat.

"Nice to see you again Mr. Templeton," Blade said as Templeton blinked awake.

"Holmes."

Blade tied Templeton's hands behind his back, walked him over to the buggy, cinched a rope around his waist and secured him to the buggy seat. Blade, still sore and mad, shook his head in disgust and tore the Pinkerton badge from Templeton's new shirt. As an extra precaution, he tied the squat man's legs together, ran the rope under the seat, wrapped his wrists, again, and then pulled the rope back under the seat and tied it to the back of the buggy. Blade would not let anything go wrong, not this time. With Medicines saddle strapped on the back of the buggy and the big Appaloosa tied alongside they started the slow ride back to Cheyenne, and to the jail inside the U.S. Marshal's office.

As they rolled along Templeton's silence showed he'd resigned himself, he had reached the end of the line, and in all likelihood would be hanging on the gallows of Cheyenne within a fortnight. When Blade loaded Templeton's belongings, he counted five handguns, two rifles, and a knife. He also had a wad of cash as big as Blade had ever seen at a gambling table. The hard work was over, the sun was halfway above the horizon in the east, and Blade started to relax and dream of Emma, and Kansas City. The rhythmic sounds of the buggy wheels turning were more mesmerizing than sitting a horse and riding, Blade fought hard to keep from dozing off even with a murder tied beside him.

A shot echoed off the high rock walls on the east side of the trail. Sounded like it came from behind but Blade couldn't tell, not for sure. The slug struck Templeton high in the back, he didn't fall, instead continued to sit upright because of the hog tying Blade had done on him. Blade turned the buggy at a ninety-degree angle and whipped the horse for a quarter mile, trying to keep both him and his prisoner low with some protection from the buggy seats thick wooden back. He raced the buggy through tall grass speckled with sage, bouncing toward a group of small hills protected by a tiny stand of cottonwood and aspen. While the buggy bumped and bounced along four more shots rang out the last striking the buggies horse in the neck a few steps before they reached the protection of the trees. Blade slashed the rope tethering Medicine as he pulled his big rifle from the saddle scabbard and flattened out on the hillside peering under low branches in a tangle of small aspen. The minute he got comfortable he wished he had his field glasses.

He didn't see anyone for the next few minutes and decided to crawl back toward the buggy. Keeping the side of the buggy between him and the place where the bullets came from Blade pulled the field glasses from his saddlebags. Blade crouched and dashed back into the grove, flattened out in the shadows and took a deep breath. Even as close as he was he used the binoculars to check up close first, Templeton was secure and looked to be unconscious, but he was still breathing. Medicine had been around shooting since Blade started to train him, and the shots had not scared him much, he stood unfazed munching grass among the aspens within a hundred yards.

It took the better part of ten minutes, of study glassing, before Blade found them, but there they were, like tiny little two-legged bugs far out of rifle distance. Blade relaxed and stood, steadying his arms on a limb to re-focus the glasses, guessing the shooters were at least three-quarters of a mile away. The two men were on foot, sneaking through a small boulder field ducking in and out behind the tall sage as they made their way south. Now through the clear view of the field glasses Blade could see two horses tied a few more steps from the shooters, he wondered if there was anything he could do? For a few seconds, Blade looked down the barrel of his rifle lining the men into the notch of his sights trying and hoping for one good shot. Then he thought better of it, realizing it was too far, even for him. Blade laid the big rifle aside and walked toward Templeton. He stopped and took one last look through the glasses, watching the shooters, now on horseback, galloping to the south. They're leaving and right now I can't do a thing about it, Blade thought, as he turned to get his horse.

Medicine looked contented, grazing now about two-hundred yards from the buggy. The rental horse stood on wobbling legs in a pool of blood next to the buggy and needed some immediate attention. Blade took one last look to the south toward the shooters but could see nothing of them. They would have to wait. Both a man and a horse needed his attention. Blade looked over at Templeton, unconscious still tied securely in the buggy, and then he looked at the horse. The buggy horse was down on its front legs, knees on the ground, with its hind legs stiff as if locked in place to hold the body upright. She was losing too much blood to last much longer. Blade decided to attend to the horse first, looked like it had the better chance of survival.

Roy Tibbs sat his saddle, all smiles, as he and his partner ran their horses south, he knew he could make the shot, and he had. Now he wished he'd taken out Holmes also, but the fast-moving buggy shot proved too difficult, besides waiting one more day for him, after all these years, really wasn't too bad. He and his partner slowed to a trot and then to a walk. Tibbs convinced himself the sharp turn Holmes made with the wagon was the reason he missed him, not a bad shot. He knew the first shot, the head-on three hundred yard shot that hit Templeton, was much easier, and many a shooter could have made it, but he couldn't admit it to himself.

Blade Holmes was accomplished in many things, but his doctoring skills were never a strong suit. He started thinking about the past few days while he packed mud and milkweed cotton into the wound on the horse's neck. He needed some time away. Some time at a card table or time at home in Kansas City, if he still had a home there. The bleeding from the horse's neck had started to clump and slow, looking like it might stop, and Blade turned his thoughts back to what he felt were his strong suits: diamonds, hearts, spades and clubs and the new suit Emma started making for him before he left. Odd connections, Blade thought, and despite the circumstances he felt a smile crease his face as he let his mind race. Then he laughed, maybe a laugh of relief or one of comfort, "I'm not really much good at cards," he said and looked over toward the slumped man on the buggy seat.

He turned his attention now to the passed out Templeton. Blade decided to do the best he could for the no account. The poultice he packed on the neck of the horse he'd learned from the old mountain man and now he was trying to save his murder. Sometimes life made little sense, Blade started tending to Templeton, deciding if it helped the horse, it might do the same for him. He took his time doing the best he could, despite feeling he would feel much better if he left him for the buzzards. Finishing all the doctoring he knew, Blade walked the few steps back to the small aspen grove, sat down, and leaned against one of the white trunks. He took off his hat, laid it on the ground, and closed his eyes. Today had been a long day, as long as any day could be.

Chapter 32

A deep dreaming sleep came within minutes. In a moment, his sleeping mind took him back seven years and over a hundred miles north, north to Fort Laramie.

At nineteen, Blade Holmes was the youngest scout ever to work out of the fort. The sun was warm and the snow in the flats was mostly gone, tiny white flowers and dark green grass were showing along the Platte. The second week of April and winter was, at last, giving way to spring. Blade was getting itchy; time to move again, he had been here for the better part of four months. Walking over to the post store to check what he could buy with a winter's savings Blade looked up and saw something out of the past. He had read dime novel Mountain Men books as a kid growing up in Ohio, but here was a real Mountain man, riding into the fort leading two pack horses. Two packs loaded with furs, looked like wolf and beaver pelts as he ambled by looking mostly down and ahead, but nodding his chin to Blade, then smiled and winked a weary gray eye as he rode past.

Forgetting about the supplies, Blade never one to talk much when he stayed at the fort, wanted to talk, he wanted to talk to the old Mountain man. Blade walked across the grounds and caught up with him near the stables as the old man led his horses to the corral. Standing a few feet away Blade found himself tongue-tied, unable to say a word. The old man in front of him seemed to turn back time, taking Blade back years to Ohio.

The old man in front of him looked to be straight from the cover of one of the dime novels Blade remembered reading years ago. Except now it seemed those years were not so long ago, and he finished reading the novel yesterday. The old man was John Ryan, Blade was sure. He had read and re-read, *John Ryan-Laramie Peak Legend*, so many times the book fell apart. "Hello son, wanna give me a hand here?"

Still silent Blade helped unpack the horses, after a while managing to utter an embarrassed, "looks like you had a pretty good year."

John Ryan was widely known throughout the mountain west, he had wintered at Fort Laramie and he had summered at the fort. He was a man of his own mind, seemed to work for years at a time and then at the most unexpected times show up. He had stayed at the fort for as long as three months and for as little as two days. But no matter when he showed up he was always welcome.

Over the next three days, the two spent most all their non-sleeping hours together. On the fourth day of his stay John Ryan asked Blade, "you interested in headin' up to the Laramie Peak area with me, hunt, trap, swap a few tall tales, and tell each other a lie or two?"

Blade didn't need to think the invitation over, he shook his head yes, and two days later, an hour before daybreak, the two rode out of Fort Laramie heading due west, without a word to anyone.

Somewhere a coyote barked out a mournful howl waking Blade with a dream smile still on his face. Standing and stretching he said, "those really were the good old days," he laughed a slow, relaxed laugh as he heard himself saying the words, talking to the night in the Colorado foothills.

But the good ol' days were only seven years ago. Seven years ago when Blade spent eight months in the rugged Laramie range and on west, the best eight months of his life, and most of the time he spent with his friend and mentor John Ryan. Now looking toward the buggy John Ryan's killer tried to move, leaning a little more forward and to the left. Then he managed a weak moan, looked and sounded like he was on the verge of a revisit to conciseness. Blade hated thinking it, but now looking at Templeton he wished whoever shot him would have been a better shot. If anyone ever needed killing it was the wounded man he patched up an hour and a half ago. In one season in the mountains, old John Ryan became as close to Blade as any man since he left the bottomland farm in Ohio. In many ways, John Ryan seemed real and his parents, now ten years and a thousand miles away seemed more a part of his imagination.

Blade checked the buggy horse. She was standing, unsteady, but standing and appeared to be improved, maybe his doctoring worked better than he thought it would. Blade moved out to where Medicine grazed and walked him back toward the buggy. Now Templeton looked like he had slipped back into his gunshot dream world. Blade slid Templeton's eyelids open with his thumb, and then moved back into the trees and sat down to think, and to remember his friend, the old mountain man John Ryan. Blade drank from his canteen, scooted away from the trunk of the Aspen so the sun could catch part of his face and chewed on a piece of jerky, thinking back.

It was the fourth of July 1881. Blade and Ryan fished in a beaver pond, a handful of bighorn sheep watching from the side of a sheer granite wall less than a quarter mile away. Something spooked the sheep and Ryan and Blade moved away from the stream and into the shadows. They stood unmoving listening for something or anything. Horses sounded like a herd of wild horses running. The two moved back toward the pond and Ryan mentioned it was unusual to see horses this high, too many bears, but he had seen them up here before, but only one time.

Forty minutes later the horses grazed in a high mountain meadow resplendent in yellows, blues, and greens. The sun shone bright, now passing the half-day mark, day-sky and seemed to be shining on only one horse. A magnificent blanket appaloosa, he looked to be no more than a three or four-year-old, grazing among the rather drab browns, pintos, and two smaller appaloosas. The two men looked at the horses then looked at each other. John Ryan knew which horse Blade had already picked out," if you got the medicine son, he's yours, wild horses pick us, we don't pick them."

Blade spent the next two hours, crawling, sometimes flat on his belly, and walking where he could find shelter until he reached a clump of low growing junipers less than a hundred feet from the big stallion. He was downwind and except for two nervous yearlings they were all grazing, heads down into the wind. Blade loosed the rope from his belt and made a loop. He would get one chance, probably one chance in his life, to grab the big stallion.

Oowwweee — with one cry of a lone wolf the horses were gone. Now up on one knee Blade watched them run, all but one. The big Appaloosa had trotted a few hundred feet and stopped, turned and looked at Blade, then went back to grazing. Maybe he's crippled or something else is wrong with him, Blade thought. He measured the possibilities in his mind and then took an uncalculated chance, standing up he walked toward the big horse. Blade crossed his hands behind his back, he wasn't sure the big horse would know what nonchalant looked like but hoped he looked both friendly and unafraid.

Blade had strolled almost within rope range before the horse moved another hundred feet put his head down and continued grazing. Over the next three-quarters of an hour, Blade and the big stallion continued to play the game. Blade walked toward him, the big stallion waited and moved away, suspicious but unconcerned, and then the big horse simply stopped. Blade moseyed up to him, he reared one time then let the loop slide around his neck. It was over; Blade could not believe his good fortune.

He walked his new horse toward John Ryan, now setting high up on a red sandstone outcropping smoking his pipe. When Blade got within one or two city blocks distance, Ryan got to his feet and walked to meet them. "I've seen some strong medicine in my life and I have seen things I didn't even try to understand. But this, son, this was so far-fetched I sat rubbing my eyes wondering if I was dreamin'. It isn't just powerful medicine you got, I sat and watched you walk up to one of the wildest horse's I've ever seen, and you patted him on the rump and put a loop around his neck and lead him away. What you got is special and I don't mean the fact you're better with a gun and knife and horses now than anyone I ever seen, and I've seen a heap of um. It's so much more, no one I ever knew has what you got son, and much as I hate it, you gotta get out of these mountains and make something of yourself. You got power, power like Sitting Bull or Crazy Horse, maybe more, and I knowed um both. I been watching you since you walked over to me at Laramie, I'm proud to call you my friend. But I'll tell you right now I surely don't know what it is you have or what you are. Never seen anyone with the medicine you got Blade, no one, no one, not never."

In more than a half year in the mountains, this was the longest Blade ever heard Ryan talk at one stretch. Blade didn't know what to think or say. He nodded not sure what else he should do, then said, "Thanks," and wondered what he was thanking the old mountain man for.

The next two weeks Blade spent all the daylight hours training and riding his new horse. One week into the training the old mountain man gave the magnificent, near seventeen hand high, appaloosa a name he felt deserving of both horse and rider, Medicine.

During two weeks of training, Blade and John Ryan talked more than they had in the months they'd spent together. One evening, sitting in front of a spit roasting rabbit, Blade tried his best to thank the old man for all he had learned from him. Things he may never have known without the mountain man. Mostly about, tracking and surviving in the harsh weather of the mountains, but also about living and being thankful for things around him. The old man would have none of the thanks. He waved his hand and said, "Blade when we're together you make me feel twenty years younger. I'll tell stories about you for the rest of my livin' days. Never knowed anyone like you before and never will again, don't spect there is anyone else the likes of you, let's eat some rabbit."

The next morning they both knew the time had come. In silence, Blade saddled Medicine and swung into the saddle. John Ryan walked over from the fire where he'd started coffee.

"Blade I been thinking about it some, thinking about you, who you are, there's only one place anyone could get what you got."

"I think I know what you're talking about," Blade said.

"I'm not a real religious man Blade, went to church some as a pup, too many things in life to sort out for me, too many things there ain't no answer to, gotta be someone watching over everything, I know it. There's someone special looking over Blade Holmes. You been touched by the hand of God almighty his self, son, don't you ever believe otherwise, the big stallion got brought here for you, kinda like a matched pair, the two best I've ever seen." Ryan touched Blade on the leg then turned away walked back to the fire and poured from the Arbuckle's can into the coffee pot. Blade nudged Medicine with his knee and left at a trot heading south and east, not sure where he would end up.

Blade realized he was awake, daydreaming, not sleeping any longer. He felt better, rested, looked over at Templeton who seemed to be coming around for a second time. Blade's thoughts raced through his mind. He needed to find out why Templeton killed his friend the old mountain man? That old man taught me about everything I know about this wild country, did he do it for his horse and nothing else? The kind of man Ryan was he would have given Templeton the Pinto, his pack horse, if he thought Templeton needed it. Ryan's Pinto would have been the best horse in about any man's corral. The more he watched Templeton moaning and starting to regain consciousness the more he wished he would not have survived.

Blade rode at first light, back on the trail north. He had Templeton hogtied in front of him on Medicine's back but still moved along as fast as he could without risking the health of his horse. Once in town he figured he could send someone back for the horse and buggy. The horse with the rental buggy still looked weak and appeared to not have enough strength to even walk herself back to Cheyenne. Now turned lose she had both water and good grass. Possibly with a few days rest she would get enough strength back and it might be possible the old horse could make it back and continue her recovery in town. With a little luck, she might live to pull again, at least around town.

It took most of the day for Blade to reach Cheyenne, the last hour Templeton alternated his moaning with some almost coherent speech. Blade tied Medicine to a post in front of the U.S. Marshal's office and drug a now lucid and whining Templeton inside, took him down the hall, pushed the sniveling criminal in the first cell and slammed the iron door. Blade walked back to the office fell into an ancient, straight back chair, pulled it up to the Marshal's desk and started filling out paperwork for the reward. He should have taken Templeton straight to the hospital, but under the circumstances he guessed the cell in the Marshal's office would be good enough. He felt a little better now, knowing Templeton would never get out of jail, but his killing spree still made Blade sick when he thought of it.

It was tough trying to sort out the emotions he felt right now, especially thoughts about John Ryan and his murder. Templeton was a cold-blooded killer who needed to be caught, caught and hanged. But Blade wasn't thinking about the killing right now. It was the reward bothering him. Profiting from this did not seem right. He didn't need the money, not yet, when he got it he would spend it on Emma if she were alive, and if she still wanted him. His friend John Ryan would like that. He hoped Emma would take him back.

John Ryan had lived a decent and free life, he didn't deserve to die at the hands of a petty adult delinquent from Chicago and Kansas City. A man out here on a thieving and killing spree who thought everything was his for the taking. Blade walked outside and sat down on a plank bench in front of the dry goods store next door. Watching horses, buggies, farm wagons, and pedestrians pass by he tried to make sense of what had happened over the last two weeks. The reward money was deserved, he decided.

The sun shone bright and the ever-present Wyoming wind had switched to the east. The breeze brought the smell of wood smoke, horses, dirt and people, city smells. Not like the country where smells and sounds came one at a time, John Ryan had taught him that. The wind freshened and the sun slipped in and out of the scattered clouds. Far western skies were darkening, taking on hues of blacks and grays, must be a storm coming in. Blade slid the bench out a few inches, tipped his hat down low to shade his eyes and decided he deserved a rest.

He was tired, his eyes fluttered from open, to shut, to open, and then sleep overtook his tired body and mind. He dreamed of the day he left the mountains, leaving John Ryan behind. It all seemed like so many years ago when he rode away from John Ryan. Blade traveled less than a quarter of an hour the first day before turning from southeast to the west. The next day he turned northwest. Blade wanted to see the Nez Perce, or at least what was left of the Nez Perce.

John Ryan had told him, more than once, the story of how he had wintered, several times, in the Pacific Northwest some years ago. The mountain man spent the entire year of 1873 with the tribe in Idaho and had been in the village when Chief Looking Glass led his warriors into Montana. Looking Glass and his band helped the Crow whip the hated Sioux at Pryor Creek a battle spoken about with great reverence for many years among the Nez Perce. He asked to go along but knew as a non-tribal member it was unlikely they would allow it, as expected, he was told it would be best, for him, to stay put.

Ryan claimed Medicine, the great stallion Blade caught, or the stallion that caught Blade was a remnant of Nez Perce tribal horses. According to his story, Lewis and Clark noted in their journals many fine appaloosa horses among the tribe. Blade felt, through Medicine, an attachment to the tribe, an attachment that lasted two and a half months in 1882.

The reservation in Idaho was not at all what Blade expected. Instead of a proud people, full of life, it was a bleak and sad life the people were living. Their lives centered on what had been rather than on what could be. Chief Joseph's journey, five years before, was still the talk of the tribe. The tribe owned some beautiful horses, but only a few Appaloosa and none as fine as the ones of tribes past. The people once numbering several thousand now numbered a little more than one thousand. During his stay,

Blade was embraced by the people, and in turn soaked up the past and the culture of the tribe, leaving with feelings he did not understand.

Blade woke up, re-crossed his legs, smelled rain in the air, reached inside his shirt and felt for his medicine bag, tipped his chair back and promptly fell asleep, again.

John Ryan made the medicine bag hanging from a thin strip of grizzly bear hide under Blade's shirt. He gave it to Blade as a going away present. Blade suspected Ryan had made it for himself then felt Blade needed it more than he did. He'd worn it since the day he rode away from the Laramie Peak area and the months he spent with his friend and mentor. Over the years Blade added things important to him to the medicine bag, now it carried five items.

Two smooth rocks from the creek on his Ohio farm, a gift from his mother the day he left, he had carried them in his pocket and then the medicine bag every day since he left. When he touched them, he thought of the family farm in the Ohio Valley. Sometimes Blade felt self-conscious about carrying around two small rocks for so many years but he never gave them up. He liked remembering his boyhood and still thought he might go back for a visit someday, but he kept putting it off, maybe someday. He also carried a pinch of sweet grass from a Nez Perce horse ceremony, a handmade leather button from Emma's Haberdashery in Kansas

City and a small black cross, hand-fashioned from a bear claw, given to him with the medicine pouch by John Ryan.

Maybe his medicine bag carried his power, mountain men and Indians would have believed it, Blade didn't know. But he did know his mom; the Nez Perce, Emma, and John Ryan all played a big part in his life, and his luck, past, and present.

Chapter 33

Emma opened the shop a little past seven. She laughed when her eyes fixed on the wall clock, seven-twenty. Blade would have known without looking. When they first met, she was more than a little perplexed that he always knew what time it was. She could lose herself for hours in a project or a good book and often didn't know within hours of what time of day or night it might be. Not Blade, he always knew.

Emma felt better today, maybe just thinking about him. The day seemed special and today she felt like a special person. Maybe because it was Monday, and Monday's were her favorite day of the week. Today something seemed different, she worried about Blade every day but today, after so many weeks, the anxiety had gone away, she wasn't worried, not at all. No worries about Blade, none about their relationship or their future, nothing at all, today she was in a state of happiness she hoped could last forever. Since late yesterday she had felt like this, she'd always felt better after church, listing to a good sermon, but by Monday she normally was back to the same old, worrying again, Emma, but not today, not right now anyway. Blade would come back, he was alright, she could feel it. And because she was sure of it, she was alright too.

A continual flow of customers came into the shop, some for business and some to talk for a while, they ordered or didn't order, but it was a steady stream all day long. Emma was contented and cheerful today and it would be the first of many days that started to pass more quickly for her. She had more orders than could be completed in weeks and a few things she needed to finish up today. Instead of completing projects she hurried up the stairs and brought down the white leather jacket she had made for Blade.

On an impulse, she took the navy jacket from the show rack in the front window and replaced it with Blade's new jacket. It looked good, no it looked great. Every time she looked at it, she thought of him and smiled.

A few minutes before closing a dour looking young couple came through the door. The man blurted out an explanation of how he needed a new suit because of his recent promotion from teller to loan officer at the First National Bank of Kansas City. His wife was along because it was obvious, he needed help. The three small talked for a few minutes until the young man noticed the white buckskin jacket. "Wow, this is beautiful, couldn't wear it to the bank though, is it sold, who's it for, looks something really special?" As he spoke for what seemed a bit too long his young wife poked an elbow into his rib cage embarrassed over his enthusiasm for the leather jacket.

Emma looked at the young lady and smiled, "It's alright, I don't mind."

Then she looked at the squat young banker and answered, "It's for a special man, a man named Math-a-, Blade Holmes."

"Blade Holmes," the young man blurted out, "you know Blade Holmes, he comes in here, he's famous. I've read all the books and newspaper stories, some of them I read twice or more, I thought he might not even be real, but he must be, real that is, real if he comes in here."

"Yes, I know him. He asked me to marry him and we will be married if he ever comes back long enough to stand up before a preacher for a few minutes."

"I guess you do know him, I sure would like to get introduced."

"I'll see if I can get Blade to stop in over at First National and you can meet him," Emma said. The young bankers face flushed, then smiled with pride.

After a few more minutes of small talk, most of it about Blade, and with his wife's elbow, once again, planted firmly in his ribs, the two said their thanks and left. Leaving the shop the banker's wife, her face, bright red with embarrassment, scowled at her husband who seemed ecstatic. Emma whistled a happy song.

That evening, and for part of the night Emma sat at her bedroom desk writing a letter to Blade. Not a letter to send, but a letter to put away, a letter to save. Emma didn't consider herself much of a writer, but then no one would see this letter but her. She dipped her pen and on her best stationery started to write.

She started by saying how much she loved him and how excited she was about spending the rest of her life with him. She talked about her faith in God and the strength she got from her beliefs. In great detail, she wrote about why she'd worked so hard to succeed in business, her own business. Emma ended by promising both Blade and herself she would never hold him back.

Emma blew on the still wet page and damped it with a blotter, folded the fine paper and placed it in the narrow top drawer of her chest of drawers. She walked across the room, pulled back the edge of the shade and curtain peaking out at the street below. "I know you will always be going, you're not a man to be harnessed or tied down for long. I'll never stop you. But you must promise, promise me you will always come back," she whispered.

Chapter 34

"Mr. Holmes," Blade leaned forward, pushed his hat back and blinked his eyes wide open.

After sitting in front of the dry-goods store next to the Cheyenne U.S. Marshal's office on a sun-baked bench for the past three hours he really wasn't sure if someone spoke to him or he answered a dream person. "Yes," was all Blade could say, waking up from what must have been a very pleasant nap.

"You probably don't remember me, but."

Blade eyed the U.S. Marshal's badge pinned on the cowhide vest of the man addressing him and interrupted, "I remember Marshal, the riverboat, about a year ago."

The Marshal took off his sweat-stained hat, ran the back of his arm across his forehead and sat down on the bench beside Blade. He turned to Blade and in a soft voice as if he worried someone was listening said, "That's what I needed to talk to you about Mr. Holmes, you got a minute?"

"Blade's fine Marshal, call me Blade, what about the riverboat, I'm not real busy at the present, sitting here enjoying the sun and waiting for some reward money. Sheriff Watson said they likely would have it for me later today. So I guess I got plenty of minutes to give you but when I get the money I'm heading back to Kansas City."

"I'm Tom Andrews, and I've been appointed the new U.S Marshal in Cheyenne, started yesterday morning. Part of the reason I got sent here was to protect you."

"Protect me?"

"After you turned over Big Ed Whitten to us in Kansas City he somehow got the word out he wanted you dead with a big bounty for whoever got ya. Looking back, maybe we let him have too many visitors. He had money, money and connections to the outside. Blade, he hired killers to get you, and there may be others. Doesn't look to me like you need any help or protection, the doc and I hauled Templeton out the back door and over to his office just before I sat down with you. Doc says he's in pretty rough shape, might make it, and might not. And that's not all, Templeton's Big Ed's nephew. Big Ed came out here from Chicago in sixty-one to avoid the war, ended up settling in Saint Joe or Kansas City. The reason Luke Templeton came west was because of his Uncle Ed, told him this area was full of free and easy pickings."

Blade smiled despite the fact this news was not good. "You mean I've spent the last week chasing a man who was chasing me? Should have sat back and waited for him, some people are dead on account of me chasing after him, or him after me."

"Lot of people dead everywhere he goes seems like, come on in, I got your reward, part of the reason I'm here, need you to sign some paperwork."

The Marshal surprised Blade when he counted out a pile of seventy one-hundred dollar bills. "Seven thousand dollars, the guy, was wanted for seven thousand, I thought the reward money was twelve or fifteen hundred, then was told might be $2.000, figured it would end up less, five or six hundred at best. Not sure I can spend seven thousand dollars."

"Thought you might spend it on your new wife if you ever get back to Kansas and marry her," the Marshal answered.

"She's alright then, I knew she had to be. I'm on my way tomorrow, soon as I resupply. And I'm planning on marrying her as soon as I get there."

"Yea, she's okay, got word from the Pinkerton's down there, they thought you might like to know she was alright. Darndest story I've heard in a long time seems she was holding a bolt of cloth when Templeton shot her, the bullet hit it solid. Guess it knocked her over backward and gave here quite a bump on the head, but the shops open, she's working and likely wondering when you're coming home."

After spending a restless night in one of Cheyenne's best hotels Blade walked two blocks and settled in at a corner table in the Railroad Cafe. It seemed like a long time since he'd relaxed and eaten anything at his own pace. He loved town eating places, all the work, and commotion. He looked out the window as the day's activity started to kick in. Smelling the hot grease of breakfast cooking, baking bread, strong perfume, and tobacco smoke all mingled into one reminded him how happy he was to be finally over with the chase. Done with it, done with Templeton and heading home to Kansas City, he smiled and looked up at the menu on the square of black slate.

Bacon, eggs, biscuits, coffee and fried potatoes with onions were the menu special and Blade ordered the special, the sign outside called it the *Railroader Breakfast Special.* After finishing the steaming plate of food, he scooted his chair back from the table, patted his full stomach and asked for a third cup of coffee. Blade reached across to the now empty table to his right and picked up the "Eagle," Cheyenne's newest newspaper. Deciding it might be nice to see what else was going on in the city. The first thing Blade saw was a picture, a photo of him, the only one in the paper. A drawing, but a pretty good likeness, embarrassed Blade looked around, folded the paper inside out and slipped it back on the same empty table where he'd found it. He picked up his hat, paid the bill and walked out the door.

Turning left as he walked through the door Blade strolled along the rather new looking pine board-walk. He took his time looking in store windows and exchanging greetings with shoppers as he walked. He pushed open the door of the general store, a block north of breakfast, and next door to the sheriff's office, and was greeted with the ring of a small bell.

If he was going to leave today, it was time to re-supply. His mind traveled well ahead of Cheyenne and he hoped slowing down this part of the morning might prepare him better for the trip than hurrying around. It didn't do much good once he was inside the store. He bought what he needed, carried it to the livery stable, packed his saddlebags saddled Medicine and pointed him to Kansas City. Twenty minutes after breakfast he was on his way out of town riding the well-traveled South trail.

On this trip, nothing else would get in his way. Long hours in the saddle always gave Blade time to think, and today he had plenty to think about. He still wondered why Templeton kept the Pinkerton Badge, even after he had been found out. He must have thought he would get clean away and be able to use it again. Or maybe in his mixed up mind he thought he might be some kind of avenging angel detective. Well, no matter, now he would either die from his wounds or get better and hang, wouldn't need the badge for either option. Why did someone shoot Templeton and who shot him, those thoughts overwhelmed Blade's mind today as he rode. Then he thought, maybe they were shooting at me, not Templeton, but he didn't think so. Those thoughts and many others raced through his mind, and then, what would Emma think of him when he got back, would she want him back? He thought so and prayed she would.

Blade rode until the creeping black, of what looked to be a moonless night; made it too difficult to continue, finding a secluded spot with cover from the south and east he needed to stop for the night. The site would do as it allowed him to see along his back trail. Riding for another five minutes he turned into a sparse stand of juniper and went back to the campsite. The tiny hillside was eaten away, as if someone, long ago, tried to make a dugout or maybe nature dug the side of this hill away.

A few hours back Blade started thinking about the danger he might be riding into. He picked his campsites carefully, and this was the most secure place he had seen in the last three or four hours. But he was starting to get the feeling he might not be alone, he was safe here, but someone else was around, and it made him careful and more than a little uneasy.

A tangle of roots, soil and sand from ages past were layered one on top of the other until the dugout cut reached a height of eight or ten feet. Plenty tall enough, Blade thought, to hide a man and his horse. Someone had shot Templeton, but he didn't die, would the shooters unfinished business lead to Blade or back to Templeton? Because of the kind of man Templeton was Blade wasn't sure he cared if bad things went his way. But Blade had important things ahead of him in Kansas City and would be extra cautious on this trip. He started to feel a little paranoid when he skipped the fire and settled into a cold camp.

After a fitful sleep filled with the demons of Luke Templeton, hidden shooters, and dead bodies, Blade awakened at four a.m. An odd time of day, not yet light, but much of the night had passed. The black on black of the night would soon turn gray. At this time of the morning, Blade felt safe building a small fire. The wood was already in a neat pile where he'd placed it a few hours earlier. In a few minutes, Blade had a small but efficient fire burning. He filled his coffee pot half full from one of his two canteens and dumped a generous amount of Arbuckle's into it. Blade wished he had some eggs to scramble and shells for the coffee, but he didn't, so this would have to do. Taking hardtack and a can of peaches from his saddlebags he poured a tin cup full of boiling coffee and leaned against the bank, out of the firelight, to eat his breakfast.

An hour later the morning skies showing the first streaks of gold and yellow as the new day pushed the night away, Blade rode south. It would take ten days maybe two weeks, depending on how hard he pushed Medicine, for him to reach Kansas City. For a while in Cheyenne he thought about taking the train, he could be in Kansas City in two or three days. Thoughts of the train passed when he decided the ride would give him time to sort out his thoughts and prepare for the rest of his life. He wanted to hurry, but not such a hurry he would need to take the train, and not in a big enough rush where he might risk the health of his horse. Two weeks it would need to be two weeks. This would let Medicine enjoy himself, like being out on a Sunday afternoon stroll. Along the way, Blade would have time to hunt a little, maybe do some fishing, and most of all hours for a lot of thinking.

Three eventless days later Blade and Medicine were in Denver, time to take a break and relax. It no longer seemed like someone was following, Blade had relaxed the past two days as much as he'd been able to in weeks. He put Medicine up at City Livery and rented a room around the corner, time to eat a good meal, relax and maybe even enough time for some cards. It had been quite a spell since he had sat at a card table and tonight seemed to be the perfect time. Blade enjoyed the steak, but he liked watching the people coming and going more. He took extra time, ordered peach pie and coffee, so he wouldn't be so noticeable sitting alone with an empty plate in front of him. After an hour at the table, Blade walked through the bar and into the high-stakes poker room in the back.

He watched for a few minutes, turned and left. For the first time in his life he understood what it was he liked about playing cards. It was not about the money, it was about the people. Blade could read them like a book when playing cards. He lost because he was a bad poker player, not because he did not understand his competition. Sitting at a table he could tell good men from bad, happy from sad, and touches of each player's life stories. He left the game tonight because he did not have to play, not anymore. Blade was in the saddle by five thirty in the morning.

Today he had mixed thoughts about the night before. He'd thought about a big meal and playing poker for three days before reaching Denver. When he had the chance he ate and choose to make an early night of it, went back to his room and turned in. The steak and potatoes were good, the pie and coffee excellent, but what he most wanted, he now knew, was to get to Kansas City. He surprised himself yesterday by passing up the cards and he surprised himself now as he loped along because he hadn't missed it. Maybe now he could put the cards away for good.

In midafternoon, a crystal clear foothills lake caught Blade's eye and he decided to spend the rest of the day fishing and relaxing. Blade had left most of his worrying behind in Wyoming, but never the less he wanted to be careful where he decided to fish. He skirted the lake to the south, away from the main road, for an hour and a quarter before tying Medicine with the long rope beside a stand of Aspen a few feet from the water.

With the confidence of a good fisherman Blade unpacked his frying pan, gathered firewood, and built a small fire before concentrating on the fish. Tonight he would eat trout or jerky depending on either luck or skill.

Blake was shocked at how hungry he felt, even though he hadn't eaten since last night. He'd been thinking so much about Kansas City he didn't feel the hunger until the smell of the fish frying woke up his senses. Devouring the three small trout in five quick minutes helped the hunger subside. Blade chuckled thinking how he spent fifteen minutes getting the fire going, a half hour catching and cooking the fish and then devoured them in a few quick bites. Smiling, he thought how life was like that sometimes. You work, and work, and work, and often the reward for all the hard work is small, fast and forgotten.

But not this time, not this trip, this time he was heading home with money in his pocket and a plan in his mind. This time, the reward had been worth the journey, but not for everyone. Blade felt satisfied both from the fish and with the plan. Where his life headed now sounded much like the life lessons John Ryan had taught him up in the Laramie Peak area. Thinking of the old mountain man made Blade sad, but he smiled, despite himself, thinking about those good times.

Blade relaxed back away from the fire and the lake shore. Settling for a clump of small trees where he leaned back against a twisted cluster of undersized Aspen. The last rays of the setting sun felt good warming the side of his face and Blade wished it could last a while longer. At the moment everything was going his way, everything seemed great. It felt good to relax again. Nighthawks buzzed the dying fire, tree limbs swayed in the spring breeze, and the temperature cooled. The sound of lake water lapping against the smooth rocks mixed with the buzzing of early spring insects created a symphony of sound as pretty as any music Blade Holmes had ever heard. The evening was so perfect Blade almost fell asleep before he had time to get out his bedroll.

Reluctantly Blade rose, stretched, walked over and picked up his bedroll, carried it fifty or sixty feet back into the trees leaning it against a downed cottonwood limb. He swept away pine cones and a pile of hardened brown needles, snapped the dust from his ground blanket and arranged it on top of a thick bed of soft green pine boughs. Blade felt contented, it had been a good day. Now as he started to feel safe, thoughts of Emma overwhelmed him, he couldn't sleep. Blade knew it would be hours before he could ease his mind and find sleep. He walked back to the break in the trees where Medicine grazed and rested. Stars were out now, it was clear and Blade could see pretty well. He saddled up, hung his Colt on the saddle horn, rolled his blankets and went back to get his skillet and coffee pot from the dying fire. He sat down and poured the last of the coffee into his cup, deciding to enjoy the last half cup of the still warm coffee before riding south and east. No use lying around when I could be moving, Blade thought.

Blade felt the burn before hearing the report of the rifle and then the echo. The slug buried itself high into his back, up near the top of his left shoulder. Blade felt himself slump, reached for his missing Colt, heard the lake water still slapping the rocks and started to lose consciousness. Another shot echoed through the trees and then another. Blade did not hear either; the first shot had done its job. The second shot hit between Blades ribs and his outstretched right arm boring through the fringes of his white leather jacket but not hitting flesh. The last shot should have ripped through his neck but instead ricocheted off the ten-inch knife tucked in his shirt collar. Blade had been saved, at least for now, because he was never without the namesake knifes.

Roy Tibbs smiled, focusing his binoculars on the still shape of a body four hundred yards straight away and below him. Then he burst out laughing. "I think I hit him all three times, matter of fact, I'm sure of it," he said while he and his partner mounted to ride down and make sure Holmes was dead. He was happy but wished there was a little more light, enough good light to make sure Holmes was dead, and to do it at a fair distance. He was confident but still nervous.

"This will be nothing but a waste of time, he's dead. Why I ever got mixed up with Big Ed and hired that lunatic Templeton, I must have been crazy. He got himself shot up and stuck in jail or dead by now. It was so simple. I ride out here and kill the great Blade Holmes. He thought he was so high and mighty, died like all the other man I've killed, quick and easy."

Tibbs partner nodded twice and forced an uneven grin when Tibbs looked over at him but continued along in silence. The two took their time picking a way down the steep shale covered hillside and then through the tall sage and cactus as they reached the flats nearer the lake. Approaching the southwest corner of the lake the pair reminded each other to be careful, just in case, but they were sure no danger waited ahead, not from a dead man.

It took more than a quarter of an hour to get near the lake, still only halfway to Holmes and darkness settled in. They would not be able to see the body, especially with the little starlight available until they were nearly on top of it, and for some reason that thought unnerved both Tibbs and his partner. Tibbs thought for a moment about going back and waiting for the morning sun.

The smallish man partnered with Tibbs had the look of a man who wanted to run. Thoughts raced through his mind; maybe the stories about Holmes were true. He might be able to resurrect and kill them yet, or maybe he was like a cat with nine lives.

Holmes, as usual, had picked this campsite carefully. Roy Tibbs had been able to see Holmes and the last embers of the fire from his vantage point at four hundred yards but the closer the pair rode the more difficult it became to see the camp. The site was all but inaccessible except straight on, and then a small rise fifty yards out hid it from sight. Blade had stopped here with some concern for his safety, but not a deep worry. Not the kind of worry that would have him pass up this site, a site too close to water and too low. But his innate ability led him to still choose a camp where he was well hidden, a campsite better than most men could find in a lifetime.

Tibbs dismounted and waved his arm, letting his partner know they would walk the rest of the way. It had taken them the better part of an hour to get to this point and Tibbs was starting to doubt his own courage, something that brought on a murdering rage in other times and places. The two stepped as soft and slow as they could, still afraid to take a chance. With six-guns drawn the partners more crawled than walked over the last rise. A cautious few steps, the two men stopping to listen down on one knee, a few deep breaths and then they took a few more steps. Time crawled at a pace slower than minutes and seconds as the killers approached the camp.

The embers of the dying fire reflected an eerie dull orange against the stone circle of the fire pit. The flat top of the rocks mirrored the breaking silver light of twinkling stars high in the clearing sky. Together they cast enough light to see the coffee pot still on the coals and enough light to see most of the campsite. The night was casting long shadows of tree-filtered light, enough brightness that when Tibbs and his partner reached close enough they could see the entire camp. Blade Holmes was gone—vanished.

The two outlaws spent the next fifteen or twenty minutes looking. They looked until they gave in to total clouded darkness. It was impossible trying to find any sign of a dead Blade Holmes or a living Blade Holmes. The dark allowed for no tracks.

No sign and Tibbs and his partner were afraid their prey of a few minutes ago could now become their hunter. The Denver thug who Tibbs brought along as his partner was scared, he asked for the ten dollars he was promised for two days work, saying he wanted to be on his way back to Denver. For a moment Tibbs considered paying him off so he would shut up, but then thought better of it, pulled his rifle and shot him in the back of the head while he turned to check an imaginary sound near the water.

Blade heard the shot, it didn't worry him, but he did wonder what was going on.   He guessed his attackers were arguing and maybe two attackers were now only one. Or maybe they were spooked and shooting at noises in the night.

First light in the morning would tell the story. Blade hadn't gone far, only about a quarter of a mile. Roy Tibbs and Holmes had traded positions. Holmes now sat within a few feet of where Tibbs and his ex-partner sat when they shot him and Tibbs stared into the dead embers of Blade Holmes campfire. Now Blade squinted, looking down on his own camp but it was too dark to see anything. He'd recognized Tibbs, in the dying light, when they passed within seven or eight feet a half hour ago. Blade had not thought of Tibbs for years and now wondered why he tried to kill him. But thinking back Blade realized nothing about Roy Tibbs should surprise him.

Instead of running from his attackers in the dim of the starlit darkness, Blade, after a moment of lost consciousness, had gone in a direct line, right at his attackers using long shadows and darkness to hide. He could have killed them on any other day but today the exertion of throwing a knife was too much. His pistol and the big rifle were on Medicine and Blade wasn't sure, even if he had either, he could have held steady enough to hit a target a few feet away. Blade managed to cut Medicine lose before he started his slow exchange of positions with his attackers, and true to the magnificent horse's name he now stood within inches of Blade. He cut him loose, but couldn't reach high enough to get either of his firearms. It seemed a mere stroke of luck that he had finished saddling Medicine and packing up camp to leave and ride a night trail. Now thanks to Medicine he had bandages, medical supplies, food, water and his weapons. Maybe he did have the medicine, maybe his old friend John Ryan was correct in his thinking; maybe he did have something, inside him, others did not have. One thing he knew for sure—he had one great horse, and he was thankful he did.

Morning would be soon enough, Blade thought, as he packed a larger bandage into the hole in his back. When it became too dark to worry about being seen Blade removed the bandages, grimaced when he poured the bullet hole full of whiskey then tamped it full of leaves from a nearby aspen and bound a cloth around his body. Despite the pain, and the desperate situation, he stretched out on his side against a large sandstone outcropping and fell asleep.

Blade woke in six hours, rested, hurting bad, and weak. He had slept and despite the pain slept soundly. It was between three thirty and three forty-five, too dark to see if the ambushers were still in the area. Except the fire was burning, someone was feeding it. Bad as he felt, Blade was more curious than mad. Why Tibbs shot him, it hadn't been a mistake, not a chance. First light should be interesting, someone hiding and keeping a fire going at the same time was either worried, scared or both. Blade moved away from the rock bank, propped himself up against a cottonwood fall, tried to make himself comfortable, and waited. He slept off and on for another two hours. Now awake and alert, he felt pretty good. Aching more than before, but stronger and fortunate to be alive, he knew now for the first time, he would not die, not this time, then he thought of Emma.

First light was breaking, a quarter mile away a fire burned, a fire Blade thought must be tended by an exhausted Roy Tibbs. Tibbs had envied Blade, and now it looked like he had turned his envy into hatred. There could be no other reason. Blade had little doubt Tibbs had shot his own partner, probably so he would never talk about the killing of Blade Holmes. A smile creased his face despite the pain in his back as Blade realized this battle was one he would win. Then he wondered again why, after all these years?

For the third time in a decade, Blade pulled the big Sharps rifle from the scabbard. He hefted it and then curled it in the crook of his right arm. He always liked the feel of the big gun. Blade rubbed his palm down the barrel then raised and pointing it toward the distant fire and sighted down the barrel.

Tibbs always was a pretty good rifle shot, but last evening not quite good enough. This morning Tibbs lay partially hidden behind the nearest tree to the fire. Blade could shoot him in one of his legs right now. He considered it but waited for more light. Blade cracked open the breach of the big rifle slid a cartridge in and snapped it shut.

"Finish each day and be done with it. You have done what you could; some blunders and absurdities have crept in; forget them as soon as you can. Tomorrow is a new day; you shall begin it serenely and with too high a spirit to be encumbered with your old nonsense."

"Thanks for the words Mr. Emerson, tomorrow is here," Blade whispered, then smiled and winced in pain as he tried to get comfortable.

He almost laughed as he, pondered how many people quoted Emerson after getting shot and waiting for the shooter to come to them.

Chapter 35

Tibbs knew he was in trouble. Blade Holmes was by himself, no one could have helped him or the big Appaloosa out of there. Tibbs was sure he hit him, thought he hit him all three times with the Winchester, matter of fact he would bet his life on it, perhaps he already had.

How could he have gotten away? Tibbs spent a sleepless night behind an ancient split cottonwood, alternating sneaking out to throw more wood on the fire and hiding in the trees. Once he thought about letting the fire die but he liked to be able to see, even if it was only a few feet. He tried to believe the fire helped keep him warm; after all he could feel sweat running under his arms and down his ribs. Admitting he might be afraid of Holmes lurking in the dark was out of the question, but he couldn't push the idea from his mind. He dozed for a few minutes several times, once awoke from a dream shaking and kicking, his shirt as wet as if he had fallen in the lake. Even dreaming about Blade Holmes made him nervous, he looked around and saw nothing but the last of his campfire and day starting to break.

A jumpy Tibbs moved away from the fire, back into the dark of the aspen grove. Setting behind an ancient cottonwood in a futile attempt to find protection from every direction Tibbs seemed to have a nervous tick, always moving his head, looking for unseen enemies. Thinking back he knew he made mistakes, grave mistakes. Right now he most wanted to get lost from this place and get lost from the man he thought should be dead. A man he killed last night, a ghost in the dark, somewhere in the dark, coming after him.

Tibbs had come west two and half years ago. He'd needed to get away from the day to day grind of life on the farm in Ohio. And it had been a good move. He found freedom out here, not only from the farm but freedom from his wife, in-laws and his father, seemed like none of them would ever leave him be. Now he was where he wanted to be, away from them, but now this.

Meeting Big Ed had been a stroke of good luck, better than anything Tibbs could have ever hoped for. Big Ed got him into the Pinkerton's, a desk job at first, but it was the Pinkerton's. Once inside he had been able to scheme and scam his way to a few advances and into some really good money. He also worked hard at his job and put more than a few men in jail with his ability to investigate. Found them and turned them in, as long as Big Ed gave him the go ahead. He didn't mind Bid Ed having the final say, he was good to work with, and he more than doubled his monthly Pinkerton check. He also liked that the Pinkerton's did some strike breaking and strong-arming from time to time. He liked their style. Liked busting heads. The Pinkerton job made him feel important, superior to most people, not like being a farmer in Ohio. A good job, one he was satisfied with until he saw the first of two books about the great Blade Holmes. And until Big Ed hooked him up with the half-wit, Luke Templeton.

They were writing books about him, books, who did he think he was anyway? He flushed hot every time he thought about him, it was always about him. That's when he'd decided to kill Holmes. Maybe someday dime novels would be about him. *Roy Tibbs of the West,* sounded good, real good. He would show them, show all of them. Right now he could feel his heart beating against the walls of his chest, beating like it wanted out. Sweat ran in small rivulets down his back again, he took off his hat and wiped his forehead and the top of his head. He was scared, he hated being scared, and more than anything he hated Holmes because he scared him. It sounded like such a good idea and one Big Ed really liked, killing Holmes. Now Tibbs wished he'd never heard of Holmes, Big Ed, Templeton or the West, in general, he hated it all. Jumping at every sound, Tibbs now knew he was afraid, terrified of Holmes, afraid of Big Ed, afraid of the west. He felt a chill, pulled his collar tight and moved deeper into the aspen.

Still too dark to leave and he had no intention of trying to find Holmes in the dark, or for that matter in the light, if he could avoid it. Roy Tibbs thought only of survival, he had to get out of here, the sooner, the better. Then he thought about death, his own. Tibbs was letting his nerves get the better of him. Ducking behind a large deadfall pile he took a chance, built a cigarette and lit it, cupping it in his hands to cover the glow.

He was in a tight spot and thanks to Holmes; Big Ed could not be here to help him out of it. How did Holmes get away? "Maybe he's dead, crawled somewhere and died," Tibbs whispered to the glowing end of his smoke. Then he shook his head and crushed the cigarette on his forearm.

Three or four times he'd had a chance to kill Holmes. He was an easy target in Kansas City sashaying around with the beautiful rich lady. Once Holmes gave him the slip as if he knew someone was following. He'd followed him as he walked down the alley behind the haberdashery shop, seemed to be taking his time, not paying attention to anything and then he was gone, disappeared. Tibbs really hated it when Holmes did things like that, and he hated it when he felt like Holmes was playing with him. The alley had been his best chance at Holmes, dark and noisy with the wind howling out of the west. His best chance, best opportunity until a few hours ago, to kill the man he hated more than anyone or anything in his life, Blade Holmes needed to die, and he needed to be the one to pull the trigger.

"Maybe he did crawl off and die. He isn't immortal, everyone dies. Guns kill, they can kill anything or anyone, so where is he? When it gets light I'll look around, he's likely dead behind one of these trees, I hit him three times, and if he got away he's running slow and hurt bad." Talking to the pile of dead trees helped, but not enough, he looked around for the man he killed a few hours ago.

Tibbs crept over toward the body of yesterday's partner put the heel of his boot against the corpse and rolled it into the lake. He couldn't help himself, he laughed, but not loud enough for anyone listening to hear. Feeling exposed, he turned and rushed back into the aspen.

Hiring Templeton had been a mistake. The guy was clumsy and dim-witted, but lucky, and Tibbs, at the time, thought maybe, just maybe, he could do it. Templeton killed his useless Pinkerton partner for him and it only cost two hundred for one nice little murder. Two hundred dollars and one Pinkerton badge that is. Templeton seemed fascinated with the badge, maybe because his partner's last name was Pinkerton, no relation to the agency, but Templeton really wanted the badge. Tibbs let him keep it and the oaf flashed it at everyone he came in contact with, strangers, friends, good and bad, it didn't matter to him. But it did to Tibbs, Templeton was an embarrassment. So he got rid of him, sent him out of town after Holmes.

Tibbs thought he could see a little better now; sunlight was breaking up the grayness of morning. Out in the open near the lake he could see the sandy ground through light reflecting off the lake water. He knew he would not look for a body, didn't need to look for Blade's body. He was sure there was no body. He planned on running, running hard and fast. Right now anywhere but here would be the best place to be. Now the time had come to get out of here. He walked back into the trees to saddle his horse and get ready to run. Maybe California, he thought, or the Oregon country, no too many farmers in Oregon. But West, it had to be somewhere to the west.

"Just like when we were kids," Tibbs muttered, as he crept back closer to the dead campfire to retrieve his belongs, careful to stay as much in the trees as possible.

Ten minutes later he crawled back to his horse, mounted and tried to stay quiet, riding out of camp under the cover of early morning shadows and the start of a slight misting rain. "Must have lived these last few years in the city," Blade whispered, watching Tibbs trying to sneak out of the trees riding a slow winding path through the low areas then riding straight toward Blade and the big Sharps.

"Should have gone deeper back into the forest, then up in the mountains, take a month to get out and he would have gotten out. Not ride out toward the main road at first light," Blade looked at Medicine and shook his head, believing his horse already knew what he just told him. The corners of his mouth turned slightly into what Emma used to refer to as the Mathew smile. A smile, he wasn't happy, but he was amused by Tibbs, a greenhorn about to be caught.

Blade continued watching as Tibbs rode, gun drawn, coming directly at him. Typical city folk mistake, Blade thought, ride out the way you came in, like the main road in and out of town. Farmers and businessmen always took the shortest route and often the same route. Old habits die hard, Blade thought, as he watched the unsuspecting murderer riding to him like they had prearranged a business meeting. Blade seldom left any place, even towns, the way he came in, often spending a day or more backtracking and circling just to be safe. But it never surprised him when others made the mistake of becoming too predictable. They were not taught life lessons by a mountain man like John Ryan. Blade guessed Ryan gave him a one up on most everyone.

"Drop the gun and get down," Blade shouted at Tibbs from less than fifty feet. Tibbs fired once, then twice more. The Big Sharps roared, Tibbs' chest ripped apart. Blade felt fire race through his body from the kick of the big rifle the moment before he passed out. Tibbs was dead before he hit the ground.

Chapter 36

Three weeks later, to the day, Matthew (Blade) Holmes and Emma Marja Fick were married in the magnificent drawing room of the commanding officer quarters at Fort D.A. Russell southwest of Cheyenne, Wyoming Territory. Much to Blade's surprise Civil War hero and friend Colonel Henry Clay Merriam made the hard two-day trip from Fort Laramie to perform the service. Sheriff Watson had telegraphed the Colonel when Emma arrived in Cheyenne and in less than a week Merriam reached town. The entire ceremony, which Blade thought would be small and significant to his new wife and him, but no one else, turned into something the citizens of Cheyenne would talk about for weeks, then years.

The entire Eleventh Infantry of D.A. Russell attired in their best uniforms stood at attention during the fifteen-minute ceremony. Two years earlier Blade had spent some time at Fort Russell when the Ninth Cavalry, better known all over America as the Buffalo Soldiers, arrived at their new station in Cheyenne. Blade smiled and nodded to several of the men he knew from two years ago, they sat silently on horseback forming a path of nearly one hundred yards to the front door of the officer's quarters.

But the biggest surprise came with the ceremonies closing hymn. Blade heard the first words of, *"What a Friend We Have in Jesus,"* coming from the back of the drawing room. He and Emma looked at each other then turned to see from whose beautiful voice the words were coming. In the back of the room, near the door, stood Parson Joshua Christie in a rumpled black suit singing in a deep baritone, Blade looked into Emma's beautiful face and winked. He'd known the parson for only a short time but now looking at him and listening to him sing he seemed like his oldest friend. Somehow this man appeared to be his personal frumpy guardian angel. An angel who kept turning up in Blade's life, turning up when he least expected it and most needed it. Maybe turning up when both of them least expected it and needed it. Blade made a mental note to catch up with the country preacher later then turned back to Emma and together they listened to the words as he finished the hymn.

"Soon in glory bright unclouded there will be no need for prayer
Rapture, praise and endless worship will be our sweet portion there."

Today was Emma's special day. Emma and his, but the closing verse made his mind escape bringing back memories of his friend and mentor John Ryan. He squeezed Emma's hand and briefly thought ahead to the rest of their life together.

When the couple left they were astonished that more than seven hundred Cheyenne citizens were standing outside, waiting to cheer the newlyweds when they came from the officers' quarters. Less than a week later Blade and the new Mrs. Holmes were ready to leave Cheyenne for their home in Kansas City.

Blade would never understand or know how much Emma cared, how much she worried and how in love Emma was with him. She'd boarded the train the morning after word reached he that Blade lay unconscious and critical in the Laramie County Hospital in Cheyenne. Two days later she sat in a chair a foot away from the sleeping Blade. He'd started to regain conciseness the day before Emma arrived and asked her to marry him the moment he realized she actually sat waiting at his side. She laughed and said he would need to ask her again when he woke up. He asked her three more times that day and the next morning she said yes.

Now the husband and wife of four days were heading home, against doctors orders, heading home to Kansas City. Blade had never been one to sit around, he was healing and despite the fact he felt sore and still a bit stoved up he wanted to get on with the rest of his life.

They took the train from Cheyenne to Denver then switched trains to Kansas City. At each stop, Blade and Emma walked back to check on Medicine. He rode in relative luxury, a boxcar just for him; nice bedding straw and oats and a bucket of water every few stops, all compliments of an anonymous donor, a wedding present from someone in Laramie City. Blade didn't believe Medicine liked the ride, but the horse took it as he always did something that had to be.

Blade and now Emma were celebrities when they got home to the apartment above the haberdashery. Everywhere they went young people and old pointed, watched and whispered. People he had never seen before greeted Blade on the streets and asked for autographs. Within weeks three new dime novels about Blade were in stores all over town, one of the books told about his escapades in California, a state Blade had never been within several hundred miles. He was offered jobs, most in law enforcement, but also in banking and a variety of small businesses, even a speaking tour to Europe, something he dismissed with an embarrassed and somewhat forced laugh.

Now, five months later, Blade with regained health, managed to avoid gainful employment. The reward money would last for quite a while, but sooner or later he would need to find a job. He didn't want to feel like a kept man. Emma went back to her normal workday a week after they were home. She didn't expect what greeted her when she went back to work, business became more than she could handle, hiring a young apprentice helped her keep up. Blade occupied his time building a new picket fence around the shop. It looked good and Blade thought for an hour or so about becoming a full-time carpenter but then let the thought pass.

The couple spent months living a storybook existence. Their lives became something others wanted to know about, newspapers tried to keep the public informed about their every movement, and every involvement. Mr. and Mrs. Blade Holmes spent time dancing and dining, loving and talking, talking about family and children and the future. They helped the less fortunate volunteering where they could. They resumed their attendance at the poetry readings, joined the neighborhood Methodist church, and checked out the latest books from the local library. Never had there been a happier couple in Kansas City, now all Blade needed to do was find a job, one where he felt fulfilled, and life for the new couple would be perfect.

Another dime novel appeared this one not about Holmes as much as it told the story of an old country preacher named Joshua Christie. The eighty-page book told the story of Christie riding alone enjoying the day and all of God's wonderment in the foothills. In the sunshine of early morning, he found the wounded Blade Holmes unconscious and near death. And a dead man lying nearby, a man later identified as Roy Tibbs.

Christie re-dressed a large gunshot hole in Blade's shoulder and patched a more recent deep gash crossing the outside of Blades right leg two inches above his knee. He tended to him for a day and a half before leaving the area. Christie said he wanted to bury Tibbs, thought it would be the decent Christian thing to do. But he was old and tired and didn't have the energy. He settled for covering the body with pine boughs and rocks.

Preacher Christie did take the time to read and sermonize over Tibbs's body. He'd preached many funeral sermons in his life and either felt Tibbs deserved one, or he was going to hell and needed one. He loved *Ecclesiastes* for times like this. He quoted, he paraphrased and he put his own thoughts between the lines as he preached from *Ecclesiastes 3:1-8*.

There is a time for everything,
And a season for every activity under heaven:
A time to be born and a time to die—

"And for the deceased whose name I am unfamiliar, it looks like it was your time and I do know Mr. Blade Holmes name, and it looks like it was him that sent you away so I would guess you deserved it."

A time to plant and a time to uproot,
A time to kill and a time to heal and

"God in heaven, looks like our son Blade

here is in need of some real healing—please put your hand on the boy, he needs some more time here there's a lot of good to be done, and this boy has it in him to do more good."

A time to tear down and a time to build
A time to weep and a time to laugh,
A time to mourn and a time to dance,
A time to scatter stones and a time to gather them,
A time to embrace and a time to refrain,
A time to search and a time to give up,
A time to keep and a time to throw away,
A time to tear and a time to mend,
A time to be silent and a time to speak,
A time to love and a time to hate,
A time for war and a time for peace.

"Looks like this here war is over Lord please excuse me for not being of good enough body anymore to bury him proper. But we all know there are plenty of critters here and they all need nourishment, and I pray this man's body can finally do one good deed by taking care of those critters eatin' needs.
Amen."

People liked the story, thought it was good, except for the part where the sixty-two-year-old, one-hundred-pound preacher lifted the two-hundred-pound Holmes onto his horse, tied him in place and hauled him for two days over some of the roughest ground God ever created to the hospital. Seemed like everyone in Cheyenne had read the book and when folks asked the couple about the story, Blade looked right into Emma's beautiful face and winked.

Life was good for the newlyweds and a time for Blade and Emma to enjoy all things.

Chapter 37

Blade blew out a long cold breath and watched the air turn to steam as he tugged the collar of his new white buckskin coat up under his chin. The old back wound ached and his shoulder still hurt all day long. The bite of the October wind only made the old injuries worse. Blade had spent, ten years, much of his adult life, in Wyoming and right now he felt home again. It was dark, but the light from the new day was trying to battle its way through the darkness.

He'd broke camp and saddled Medicine early, knowing October weather could be unpredictable on the high sagebrush plains. Now two days from Fort Laramie Blade squinted and let Medicine pick his way. He smiled leaned back against the cantle and tried to stretch a little, then he tapped his heel into Medicine, looked like it would be a fine day.

Neil Waring lives in Guernsey, Wyoming – less than a mile from the Oregon Trail & 14 miles from Fort Laramie

About the Author

Neil Waring, born in O'Neill, Nebraska and raised in Fairbury, Nebraska was educated at Peru State College, Wayne State College and the University of Wyoming. He spent 42 years in education, teaching, American History, Wyoming History, and Geography along with a variety of other social science and English classes. Although the majority of his career was spent teaching at the high school level, he also taught Wyoming History, as an adjunct professor, for area community colleges for twenty years.

In addition to this book Mr. Waring has published a nonfiction book about the Civilian Conservation Corps and the building of Guernsey State Park. Also to his credit are two young readers, growing up books, *Melvin the E Street Ghost,* and, *"Then Mike Said, There's a Zombie in Our Basement."* Book two of this Blade Holmes's trilogy, set in and near Laramie Peak, is scheduled to be released winter 2015.

Neil has also published multiple short stories and historical pieces both online and in print. He writes a popular Wyoming blog, Wyoming Fact and Fiction, at http://wyoming-fact-and-fiction.blogspot.com and can be followed on Twitter @wyohistoryguy.

Neil and his wife Jan live in Guernsey, Wyoming near Fort Laramie, the Oregon Trail, the North Platte River and beautiful Guernsey State Park. When not writing Mr. Waring spends time, reading, gardening, playing golf, fishing, traveling and hiking in Guernsey State Park.

-Other Books by Neil Waring-

~ *The CCC & the Building of Guernsey State Park - With Folktales of the Park*   (nonfiction)

~ *Melvin, The E Street Ghost*   (young reader)

~ *Then Mike Said, "There's a Zombie in My Basement*   (young reader)

All books by Neil Waring can be found or ordered through your favorite bookstores.

Neil's books are available in book or EBook formats and can be found at all major online bookselling sites. Books can also be found or ordered at many brick and mortar locations both in Wyoming and nationwide.

Books are also available on my publishing site - http://oldtrailspublishing.blogspot.com

*Like a signed copy? All books purchased from Neil's publishing site will be autographed. If a reader has purchased elsewhere and would like a free autographed bookmarker, request from the old trails publishing site and one will be promptly sent.

www.ingramcontent.com/pod-product-compliance
Lightning Source LLC
Chambersburg PA
CBHW051946240626
47153CB00005B/1647